BAD BOY PLAYER

KAT T. MASEN

Kat T. Masen

Bad Boy Player

A Brother's Best Friend Romance

ISBN: 979-8691795473

Editing by Swish Design & Editing
Cover design by Outlined with Love Designs
Cover Image Copyright 2019
Second Edition 2019
All Rights Reserved

PROLOGUE

*"There are two voices that exist,
my head and my heart."*
~ *Emerson Chase*

"And five... four... three... two..." our producer Cliff calls. "Action."

Within seconds the cameras begin rolling. There's three of them surrounding us, inches away as they zoom in close attempting to capture every second of this moment.

We're standing in front of the Eiffel Tower at some godawful hour in the middle of winter. I'm a summer girl myself, but something about this place is magical during this season. Perhaps it's the beautiful snowflakes falling around us or the twinkling lights from the tower. There's also the sound of heavenly peace.

I breathe it all in—the beauty, the silence, and the man standing in front of me wearing a black Versace suit with no overcoat. Bearing the cold, yet still as dashing as the first moment I laid eyes on him three years ago.

"Em, there isn't a day that goes past when I don't imagine you in my life. We've been on this journey together, and the moment you walked into that restaurant I knew you were the one. Wearing that red dress... you looked absolutely breathtaking." A puff of cold air escapes his mouth, followed by a nervous bite on my lip. "I want to spend the rest of my life with you, and only you."

Wesley lowers himself to the ground on one knee, eyes fixed on me as he produces a small, black box. He flicks it open and inside sits a beautiful diamond ring. His eyes glaze over—a signature move he often does when he chokes up. And for a moment—if only a few seconds—I forget the world is watching. It's just him and me standing alone during this very intimate moment.

"Emerson Chase, will you do me the honor of being my wife?"

The camera zooms in closer with Cliff watching behind the lens, his arms crossed. I try not to pay attention to the way his face has tightened or how his lips remain flat. Never a good sign.

Somewhere, deep inside, my heart asks if this man is the love of my life. If marrying Wesley is the best thing to happen to me. It's all about relationship progression.

'We can't stay boyfriend and girlfriend forever.' *Words spoken by our publicist.*

I begin to blink my eyes, and within moments, the tears build and one falls graciously down my cheek.

I smile through the lonesome tear. "Yes."

Wesley's face lights up with joy. His messy, brown hair flicks against the slight wind as he pulls the ring out of the box and slides it on my finger.

It's beautiful.

I stare at it in complete and utter awe. The rock is huge, no doubt some designer looking for a promotional opportunity. The second this image hits social media, the ring will be sold out everywhere, and the designer will be laughing all the way to the bank.

In a swift and overexcited move, Wes pulls my body against his and kisses me deeply, moving his warm tongue against mine before pulling back with a grin on his face.

Wesley Rich is an attractive guy. Sweet, yet at times, arrogant and a know-it-all. The fans *love* him. The ultimate pin-up boy every girl has in her bedroom and imagination. Yet, his boyish grin coupled with an exuberant attitude to make me his wife rubs off on me as the excitement slowly sinks in.

Holy shit! I'm getting married!

I take another look at my ring, glancing sideways to read the white cardboard which Cliff is holding up. I should have practiced my lines, and Cliff's annoyed face tells me he thinks the same.

"It's such a beautiful ring," I comment with a sheepish smile. "Where? How?"

Wes quickly kisses the tip of the ring while not letting go of my hand, holding them preciously as if they belong to him.

"Harry Winston, of course. Nothing less for my fiancée."

"Fiancée." I beam without effort. "I really like the sound of that."

Wes runs his finger along the base of my jaw, tracing it with his eyes before raising them to meet mine.

Closing my eyes briefly, I take a breath and allow myself to feel this moment. *This is it.* The moment you imagined your entire life. The man you love proposing marriage. This is what all little girls dream about—Mr. Prince Charming, sweeping you away and creating this perfect memory to set the foundation for a happily ever after.

"I love you, Em. Nothing will stop you from becoming my wife."

"I love you, too," I breathe slowly.

We both lean in for another kiss, lingering until Cliff yells, "Cut."

Wes pulls away first but maintains his position. His body begins to shiver with the brutal cold finally settling in. "You like it?" He strains while his teeth shatter uncontrollably, cradling my waist in his arms and using my body to warm himself up.

"It's beautiful," I respond almost speechless and mesmerized by the exquisite piece of jewelry now sitting on my finger.

"Great work, guys, but we have one problem. Wesley, for fuck's sake, you got the dress color wrong," Cliff shouts, disgruntled, shoving his coffee cup into the chest of his assistant, causing the brown liquid to spill all over her white coat.

"I did?" Wes replies with a half-assed laugh.

"That's right," I confirm, remembering the moment we first met. "It was white."

"Oh..." Wes' face drops, his devilish smile disappearing quickly. "That dress."

The dress which caused our first major fight and ended up in the tabloids. It all started because his jealousy reared its ugly head when he caught an ex-cast member commenting on how I looked 'fuckable' in that dress.

"Sorry, guys, but since we have that first episode aired

we need to get the facts straight," Jenny, our co-producer, informs us.

"You mean I have to do this again?" Wes complains, removing his hands from my body, folding his arms while kicking the snow beneath his feet.

"Wow," I drag. "God forbid you have to propose again?"

"C'mon, Em, I didn't mean it like that. I just want this over with."

His face softens, and perhaps I'm a bitch for pointing out my feelings are hurt. But like everything that's happened in my life, it all feels staged. And this so-called perfect moment suddenly feels very imperfect.

The cold becomes unbearable. My feet are frozen in the expensive pair of boots I'm wearing. The dress I have on has long sleeves, but because we have to get this proposal right, the designer requested I didn't wear a jacket. The million-dollar diamond necklace adorning my neck feels like cold steel against my already-frozen skin.

I should have taken it as a sign.

Everything about this is to bring in ratings.

To make the television network rich.

And somewhere amongst this scripted moment, Wes and I are supposed to make it come alive. Show everyone what true love is all about.

I do love him. We've built a life together over the last three years. We purchased our first home, moved in together, and spent the previous year growing our fitness line. We've even adopted a dog—George Puggington.

Everyone refers to us as the 'unstoppable duo.' We're taking the world by storm and at the ripe old age of twenty-six. *Forbes* predicted we would be billionaires by the time we reach thirty.

It's win-win in everyone's eyes.

Everyone's but my own.

There's a commotion around us, the crew touching up my makeup and hovering over me while my knees shake with the cold.

Wesley taps his foot, frustrated and impatiently waiting for them to finish when the ring box slips out of his shivering fingers and onto the pile of snow in front of me.

I don't know what compels me to bend down and pick it up. As I lean down, ignoring my fingers stiffening from the cold, I lift it toward me until my focus moves to the scar on my knee. Three stitches from when I fell off a zip-line at the age of ten. When I didn't have a care in the world. When life was nothing but unicorns, rainbows, and making my brother's life hell.

The good old days before life became a circus show.

But who do I have to blame?

The man professing his love to me in front of the entire world?

The millions of fans who tune in at seven every Monday night?

Or myself, for thinking I had to prove a point?

Cliff directs the cameramen to take their places. With everyone positioned as before, Wes stands on the black cross —taped to the ground—and I follow his lead.

"And five... four... three... two..."

"Em, there isn't a day that goes past that I don't imagine you in my life..."

ONE

"There are signs everywhere you look. You just need to ignore the bullshit that clouds them."
~ *Emerson Chase*

"What is it like to be the hottest couple on TV?"

I should have seen the question coming.

A frenzy that can only be described as pure madness.

My publicist, Nina, had warned us this would happen. The producers and network executives knew they would top the ratings with the proposal episode.

Now everyone's on a high, including me.

"We simply go on about our lives as if the cameras aren't watching. Hottest? We honestly don't think that of ourselves." Wesley laughs, resting his hand comfortably on my thigh.

What a load of shit. I hold back the predictable eyerolling as Wesley charms the reporter from *Hot Enter-*

tainment News, the biggest entertainment program around the globe.

We've been asked this question numerous times, and each time Wesley lies through his teeth that labels aren't important.

Let's clarify—they aren't important to me.

I couldn't care less.

But Wesley has this desperate need to be number one in everything he does.

When we first met, his competitiveness was a major turn-on. Now, I simply ignore his immature behavior.

The proposal was filmed two months ago and aired only last night. We were under strict contractual obligations to not let it slip, which meant I was forced to keep the beautiful ring in my closet and not showcase it like a happy, newly engaged woman normally would. Aside from our parents and entourage of management, no one else knew.

But last night, at precisely 7:42 p.m. the world watched on, and social media blew up.

Many congratulatory messages from fellow actors and fans rolled in and then, the trolls started.

How dare I marry Wesley Rich?

Emerson Chase is nothing but an ugly, gold-digging whore wanting to tie him down and ruin his reputation.

I was also called, too fat. Too skinny. And, *oh my God, I hate her hair!*

I've heard and seen it all before.

Ignoring the nastiness and avoiding social media at all costs is on top of my list—that was until Wesley read the tweets to me late last night.

"Babe, check it out... this chick has Photoshopped you onto a cow's body."

I grabbed his phone to look at the photo. It was kinda funny, but it still hurt my feelings.

This industry calls for a tough skin. I just didn't anticipate three years ago that our show, *Generation Next,* would be the highest-rating show for the network. They didn't predict it either.

When we were scouted on campus to star in the show, they merely wanted some college kids with different majors.

I'm not stupid though, I knew they wanted me because of who my mother is, and the fact that my brother had at the time just been picked up to play premier-league soccer in England. But nevertheless, I signed on the dotted line because I was bored and had zero social life.

College was always depicted as one big social orgy.

Yeah, I may have gone to a few frat parties and drank like tomorrow didn't exist, but for most of the part, I kept to myself with the goal of finishing my major, sober.

My attention is brought back to Donna Mack, the slutty reporter showing way too much leg who Wesley is pretending to ignore.

"According to online polls, you guys are finalists as the hottest couple on television. The fans love you. They've even started Instagram accounts dedicated to only pictures of the both of you." She's quick to smile as if she's just dished out some sort of compliment.

Wes places his arm around me, pulling my body closer while planting a kiss on my neck. I am all for affection in private, but dislike it when he purposely does it in interviews. Something he's been doing more of in front of the camera and less in the bedroom.

Perhaps that is what's causing this crabby, irritable mood. I need to get laid.

Blame it on busy schedules, back-to-back filming, or the

fact that George claimed the middle of our bed as his territory. Either way, it's causing significant friction in our relationship.

"Wesley's a very affectionate guy. We're flattered our fans take time out to praise our relationship," I answer in a confident tone.

Lies... more lies.

She asks a couple more routine questions before wrapping up the interview. When she leaves the area, Wes takes the opportunity to slide his hand along my thigh and into the slit of my dress. Attempting to push him away, I scan our surroundings to make sure no one's watching.

Someone is always watching us.

"Let me finger you, you know you love it," he begs, tempting me with his eyes.

I squeeze my legs tight, ignoring the sensations building. "Can't you wait? Seriously, they'll be back any minute."

Wes ignores my comment, pressing further on the base of my clit until we're interrupted by one of the assistants carrying two bottles of water. She spots his hand buried between my thighs, turning her red face in the opposite direction and almost crashing into the camera.

"I'm sorry..." she stammers while eyeing the floor.

Wes snickers, retracting his hand with a satisfied smirk. Annoyed at his childish behavior, I offer her a genuine smile, ignoring the voices warning me this will end up in the headlines like everything else.

The camera crew closely follow with the interviewer at their heels.

Great—*Hot Gossip* magazine.

I despise this group.

You could say the sky is blue, and somehow they will

capture the quote and make you a home-wrecking whore sleeping with David Beckham.

I manage to put on a smile as Wesley tilts his head toward me and carefully moves his fingers across his nostrils.

Breathing slowly against my ear, he whispers, "I can smell you on me. When this is over... you're mine."

Wesley Rich has a way with words. He also has a way with using them in the bedroom. I disguise my grin by covering my mouth and letting out a small cough, knowing he's suffering from lack of sex makes me feel better.

I place my hand on his, keeping it on his lap as the magazine starts interrogating our lives. We have our answers down pat, having done this hundreds of times. To add to this, we often prepped our answers to avoid being caught out. We are professionals. To the world, we are reality stars of the hit television show, but to us we are actors. Actors which happened to fall in love while filming.

An hour passes, and finally, we're done. Removing our microphones, Wes hops off the stool and pulls his phone out of his pocket the same time I do. There's a dozen notifications, but the only one which catches my eye is the text from my mom.

Mom: *Big news, kiddo. Call me when you're free.*

I love my mom, but she's the most annoying woman to walk this planet when she vague-texts me, which is something she does often to prompt a phone call.

"I'm going to call my mom," I tell Wes. "I'll meet you outside?"

He nods, his head buried in his phone while typing quickly and barely acknowledging my presence.

I wander toward the exit, smiling politely as I pass the crew. There are a few younger kids hanging around that stop and ask me for a selfie. I happily oblige, though desperate to find out what the big news is.

At the end of the hall, there's a small conference room which I slip into, closing the door behind me. I hit dial on Mom's number and wait impatiently for her to answer.

"Kid, can I call you back? I'm just in the middle of writing this complicated scene, and my characters are screaming at me," she says in one breath.

"Uh... no," I argue back. "You don't just vague-text me and leave me hanging. Hand your characters a Xanax and tell them to chill out."

Mom laughs, letting out a sigh. It's the same sigh she often lets out when she's caught in the middle of a deadline and brought back to reality.

"Okay, you have my attention."

"Mom," I yell in frustration. "What's the big news?"

"Your brother will be in town tomorrow. He has some news, and has asked if you can come home."

My brother, Ashley, hasn't been home since last year, busy with his own life and career. This proved a point—as his twin sister—that we do not have the ESP thing going on. The last text he sent me was yesterday, and it was a picture of his injured foot which completely grossed me out.

"He's gay, is that it?" I joke.

"Your brother gay? The tabloids have a fascination with his love life which all involve women. I don't know how I raised a man-whore child."

I laugh softly. "Because it's in your blood. You write romance novels, Mom. You're a *New York Times* bestseller. Even when you're not writing, you're sending out this romantic vibe to everyone around you."

"Romance is one thing, kid, your brother is entirely another." She chuckles. "So, can you fly back tomorrow?"

My parents live on the east coast, in a small town just outside of Connecticut with my younger sister Tayla. As much as I miss being home and the quiet life, flying out is always a hassle. Over the past year, paparazzi have had a fascination with my movements and followed me wherever I go. A reason why I reduced the trips back home.

"I guess I can swing it. We're not filming till next week, and Wes is flying to Amsterdam for a photoshoot tonight."

"Great! I'll get Daddy to pick you up at the airport. I miss you, kid, it's been too long."

"I know, Mom. See you tomorrow." I sigh, then end the call.

You would think being a twenty-six-year-old woman, I'd have my big-girl panties permanently on, but on occasions like this when something seems off and not right, I miss my mom a lot. Living across the country might as well be across the ocean. We have a relationship most people envy as I can easily call her my best friend. We text several times a day, anything and everything she knows about my life. I respect her opinion, and we rarely argue about anything unless it's who might win *The Bachelor*.

Growing up with a mother who writes romance has its ups and downs. I didn't know it at the time, but Mom's one of the most respected and successful romance writers in the world. Her books have been translated in every possible language, and she often attends signings across the globe.

My first memory of her leaving us for the weekend was when I was five. I cried because Dad's a shitty cook, and I didn't want anyone to cook besides her. *Self-centered and a brat.*

As I grew older, I became fascinated with her career

and began reading her books in my teens. The only thing I skim is the sex scenes. Mom's a great writer, but some things are best left a mystery in my opinion.

People often ask her, "Where do you get your inspiration from?" and "I bet you live an exciting life."

Sure, Mom and Dad love each other, but Dad's always the beer-drinking, nut-eating dad that yells at the television when his team lets him down. He's a sports fanatic, who has very little time for romance. At least, that's my observation.

I make my way slowly to the interview room to find Wes waiting for me.

Something's amiss.

His normally styled hair looks like he's just run a marathon—it's sweaty and stuck to his forehead. He's quick to shove his phone in his pocket, focusing his attention on me. "Em, we have to go. My flight leaves tonight, and I'm not packed."

"Yeah, okay," I respond while he reaches out for my hand. "Mom called me. She wants me to fly home for the weekend."

"To Connecticut?"

"No, to the moon. Yes, to Connecticut. Something about my brother being in town with a surprise."

"I don't like you going there alone."

"Well, I don't like you going alone to Amsterdam, but you insisted," I argue back.

He squeezes my hand tighter, plastering a fake smile knowing all eyes will be on us when we leave the room. Not saying another word, we scurry past the few fans lined up and climb into the car. We buckle our seatbelts in unison then he starts the engine quickly, checking the rearview mirror before speeding off.

"There's so much I need to do for the photoshoot,

Em. I didn't work out yesterday or today because of all these interviews. I'm not in my best shape."

I am not buying the excuse, and instead remain tightlipped avoiding another argument. All we seem to do lately is argue. I'm fed up with his unorganized trips, and for some reason, he's become more possessive over our relationship which frustrates me. We've had a few fights on camera which the both of us were forced to reconcile and put on a united front. I don't know what it is about us, but I've pinned it down to the fact we're engaged, and now sitting on top of our shoulders is a wedding which the network executives are eager to pay for knowing it's their golden egg.

"Listen." He parks the car in the garage of our apartment block, resting his arm on the back of my chair. "I know things have been tense between us, but it'll all die down soon. Maybe we need a trip away? A quick romantic getaway where I can fuck you all weekend long."

I smile softly. "You're a jerk. That's the problem. Less jerk, more fucking."

Burying his face in my neck, he runs his tongue along my skin as I close my eyes. The sound of the leather seat squeaks when he shifts closer to me. I miss him already and wish he'd beg me to come on this trip. Throw all caution to the wind and be more spontaneous.

"You're mine," he murmurs. "Remember that."

Here we go again. I humor him and then attempt to rile some sort of reaction.

"I'll try to remember that and let my other boyfriend know." I chuckle.

His smirk fades, brows furrowing. "You know I don't like that joke. There's a million guys lining up for you."

"Name one?"

"I could name a dozen. You never know, Em. There's probably that one guy out there completely obsessed with you. Would do anything to make you his."

"Tell him I said hello when you find him," I say, deadpan.

"Funny. Now shut up. You've wasted enough time. Get your ass out of this car and in our bed so I can fuck you till my flight leaves."

I let out a giggle, ignoring our fight as we both laugh and race up the stairs to our apartment.

He throws me over his shoulder, opening the door with a youthful laugh until he stops and yells, "Fuck!"

Dropping me to the floor, I turn around swiftly and see only one thing—George, with a mouthful of Wes' expensive shoes.

Without saying a single word, Wes' face foretells our future.

No one is getting laid tonight.

TWO

"Home is where the heart is and memories you forgot existed." ~ Emerson Chase

There's nothing more satisfying than walking through the airport doors and smelling fresh air. Especially when the air is *home.*

Even with my shades on, fans notice and beg for autographs and selfies. It doesn't bother me since it only takes a few minutes, and they aren't as ruthless as the paparazzi. I smile—happy to oblige—then worm my way out of the small circle which has begun to grow and draw attention.

Dad meets me at the terminal, parked outside in his fancy Mercedes. The one Mom calls a *mid-life crisis.* It's a nice car—sleek, black, and shiny. For someone in his mid-fifties, Dad scrubs up well. He hasn't aged much over the years, still styling his silver-gray hair to the side with a thin beard to match. His piercing blue eyes mirror mine and my brother's, though his are surrounded with slight wrinkles when he smiles.

"I missed you, Emmy." He smiles, placing his arm around me after he loads my suitcase into the trunk.

"Miss you, too, Daddy-O. Bet you miss Ash more."

He releases a short grunt, quick to voice his opinion. "I don't know what your brother is up to by coming home, but it doesn't sound good. Especially when they have an important game next week."

"C'mon Dad, it's not like he's going to quit soccer. He lives and breathes that shit."

We both hop into the car, mindful of the parking attendant yelling at everyone delaying the traffic. In a quick second, Dad speeds off, and we're on the freeway driving home.

"So, how's Wesley?"

I shrug. "The same, I guess."

"Taking care of you?"

"Dad, I'm twenty-six. I can take care of myself."

"I know that," he states with a half-smile. "You've always been independent just like your mother. I meant... is he treating you well?"

"Yes, Dad. I wouldn't marry someone who's not treating me well."

Just like I had predicted, George eating Wes' shoes had left Wes in a foul mood. To top the night off, we got into another fight as the car service pulled up to the apartment. Wes was stepping out of the door while informing me of a party where he was scheduled to make an appearance. Normally, I wouldn't mind, but then he told me who'd be attending and I was quick to voice my concerns. The group of actors who will be there are nothing short of trouble, dragging everyone's name through the mud along with them. We left off shouting nasty words to each other and haven't spoken since.

Poor George—he witnessed the whole thing.

"And the wedding. Has the program set a date yet?" Dad asks, veering right as he exits the freeway.

"Not yet. They want to make sure it falls at the right time. The largest viewing numbers are during winter when people are stuck at home. So, maybe a winter wedding. Personally, I like the summertime."

Dad remains quiet. I know he isn't a fan of what I'm doing with my life. In fact, he's the first person to tell me I shouldn't be part of such trivial and mindless television. Of course, he'd say that—Ash's his favorite.

When I signed the dotted line to appear on the reality show, we didn't speak for weeks until I cried over the phone and told him that I loved him and needed him to support me. That moment defined our relationship. He admitted he wanted only the best and would support me as long as I was happy.

The problem now—I'm not happy.

But I keep it to myself, playing the part of the happy fiancée as I don't know any different, and because the web I've weaved for myself seems so intricate and impossible to untangle.

We drive through the leafy town of Green Meadows—a place which has been home since the moment I left my mother's womb. It's a gorgeous day—blue skies with a small array of clouds clustered in the east. The air outside is warm, so I open the window to feel the warmth against my cool skin.

Every place in Green Meadows has a memory. The corner shop where I would ride my bike and buy candy with money I stole from Ash's room, to the large oak tree which sits in the middle of the town square shading the playground equipment.

Resting in the seat, I watch the familiar places as we drive by and head toward home. Turning the corner, the streets become wider and the houses grander until I see our home in full view. It still takes my breath away. The two-story red brick dwelling is partially covered with vines. When I was younger, it looked like a mansion. It's funny how as we grow our perception changes.

Dad drives the car along the driveway until we're parked adjacent to the front doors. He exits and begins unloading my belongings.

The door opens, and I see Mom peeking her head out. "Emmy!"

Running out the door with a joyous smile, she impatiently waits for me to get out of the car. I quickly do so and jump straight into her arms, burying my head on her shoulder like I did when I was a kid. She still smells the same—lavender mixed with strawberries and vanilla. The same fruity, flowery perfume my grandmother used to always wear.

With my face buried in her long black hair, tears fall down my cheeks as the reality of being home sinks in. This is just what I need—my family. Life has been so hectic over the past year that I ignored my desperate need to be here. A place that means so much more to me than brick and mortar.

Mom pulls me back, studying my face with her palms pressed against my tear-streaked cheeks. "Hey kid, why the tears?"

"Just... I..." I stammer on my words while trying to control my emotions. "I missed you."

"Gee, I didn't get a greeting like that," Dad mumbles

under his breath as he walks past, carrying the bags inside and disappearing up the large staircase.

"Don't mind him," Mom says softly. "C'mon, I've made your favorite cake."

"The rainbow cake vomiting the M&M's?"

Mom laughs, closing the door behind her as we walk toward the kitchen.

"You make it sound so... appetizing. Go get settled in your room and come down when you're ready. And while you're up there check to see if your sister is alive. I haven't seen her all day."

I lean across the countertop, my hands moving toward the cake with delight. It's just how I remember it—four colorful layers with cream filling in between. When you slice the middle open, the M&M's pour out displaying its yummy goodness.

Another reason why it's good to be back.

I've showered and changed into a casual sundress with no plans to go anywhere tonight. And just like Mom asked, I stopped by my sister Tayla's room but was ignored.

Apparently, she's going through that teen attitude stage.

At sixteen, she's the baby of the family. Mom admitted to me one day, she was the result of a weekend away in Vegas with a bottle of Moscato.

Now that's something I didn't need to know.

The cake is calling my name, so I dig in, chatting with Mom as she stands opposite me. I may be biased, but Mom is insanely beautiful. She wears her long, black hair down as usual—her reading glasses perched on her head which pull the hair away from her face. Wearing minimal makeup, her skin is flawless and naturally bright. At family parties, my aunties all moan about the amount of Botox Mom's apparently had injected, which amounts to—*zero*. They're jealous women looking for any reason to tear down their little sister. I never understood how jealousy could be such an unhealthy obsession, but Hollywood quickly taught me just how much it drove people to do crazy things.

"So, what's happening, and what was that text last night about Wes being a moron?"

Sliding my fork sideways, I scoop another piece of heaven and bring it to my mouth.

"It's not George's fault. He's bored, and we haven't been paying as much attention to him as we should."

"Still, that dog of yours has expensive taste," Mom casually adds, sliding a glass of homemade lemonade over to me. She knows the way to my stomach.

"I think he's gay."

"You think your dog is gay?"

"He only chews on Versace shoes. Plus, one time at the dog park, he totally just sat there and watched another male dog hump the streetlamp."

Mom laughs, almost spitting out her drink. "Hollywood dog parks seem more controversial than here."

"You're telling me. Plenty of bitches. And about Wes..." I pause with a sigh, "... I'm over his immature behavior. He wants to party and hang out with his so-called friends like he's eighteen again. Haven't we outgrown this phase? I'm all for a drink now and then, but grow up already."

I air out my frustrations, not realizing how heavy it's being weighing on my shoulders. It feels good to chat to Mom in person because if anyone can understand me, it's her.

"Maybe you're taking life too seriously?"

Her eyes scan mine with curiosity as my words remain trapped in my throat. I've never considered myself as a serious person—I like to have fun, too. But lately I'm forever being the adult for the both of us, and that may be due to the pressure I'm feeling to be the next big thing. Pressure which stems from management, and myself.

"I do know how to have fun, Mom," I respond flatly.

"Last Friday night you were pairing socks, adamant there's a secret place in the universe where socks migrate, leaving you forever pair-less."

I smile, relaxing my shoulders. "There is, right? You're a mom, surely you should be letting me in on the secret of where this place is?"

Mom strokes my cheek with her hand, calming my agitated mood. "Kid, it'll forever remain a mystery, but if you ever find out promise me you'll tell me first?"

"Pinky swear."

There's a commotion coming from the hall. Doors slamming and a gust of wind flutters down the hallway and into the kitchen. Seconds later, my brother steps in with his usual shit-eating grin, dumping his bag onto the floor.

Mom is quick to wipe her hands on her apron, bringing him in for a hug. Ash towers over her, but still looks like a little momma's boy when she fixes his dirty-blond hair and parts it to the side. It's hard to believe we're twins considering we look nothing alike, aside from our blue eyes and the few freckles which are scattered over the bridge of our noses.

Throughout my childhood, I swore it was a ploy to bring us closer together and that we weren't actually twins. Instead, in my mind, Ash was adopted from some alien being, who spawned around the time I was born. It explained to me why he had the IQ of a peanut.

"Missed ya, Ma." He grins, his eyes wandering to the plate parked in front of me. It doesn't take him long to acknowledge my presence. "Well, well, well... if it isn't my long-lost famous sister."

"Well, well, well..." I mimic, "... if it isn't my annoying brother with some sort of foot fungal disease."

Ash moves around the counter letting go of Mom and wrapping his arms around me from behind.

Yeah, I kind of missed the fucker, despite how much he annoys me. He hasn't changed much since I saw him last year, still sporting some weird crew-cut and seems to be growing a mustache to hide his baby face. I don't know how he became this man-whore with that god-awful mustache. And of course, he still wears the same clothes—Adidas everything. It's like the brand threw up all over his shirt, shorts, shoes, even socks. *He's a damn walking billboard.*

Just when I think I actually missed him and it's good to have him around again, his giant man hands swipe the last bite of cake on my plate, throwing it in his mouth.

"Hey," I complain, releasing myself from his over-bearing hug.

"You snooze, you lose."

"I wasn't snoozing, you ape."

"One minute and the two of you are fighting? I thought absence is supposed to make the heart grow fonder?" Dad chuckles, placing his keys on the counter and standing beside Mom.

"Not when my dear old brother texts you a million times a day. There's no absence."

Suddenly, Ash's demeanor changes, he's almost nervous. He does this thing with his eyebrows where he twists the ends of them as if to distract himself. I know something's up, but much like Mom and Dad, I'm entirely in the dark.

I'm about to call him out on it until Logan—my brother's best friend—and a mystery woman walk into the kitchen. Logan flies through girlfriends like I go through underwear, so it doesn't surprise me she's here. Yet, I find it rude and annoying he doesn't have the courtesy to inform us a stranger will be joining us.

Logan's face breaks out into a mischievous smirk, the same one he had when he played pranks on me when we were younger. The only thing that's changed is the fact he's taller than me. Actually, he towers over me like Ash. Add to that a muscular body, instead of a ten-year-old fat prepuberty kid. And he got rid of the bowl haircut.

According to some magazine, he was named the hottest athlete of the year. I remember reading the article thinking *Logan Carrington... really?* The same boy who practically lived in our house and was Ash's Siamese twin. Let's ignore the fact that I'm his actual twin.

Age changes everyone, and despite the fact I haven't seen him in over two years, nothing much has changed except his legs are now covered in tattoos. He's wearing shorts which give me a view of the intricate patterns and drawings.

I can't get over it, staring rudely while Ash rambles on about something. I'm surprised Dad or Mom haven't said anything either. Logan's like a son to them and Dad's *anti-tattoos*. It's the reason why Ash keeps the one just under his stomach a secret. It happened on some bro-code drunken night-out, and when he tried to text me a pic, I was quick to point out the fact I almost threw up in my mouth at the sight of his pubes.

What fascinates me about the tattoos on Logan is his

arms are ink-free. Usually, the arms are the first place you have inked, not the legs. Nevertheless, I move my rude stare away from him, onto Ash and his dirty face.

Logan moves around the kitchen and stops at Mom, embracing her in a tight hug and not letting go for a while.

Something smells fishy.

Aside from the lingering smirk, his ash-brown hair is flicked to the side, styled with a line cut through the lower part. A fad that's apparently rocking this generation. He runs his hands through it, lifting his bottle-green eyes to meet mine. I jump off the stool as he walks around the counter to me, and wrap my arms around him.

In my bare feet and stretching on my tiptoes, I whisper in his ear, "What are you up to?"

Logan holds me tight, wrapping his arms around my waist. I hate to admit he smells good. Some fancy aftershave designed to lure in women I'm guessing.

Bringing his lips close to my ear, his tone is smooth. "This will send you into a tailspin."

I pull back, confused, but quick to extend my hand to the girl standing quietly in the corner. She's quite pretty—exotic with a nice fashion sense. It's my polite way of saying not everyone can rock a caftan but she certainly can.

"Hi, I'm Emerson... Ash's sister."

She smiles with nerves, biting down on her lip with her very white teeth. I'm amazed at the length of her hair, which she's wearing straight with a few blonde streaks reaching the tip of her waist.

"I'm Alessandra, I've heard a lot about you." She speaks with an accent—it's thick, and by the way she rolls her 'r' I assume she's from Spain.

"Oh," I say looking in Logan's direction. I didn't think he'd talk about me, but obviously, he does. *Odd, considering we aren't that close anymore.* "That's nice of Logan to talk about—"

"Mom, Dad," Ash interrupts me, moving closer to Alessandra and wrapping his arm around her waist. "Alessandra is my... my wife."

My eyes spring wide open, my jaw drops to the floor with a crashing halt. *His wife?* When in God's name did this happen? He hasn't even mentioned dating let alone marriage. This has to be some sort of prank. Logan's put him up to it. This isn't the first time they have done something like this. They used to gang up on me all the time and it drove me insane.

We were known as the three troublemakers in the neighborhood when we were kids, and I considered myself one of the boys until I turned fourteen. So, I can smell a prank a mile away and this one is *rotten* to the core.

"Excuse me?" Dad questions, clearing his throat. His usually fair skin takes on a beet red color, a tell-tale sign he's fuming. I glance over at Mom, she looks equally as shocked.

"We got married in Spain. Alessandra is my wife."

"Married?" Dad repeats.

Ash nods, keeping his stare persistent and not blinking to challenge Dad. The two of them are just as stubborn as each other, and the longer this drags on, the more it becomes evident this isn't a joke.

"When did this happen?" Mom asks in a calmer tone, trying to disguise her shock.

Ash looks at Alessandra, thoughts passing between them, keeping the rest of us waiting impatiently. "It happened last weekend. It sorta just happened."

"You don't sorta get married, Ashley," Dad grits, slamming his palm on the marble top. "You're too young to be married."

"I knew you'd say that." Ash raises his voice, competing with Dad. "You had no problem when Emmy announced she was engaged… and to some dickhead she met on TV!"

"Hey," I shout, quick to defend myself. "Don't drag me into your mess. And thanks for thinking my fiancé is a dickhead." I storm out of the kitchen, walking out to the backyard for fresh air. The nerve of him to throw me under the bus while he's fucking standing in front of me. My anger refuses to subside, the air not calming the heat burning through me as the weight of Ash's decision finally sinks in. He got married and didn't say a word like I'm nothing and nobody to him. I can recall all the conversations we've had over the past week and none of them alluded to this. That's what fucking hurts right now, my brother hid the biggest thing to happen to him from me.

I continue to walk further into the yard to stop myself from running back inside and yelling at him. My parents place sits on acres of land. I wandered over to my favorite spot—the hammock which swings between two large trees. Climbing in, I rock back and forth while staring at the sky.

We're twins. We shared a goddamn womb for nine months. No matter how much we fight, he always has my back.

Perhaps he's struck a nerve calling Wes a dickhead. Sure, Wes has his moments which unfortunately are caught on camera, but this isn't about Wes, this is purely about the betrayal I feel from my own brother.

"I told you it'd send you into a tailspin."

The sound of Logan's voice startles me. Yet, I continue to rock back and forth, lost in a sea of thought.

"Are Mom and Dad grilling him?"

"I walked out when Chris said 'I had more hopes for you, son.'"

"Ouch." *Poor Alessandra.* "But it's not like Ash to be so..."

"Committed?"

"Yes." I pull myself up, leaning on my elbows for support as I gaze directly at Logan. "Why didn't you tell me?"

"It's not my news to tell. Plus, I think I'm still in shock myself. Move over."

I wriggle my body a little allowing some space for Logan to lay beside me—something we often did when we're both angry at Ash at the same time. Except, we aren't ten plotting to hit him with water balloons on the way to school. *Though, I wouldn't mind finding some and releasing my anger with them right now.*

"So you think this is weird, too?" I ask.

He nods, placing his arms underneath his head. The bottom of his shirt lifts slightly and I do my best to avoid looking at his happy trail. Okay, his happy trail is damn sexy. I didn't even know it was possible to think like that— *isn't a happy trail just an extension of your pubic hair?*

"We walked into the bar after the game. He says 'she's the most beautiful woman he's ever seen,' and the next morning he calls to tell me he married her."

"What?" I sit up on my elbows again but this time in a mad rush, which causes the hammock to swing faster. "He knew her for less than a day?"

"Yes."

"And he has the nerve to say I'm getting married too fast."

"Oh yeah..." Logan half-smiles. "Congratulations by the way."

"Thanks." I kill my curiosity by asking him for the truth. "Did you watch it?"

There's a short silence while he gazes at the sky. He's one of those people that when he smiles his whole face lights up, but most notably his eyes. The color of them used to freak me out—a green that sometimes changes to brown—and when I asked him how he did that he told me he was bionic, raised by robots pretending to be human.

"You know I don't watch TV unless it's sports."

I'm not sure how to respond, so I choose to drop the subject of my engagement and focus on Ash. "What happens now? Is your coach mad?"

"Coach Bennett is fuming but he's calmed a bit. He sent Ash home to tell your parents and expects us back in three days to commence training. He said 'if this relationship ruins our game' he's out. No second chances."

"That's a bit harsh, don't you think? So what... you're not allowed to have relationships?"

"Not ones that could affect our gameplay."

"Huh," I say loosely. "Explains why you're a player."

He knocks into my arm, causing the hammock to swing faster.

"Let's go out tonight. Maybe we should celebrate his decision? I've been a terrible best friend," he openly admits.

"Really? Is that a cover for you just wanting to go out tonight and find some random chick to screw? Some Green Meadows hussy waiting for the hottest athlete to come sweep her off her feet?" I lace my voice with adoration, mocking his persona.

"You know me too well, Emmy." He grins.

"I can spot a man-whore a mile away," I point out confidently. "All right, first let's see if he's still alive."

"Good idea."

We both climb off the hammock with great difficulty. Walking back toward the house, we talk about what's been going on. As we step past the edge of the pool, I make a mental note to keep a reasonable distance from it. You learn from your past—once a prankster always a prankster.

"Lighten up, I won't push you in," Logan chastises.

"That's what you've said numerous times. Once played always scarred."

"C'mon, I've grown up. We aren't kids anymore."

Logan Carrington isn't a kid—that's for sure.

He's all man.

One that screams bad boy.

I feel sorry for the women who fall in love with him. He's your classic athlete with the biggest head on this planet next to my brother, of course. That's why they have been best friends since day one—two man-whore peas in one man-whore pod.

"I guess you're right."

I make my way back to the marble pool coping when all of a sudden I lose my balance from the nudge of his arm and teeter on the edge before my body hits the frigid water with an almighty splash. The impact of the fall drags me under the surface. The sudden cold forces water into my mouth making me swallow while I flail my arms around in an attempt to swim until my head has emerged above the water.

"You... asshole..." I yell, trying to swim to the side. It's a lot more difficult swimming fully clothed than in a bikini.

He's on the edge—squatting—staring me down. "I said we weren't kids, never said I wasn't an asshole."

I growl in annoyance, using my leg to climb over and out of the pool. With the jerk walking away, I run toward him and jump on his back like I've done a million times before. This time it's harder, his height and hard muscles make it difficult for me to latch on. *When the fuck did he get so tall?* Or maybe I'm shrinking.

"Payback is sweet... dear old friend."

He continues to walk, not fazed I'm hanging on his back like a desperate monkey. "You've got to do more than jump on my back wet to come close to paying me back."

"Oh, don't you worry Carrington, game on."

"Game on?" He laughs, mocking me.

"Game on," I repeat.

Jumping off his back, I open the door to a screaming match going on inside the house.

THREE

"There aren't enough rounds of drinks to cure the brokenhearted." ~ Emerson Chase

It's the most awkward car ride in the history of car rides. Ash has taken the wheel like a crazed maniac with Logan sitting equally agitated beside him. I sit in the back with Alessandra, making small talk to pass the time. I can't fault her. She's answered every question with ease and has even been speaking about her profession —nursing.

It all began to make sense—sort of.

She's attractive plus, she wears a nurse's uniform for a living. Ash and Logan used to kid around about nurses being their ultimate fantasy. It was during these conversations I used to tune out. They thought of me as one of the guys but little did they know I had zero interest in fucking nurses.

No wonder Ash wanted to marry her.

We stumble into Harry's Joint—a local bar with a jukebox as old as Betty White and a dingy pool table nestled in a dimly lit corner. It's ten miles from home and quiet for a Saturday night. It smells of cigars mixed with stale beer and man sweat. Three of my *least* favorite things.

Only after a minute of being inside, Ash orders a round of beers, ignoring us while he isolates himself in the corner rubbing chalk on his cue. Alessandra walks over, placing her hand on his shoulder only for him to remove it.

"Great," I mumble from where I'm leaning against the bar. "This will not end well."

Logan positions himself next to me, watching them with boredom. "You're telling me. Your dad's fuming. I could practically see the steam shooting out of his ears."

His comment prompts me to text Mom. I know the situation has upset her even though she's not as vocal as Dad. Pulling my phone out of my purse, I quickly send her a text asking if she's okay. Since my phone is still in hand I also text Wes hoping to have a quick chat with him and reconcile after last night.

A few seconds, I see my screen light up.

Mom: *I'll be ok kiddo. Just need to process.*

I let out a sigh while gazing at my brother. He doesn't know how many lives he's affected by making such a rash decision. It's fair to say we're all hurting in some way or another—the moron just doesn't care.

Logan nudges me to follow him to the pool table, carrying the tray of beers. By the time we get there, Ash and Alessandra have reconciled and they're making out like lovesick fools.

Gross. Nobody wants to see their brother making out.

Ever.

I grab a beer off the tray, almost chugging it in one go. It doesn't sit too well in my stomach. My body's used to the high-end martinis at Hollywood parties. But I don't want to be *that* person, especially in front of the boys mainly because I'll never hear the end of it.

We decide to play a game of pool. Ash and Alessandra versus Logan and me. It's great to let our hair down, and even better that the four of us can unwind in a place where no one knows who we are. In the eyes of the few patrons hanging around, we're a bunch of rowdy drunks playing pool in the corner. I crave this type of solitude. Filming a reality show means we're always followed by cameras.

Cliff believes to catch the essence of a person's life, cameras need to be around them twenty-four-seven.

Thankfully, after much negotiation, they permitted me to be camera-free for the weekend.

Ash and Logan are in the same boat. Their back-to-back wins mean they're in the public eye more than they care to be. Soccer's huge in Europe, and overnight the two of them became household names.

Side-tracked by my thoughts, I catch up to the conversation which happens to be about *Star Wars*. It forces me to walk back to the bar to order something my stomach will agree with.

"Hey, Harry," I greet in a chilled voice with menu in hand. "What do you recommend?"

Harry doesn't make eye contact, wringing a hand towel while chewing on a piece of tobacco. "You're a lightweight. Maybe a glass of ginger ale."

I scrunch my face, shuddering at the thought. "What about a martini?"

He throws the towel on the bench, resting his palms on

the edge of the counter while watching me. "You're that Chase kid."

I nod, smiling politely and putting on the charm. I don't know where this is going, but by the way Harry's watching me suspiciously it doesn't look good.

"One of," I answer, clearing my throat. "Emerson."

His stare doesn't budge making me very uncomfortable.

"You're the one that left the gate open and let Rufus out."

"Rufus?" It jogs my memory and without raising too much suspicion, I glance sideways tapping on the counter pretending it wasn't me. Of course, I let Rufus out. He was an overweight bulldog who looked sad behind the wired gate. I thought he needed to live a little. Mind you, I was eight. My perception of living meant running wild without a care in the world. How was I to know Rufus would run away and never come back?

What's that saying again? Something about *'letting something go, and if it doesn't come back it was never meant to be.'*

"So, about that martini?"

He bites down on his teeth releasing a small growl while grabbing a glass and making the martini. I take the opportunity to wander over to the jukebox. Scanning the songs, I notice there's nothing after nineteen-ninety, leaving very few choices. I settle on some Prince then head back after grabbing my martini from Harry.

"You know what his problem is?" Ash shouts, sliding the cue between his fingers and aiming straight for the red ball which is nestled amongst the others in the corner.

I shrug, looking at Logan for some insight as to what we're talking about because a moment ago it was *Star Wars*.

"He's a dick," he finishes.

"Wait, Dad's a dick?"

"Yep," he says with conviction.

"In all fairness, he's done nothing but support you. Remember when you were fourteen and you begged to do that soccer camp in Spain? Dad took time off work so you could go."

His eyes lift to meet mine, they're full of anger and resentment. "So what? He wanted his only son to play soccer."

I have a whole argument planned out—it involves telling him he's ungrateful and should thank Mom and Dad for the sacrifices they made so he could play—but I decide against saying anything.

Ash and Logan lived and breathed soccer. When they turned thirteen, it was clear their obsession wasn't going away. Suddenly, it was soccer training after school each day, and no longer the trips to the lake where we would devise our plans to prank people in our neighborhood.

That year was defining for me. It was always the three of us, whatever we did or wherever we went. I tried to play soccer with them, but didn't have their passion or drive. I found myself pulling away and hanging out more with the girls at school.

Funnily enough, you stop hanging out with boys and all the girls want to do is talk about boys. *Boys, boys, boys.* The world just can't exist without them.

Life changed after that. With Logan's dad being a deadbeat and never showing up to games, Dad took it upon himself to quit his job and travel with the boys to various soccer camps. Logan's mom, Aunty Reese, is Mom's best friend. She was having a difficult time with the divorce and worried Logan would rebel.

There would be no time for rebelling. They proved they

had the skills even at a young age. Dad, Mom, and Aunty Reese agreed homeschooling would work best given their hectic schedule leaving me alone to fend for myself in high school.

I shouldn't complain—I had fun. I dated boys, did the whole cheerleader squad thing and lost my virginity in senior high to a guy named Dick. *False advertising.* His 'dick' was all talk, no action. One of those jocks that talked the talk but definitely did not walk the walk.

Everyone was so proud of Ash and Logan. They had a bright future. I sat back and watched until my life did a complete one-eighty.

I guess as kids, none of us expect to be where we are. Our lives are constantly under scrutiny and in front of the cameras being judged by the whole world.

Alessandra is sitting on the stool beside me, drinking water and keeping quiet. Ash continues to act like a dick and goes back to ignoring her.

This isn't her fault.

She's fallen in love with a loser.

Should I even be using the word *love*?

How do you fall in love with someone after knowing them for five minutes? *Impossible.*

"I'm sorry about my brother." I lean into her trying to make my voice heard over the music.

"Your brother is... passionate," she responds with a gentle smile.

"Interesting choice of word. You can call him an asshole, it's okay."

She shrugs half-heartedly. "He's my husband. In my family we don't call our husbands that."

Averting my eyes and lowering my gaze, I try not to let my feelings show. Am I that much of a bitch toward Wes?

Here's a woman who's committed to a man she met and married the same night, and here she is telling me, in her own way, she'll stick by his side no matter what. Wes and I have been together for three years, and the engagement has me questioning everything.

The uncertainty is honestly driving me insane.

His lack of responding to my messages is driving me insane.

I pull out my phone again and tap on the message I sent him. It shows me it's been *read* but still no response. *Fucking asshole!*

"Can I ask you something?" I question, controlling my voice and pushing aside my irritation. "Since you're my sister-in-law and all."

The endearment keeps her smiling. "Sure."

"How did you know you wanted to marry him? What pushed you past your doubts? I mean, surely, you would have had some doubts?"

"No doubts," she answers confidently. "He made me smile, laugh, and feel alive. I've never felt all those three things in one moment. When he asked me to marry him, I agreed because if he could make me feel that way for the rest of my life then what a life to live."

My gaze shifts toward my brother, angrily slamming the ball and cussing at his poor shot. Logan stands behind him, heckling and calling him soft. I wonder if Alessandra feels that way now, witnessing the darker side of my brother. I just can't see what she sees—someone who makes you smile, laugh, and feel alive?

I want to ask her specifically what makes her feel alive. It can be interpreted in so many ways.

Have I ever felt alive? Surely, I must have.

Yet, as I try to think of the moments when I felt alive, I

can only think of when Wes proposed. Our relationship has been calculated from the moment we met, and maybe that's what has allowed the doubt to creep in. We're both programmed to feel or act a certain way, and by now, it's become second nature.

"Are we going to kick his ass or are you going to stand there acting all girly?" Logan hisses from across the table, watching me intensely with his eyes fixed on mine.

"Who you calling a girl?" I slam my palm onto the table on purpose, holding back the pain which ricochets up my arm.

"The person standing across the table wearing a dress with pussies all over it."

Lowering my eyes, I gaze at the pattern on my dress—it's navy with scattered kitten faces. The halter neck combined with flared skirt make it very vintage. The designer's known for thinking outside the box—something I admire about her clothing.

"Kittens. And I'll have you know that an upcoming designer gave me this dress as a present. I happen to love it," I answer defensively.

"Shit, Emmy..." Ash laughs. "Maybe you need to switch teams. Team pussy."

Logan raises his hand to his mouth, trapping in his laughter. "If you can't beat 'em eat 'em."

Ash erupts into laughter, smacking his hand against the table. Logan's no better with his snide remark and arrogant laughter only irritating me more. Just like always, they gang up on me, teasing me relentlessly about anything and everything. Some things never change, and for once in my life, I kind of missed this—letting my hair down and just being me. Pussy dress and all.

I brush it off like it doesn't bother me, walking across to

the other side of the pool table. Grabbing the spare cue, my eyes dart back and forth analyzing the game. *I have zero chance.* The orange ball's too far left and I'm not that good of a player to rebound it off the side and into the pocket. The blue one's an inch away from the black, which is positioned so close to the pocket I'll end the game for the both of us.

Fuck. I don't like to lose either, especially to my dipshit brother.

Leaning down, my body angles along with the cue, my eyes focusing in on the orange ball. I have a small chance of making the shot, and just when I'm about to push forward, I feel Logan's body lean on the back of mine. Resting his hand on top of my own, the warmth engulfs my skin as he applies pressure and directs my aim to the blue ball. "Aim for the blue ball," he whispers in my ear. "Toward the left, nice and slow."

The muscles in my stomach spasm in fits of laughter. I accidentally press back into him, connecting with his crotch. My laughter is impossible to contain, my body almost falling limp onto the table.

"Do you know how funny that sounded?" I let out between breaths. "Aim for the blue balls, nice and soft?"

I slow my breathing, still unable to hide my grin from his lame request. I think I've calmed down enough until Logan brings my body up and against his. His grip is tight and the heat of his skin is wrapped all around mine in this uncomfortable position.

"I said aim for the blue ball. But hey... nice to know where your mind is at."

The smartass applies pressure on my hand, pulling back slightly then forward as we watch the white ball roll slowly toward the blue ball avoiding any movement from the black.

I want to jump with excitement, but I'm well aware his crotch is firmly against my ass and he's far from soft.

Oh my God... what the hell is happening? It's got to be the beer mixed with the martini. I must be imagining things. Logan is not someone to admire. He's the same boy who thought dumping slugs in my socks would be fun.

"That's cheating," Ash hurls at us while clutching his cue with a tight grip.

"What does Coach always say? There's no 'I' in team, Ash," Logan notes, the amusement lighting up his eyes.

"Fuck you! It's like we're back in middle school. The two of you ganging up on me when I wanted to dress as a cowboy for Halloween, and you guys wanted to be Power Rangers."

"Dude, we were ten. Cowboys are for sissies and the last time I checked, your dick wants pussy only."

I shake my head, motioning for them to stop. "Please don't talk about Ash's organs in any type of sexual way."

"Like you're one to talk, Carrington. How many chicks came back to your hotel at the airport?" Ash asks with a menacing gaze while spilling Logan's dirty little secret.

Something holds back my laughter, watching Logan pause with a haunted smile. *What a sleaze.* Perhaps I wasn't imaging his ass probe just then. I just didn't expect it from him. Logan once told me he wouldn't make me his girlfriend if I were the last girl on earth covered in bacon and cotton candy—his two favorite things.

"A gentleman never tells," Logan answers in a decidedly odd tone.

"Bullshit. You're just saying that in front of the girls. You told me they both blew you while you poured tequila all over their mouths."

Logan's face changes, almost to anger for bringing it up.

How our conversation has changed since the days since when we were little. We could spend hours talking about *The X-Files* and aliens roaming the earth, and now we're talking about Logan being some sex god that got off on demeaning women. What the fuck?

"All right, can we move on? You're both jerks and I need another drink," I say, then yell out to Harry for another round on me. He nods, but this time I swap beers and martinis for shots of tequila.

"Like you're one to talk, Emmy. Have you seen the porn out there of you?" Logan snickers, continuing on, "Didn't realize you were that kinky."

In between my shocked expression Ash's face quickly tightens with his eyes wide and full of rage.

"Firstly, Photoshop is a magical program if you know how to use it. Secondly, I'm not stupid... I would never pose nude. I learned my lesson the time I sunbathed in Greece and had an accidental nip slip. But hey, I didn't know you like to Google naked images of me?" I reverse my shock and stare at Logan, battling with his gaze as neither one of us backs down.

"Harry," Ash shouts, breaking the awkward stand-off between Logan and me.

Harry slides the tray of shots over the countertop. Alessandra's quick to bring them over to us.

Ash puts a shot glass to his mouth, allowing it to linger while eyeing Logan. "Don't ever talk about my sister that way. You got it?"

Logan grabs a shot, tilting his head to the side with a smirk. "Emmy's a reality star. The whole world knows her business. Right, Emmy?"

"Fuck you," I fume, downing a shot until the burning sensation halts my breathing for a second. My chest begins to burn as it slowly makes it way down but then disappears as the tequila warms my entire body. "You see what the producers want you to see. I'm not the same girl you once knew and watching me on TV doesn't make you know me."

Ash raises his glass in the air. "Okay, fuck! Can we seriously just toast to something? I'm sick of this bullshit. Let's be us for the night."

I nod in agreement, lifting another glass and raising it in the air. "To us... back together again. Except, no more pranks."

"No more wet willies," Logan adds, with a disgusted look directed at Ash.

"No more swapping your chocolate for laxatives," Ash says plainly.

"That was you?" I turn to face him in shock. "I blamed Logan for that this entire time!"

"Who else knew you snuck chocolate into your room and ate it before bed?"

"Oh my God, Ash! Why couldn't you be a normal brother and like read my diary or some shit?"

He places his hand on Logan's shoulder, still holding the shot in his fingers. "I did read your diary..." he pauses for dramatic effect then continues, "Dear Diary, today I saw Logan take his shirt off at the pool. He had such big muscles and looked *sooo* hot..."

My face began to heat up, remembering the *one* time I wrote about Logan. One. Fucking. Time! I was fifteen and hormonal.

Yes, my hormones were cuckoo and smoking crack or something that day... month... year... whatever.

"I never said that." I try to brush it off while keeping my cool.

"Aww... Emmy, did you have a crush on me?" Logan teases, placing his arm around me and kissing my cheek.

"No, you douche, I was merely pointing out your transition from puberty. Now, let's drink." I pull away, avoiding this uncomfortable conversation and downing the shot in one go.

My throat's immune to the burn now, allowing the clear liquid to slide smoothly.

The boys are loud and making a scene while reminiscing about the first major soccer game they played when Ash pissed his pants on the field. Alessandra seems to enjoy the conversation, laughing along with us.

In the corner of my eye, the light of my phone illuminates my purse. It's sitting at the top, within arm's reach. Thinking it is Wes, I enter my passcode and see Nina's name appear.

Nina: *Call me NOW*.

With my phone in hand, I tell them I need to make a call, moving my way through the deserted bar and outside where the noise has diminished. The air out here is much cooler, the darkness illuminated by the sign on Harry's bar with one bulb flashing bright.

I dial her number quickly, waiting as the phone continues to ring.

"Emerson, we need to talk."

"Okay," I say. "We're talking."

"Something's happened. And before I tell you what it is, I just want to say I'm sorry and you deserve better." Her voice softens, almost into pity.

I laugh nervously through the receiver. "Let me guess, they canceled the show?"

"No. I just received a call and email from this guy who claims he's part of a paparazzi mob in Europe who follow the Royal Family. It's about Wesley."

"What about him?" I ask, moving further away from the bar.

"He's been photographed at Rogues. And the photos are not good."

"Rogues? Am I supposed to know what you're talking about?" I raise my voice, frustrated and panicky. The alcohol isn't helping me, amplifying my emotions and creating a monster ready to unleash.

"A brothel."

"A brothel?" I repeat coldly. "So what *exactly* was he doing?"

"Emerson, I'm sorry."

"Nina! What the fuck was he doing?"

She pauses, and in the background I hear my phone ding. Moving it away from my ear, I open the text message and see the photo she sent to me. I almost drop the phone, my hands are shaking and my heart's pumping so loudly I think it's going to explode all over the dirty pavement.

His body is positioned behind some woman, cock stuck inside her with some white substance laced all over her ass. There's another woman in the photo, running her tongue along the other woman's ass with a sensual gaze lingering.

My posture stiffens—arms rigid and shoulders squared as I stare into the darkness.

How dare he do this to me!

My voice is silenced by my clenched teeth, forcing me to remain quiet while processing my goddamn fucking life and how everything will change.

"Em... Emerson," Nina yells through the speaker.

"I'm here," I say just above a whisper while holding

back the tears which are threatening to escape and rationalizing the anger that makes me want to rip his fucking soul out and feed it to coyotes.

"This is bad. I just want you to know I'm in negotiation to keep this under wraps. It's going to cost us."

"Whatever. I'll talk to you later, Nina. I need to go." I have no energy or fight left within me, so I quickly terminate the call. With a sigh, I lean against the brick wall behind me.

I should have seen this coming.

All signs pointed to this.

I trusted him when my gut knew something was off. It never bothered me that women threw themselves at him online and when he was out in public. What bothered me was the way he would somehow be drawn to women at social functions where we both attended. I can't remember the number of times I would catch him talking one-on-one with some woman who he claimed was nothing more than a friendly chat.

He was always on his phone and became snappy on occasions when I asked him what he was doing. The signs all pointed to him being an ass, and I don't even know what hurts me more—his infidelity or the humiliation of the world finding out.

And they will find out.

Page six news—*Wesley Rich Caught in a Hooker Drug Scandal.*

Followed by the pity—*Poor Emerson. She deserves better.*

Then the trolls have their say—*Serves her right for trying to change him and she got what was coming to her.*

I stay outside for a good fifteen minutes, staring blankly at the ground. Dragging my feet along, I walk into the bar and plaster a fake smile calling Harry for another round. I know it's not the best idea but the boys won't know any different.

"Another round? *Fuck.* We haven't drank this hard since the night I got hitched," Ash says with a burp.

"The night you fucked up your life?" I say with a straight face staring my brother down.

"The night I fucked up my life? Wow! Thanks for the support, sis. Nice to know you have my back."

"I don't have your back. And even if you told me, I still wouldn't have your back," I raise my voice. "Marriage is for fools. Love is overrated, and you'll probably get screwed over then come running back to Logan and me to fix all your fucking problems."

Ash's face falls then switches to anger as I don't back off while I reflect my own troubles back onto him. I need a punching bag and my brother has the target smack bang in the middle of his face

"Are you done now?" he grits, standing beside Alessandra who looks disappointed by my outburst.

"Yeah, I'm done, Ash. Have a nice fucking marriage." I grab my purse and storm out, searching around for something or someone to take me anywhere but here. There's nothing in sight but a dark road and trees swaying in the shadows. I should be scared, but what's out there lurking behind the shadows should be scared of me right now.

The sticks and stones beneath my feet crackle with every footstep, and just when I think I'm alone, I'm startled by the force of hands lifting me up and throwing me over a shoulder.

Logan.

FOUR

"Love is just one pile of bullshit and I'm the one who stepped in it."
~ *Emerson Chase*

"Wh\at the hell happened back there?"

Wriggling my body out of his grip, Logan drops me to the ground as I tumble and manage somehow to not fall over on the dirt. The foliage beneath my feet crunches, echoing the silence that surrounds us.

My chest is heaving, with noisy breaths that exhale through my nose while the thumping inside—from a broken heart—fuels the adrenaline.

Why the fuck did Logan have to follow me?

I want nothing more than to be left alone and sob like a fool.

Refusing to answer him, I continue to storm off, the dirt and pebbles pushing into my brand-new wedges as my steps quicken hoping to escape him. There's a narrow pathway where town folk often walk their dogs, and with the pale moon the only light guiding me, I follow my instincts until I reach the end of the trees with the lake in full view.

In the distance, there are speckles of lights from the few houses which surround it. It's such a beautiful place and one which holds memories of my childhood. The three of us would ride our bikes into the same bush causing mischief like the rascals we were.

Dad would take the boat out, teaching Ash and me a thing or two about fishing. We enjoyed it until Dad showed us one day how to gut a fish which had me vomiting overboard—a very unpleasant memory.

Beside the rundown jetty which has many planks missing and shakes when you walk across, sits the giant rock we used to fight over. I don't know why I gravitate toward it and find myself staring blankly. Then out of the blue, I raise my foot and kick it hard with the tip of my shoe.

Ouch.

"He's an asshole," I yell, hopping back trying to control the agony sweeping through my foot and up my leg.

Logan's standing at the edge of the water with his arms folded and his eyes wandering the shoreline. His steady, muscular back is facing me and probably the best thing right now because I don't want to look at him. He's just as annoying as the rest of the men in my life.

"Yeah, sure I'll admit he can be an asshole, but don't you think you took it a bit too far?" he responds in an arctic voice but keeping his expression hidden. "He hurt me, too. This whole marriage thing may fuck up our game. You're not the only one dealing with the ramifications of his actions."

"You honestly believe all that rubbish? Falling in love?

They knew from the start? C'mon, it's impossible," I ramble to myself as Logan quietly stands there in contemplation. "You can spend a whole lifetime knowing someone and still feel unsure if the love is there or is right. Two minutes in a bar and that person is your soulmate? Ludicrous."

Logan turns his neck, body following until we're facing each other. His presence radiates with superiority, just like when we were kids. I wasn't afraid back then and I'm not afraid now. His tough-guy persona doesn't scare me one bit.

"Hypocritical coming from someone engaged to a man who swore he fell in love with you the moment he saw you?" he questions, sarcasm lacing every word leaving his mouth.

The shock of his words cripples my ability to respond with a witty comeback. We aren't having a good old laugh here, throwing worms in the bottom of Ash's school bag anymore. And my initial reaction to his cruel words does nothing to calm the sea of emotions ravaging my insides. *Logan Carrington is one of them.* They all come from the same seed—the seed of men who feel entitled.

Screw a woman.

Move on.

Fuck feelings.

And repeat.

"Knock, knock... anyone home?"

"You're a jerk," I mutter as I walk past him and toward the unsteady old jetty which is swaying along with the tide. Standing at the beginning of the broken plank, I watch the dark, murky water while the weight of Wes' actions begins to sink in. My shoulders fall, drooping and dragging the rest of my body down. My shaking hands move to the necklace sitting on my chest—a small heart Wes had given me on our first anniversary. Pulling the chain left and right, my anger overshadowing the hurt makes me remove the chain, and with one mighty yank it flies in the air and hits the water with a splash.

"What the fuck is wrong with you?" Taking giant steps toward me, Logan shouts through the quiet night, "You were fine until you checked your phone. Then you switched into queen bitch mode."

My voice remains silent, ignoring his use of derogatory names.

"So what? You're too good for us now?"

I spin around, matching his stance and moving closer to intimidate him. "I'm too good for you? How about the fact you guys think you're too good for me? After all... you left me behind." Sucking in a deep breath, I let it all go. "That call was my publicist. Wesley's been caught fucking some hooker."

His fiery, persistent stare turns to pity and the last thing I need is Logan's pity.

"A hooker?"

"Hookers." I laugh deliriously. "And sniffing coke off their asses. Because God forbid, you've got nowhere else to sniff that shit from." My lips quiver, tears threatening to fall. I don't want to give Wes the satisfaction, but emotions are a powerful thing. When you think you're strong and made out of steel, they'll make you crumble and fall harder than you can possibly imagine.

I stare at my hands, watching them shake as that trapped tear falls down my cheek, followed by another then a stream.

"I hate him!" I cry out desperately and unable to speak coherently. "The whole world will know what he did to me. I'm stupid. So... fucking... stupid... for ignoring every sign that stared me right in the fucking face."

I fall to my knees, the cold dirt grazing them instantly. "Everyone told me to marry him. He wants to get married and have kids. We argue about it all the time. I don't want kids yet. It's why we got George."

I gulp for air, sobbing uncontrollably. "He just kept pushing and telling me our brand is everything. I had no one to confide in. No one to tell me I'm an idiot for believing all his goddamn lies."

"Jesus, Emmy. Where's your fucking backbone? Since when do you listen to a guy?" Logan criticizes me.

"I don't know," I admit. "Mom knows most of it, but I've filtered out the horrible stuff. Like when he tried to switch my birth control pills to have me fall pregnant."

Logan gazes at me with a pained expression, lips taut without saying a word.

"It was never about me. It was always about the network. They needed a storyline. When the ratings dipped slightly they wanted a scandal. What better scandal than two costars getting knocked up after only one season of filming?"

"So, why the fuck did you stay with him? Do you know how stupid it makes you look?"

Logan's bluntness is exactly what I needed—two years ago. Right now though, his words hurt and my already bruised ego can't take any more. I want to crawl into a dark hole and forget the world exists. Pretend I have no life waiting or millions of fans watching my every move.

"You know what? You don't care at all. You and Ash call yourself family, yet of the few times I've reached out to you, you guys didn't give a goddamn shit."

"I could say the same thing," he argues back.

"When? When did you reach out to me?"

He keeps quiet, rubbing his neck with the palm of his hand while staring at the ground.

"Exactly. So don't tell me how *stupid* I am. It's bad enough I now have this on my shoulders. You putting me down doesn't empower me when I need all the strength I can get right now. I've fucked up. I trusted him and look where it's gotten me."

"I'm sorry. What a fucking asshole," he yells, much to my surprise. "Do you want me to call my people?"

"Your people?" I question, confused. "To do what?"

"Whatever you want."

"Cut his dick off doing a Lorena Bobbitt?"

He cringes, his posture falling over as if he knows what that feels like. "If that's your wish."

"Your people can really do that? Who are these people?"

"People."

I sigh, then let out an unexpected cry.

I hate him.

I want bad things to happen to him.

I want lots of people to make his life hell.

The bastard has hurt me more than I thought imaginable. I'm embarrassed the whole world watched me fall in love with an asshole. And now the whole world will watch as my life falls apart.

What about George?

Will he live with me?

Is there such thing as a custody battle for dogs?

Will he stay with Wes every other weekend? Poor George! He doesn't deserve to be raised in this type of environment. I wonder if there's a support group for pugs being raised in a broken home.

In the heat of the moment, I grab my phone out of my purse and throw it into the lake.

What have I done?

Oh crap!

It clicks seconds later as the ripples in the water disappear.

I run without thinking and dive straight into the water then remember the lake is filled with many creepy creatures. It's not too deep where I land, and in the distance I hear Logan's voice who's angry and annoyed, followed by the splash beside me.

I bob down again, searching for my phone with tears battling against the water and my sobs muffled. I scream, then yell, cursing at Wesley Rich for breaking my trust. For tearing my heart into a million pieces and for making me believe what we had was love. And when I pull myself up for air, Logan's standing in front of me, breathing heavily with my phone in his hand.

"Are you psycho? Seriously, Emmy!"

"Don't call me that," I shout back in his face.

"Well, you are. So, the dickhead cheated? Move on. He didn't deserve you to begin with. Marriage is for the weak. Don't fall into that whole love bullshit. You can have a good life without it."

"What would you know?" I argue, ungrateful he found my phone. "You've never been in love. At least, I took a chance."

"Geez woman, will you listen to yourself? Here's your damn phone. Don't throw an expensive phone in the lake." He pushes it toward my chest, eyes wide and fueled with anger.

"You're all the same, that's the problem," I mouth off,

not sure where I'm going with this because anger only sees one path—destruction.

"You need to cool off. I'm surprised this cold water ain't doing that. And for the record, Emmy, we're not all the same."

"Yes, you are. It's all about the pussy. The more you get the bigger you feel. There's no good men out there who actually believe in love and being faithful. Ash will fuck up. He's just like you, can't keep his dick in his pants."

"Emerson," he rasps, holding onto my wrist and watching me carefully. "You're angry. You have every right to be angry. Just don't destroy the people who love you because of how he treated you. He's the dick. He doesn't deserve you. End of story."

"Doesn't deserve me?" I laugh again. "Who am I? I don't even know who I am. Everything I do in life is for everyone else. Make everyone else happy. Entertain the world. My whole life is in the tabloids. Nothing I do is private. I'm sick of it, sick of it all! And it's my fault. Dad warned me and I didn't listen. I was so pissed off that you and Ash left me to be big stars that I wanted to rival you."

"And you did," he admits with a smirk. "You're the most wanted TV star. I know men who jerk off just talking about you."

I cringe, aware something foreign has brushed against my leg.

"That's gross," I say flatly, calming down. "Well, it depends who, but still... you really like to paint a picture and distract one's thoughts."

"I'm just saying you're gorgeous."

I keep my breathing still until the slimy, furry thing brushes against my leg again and I scream, jumping into Logan's body and wrapping my arms around his neck.

Without even thinking, I also wrap my legs around his waist scared half out of my mind.

"Oh. My. God! What the hell is that? An anaconda?"

His arms lace around my entire body, protecting me from the beast.

"Emmy," he whispers, the sound of his smooth voice calming my racing heart. "Stop living the lie. Do something for you. You owe it to yourself."

This is the most serious conversation we've ever had. I'm waiting for him to laugh, or give me a wet-willy and drop me into the beast's mouth. But it doesn't happen.

"I'm scared," I admit in the softest voice.

"Of what?"

"That you'll give me a wedgie."

The stupidity of the situation has slapped me in the face. First, I throw my phone like a tantrum-throwing toddler. Then, I find myself in the arms of Logan Carrington, who no doubt, is plotting something wicked in his sadistic mind.

Between the moon which reflects off the water and the darkness which surrounds us, the sounds of his hitched breathing echo enough for me to remain still. In some crazy way, my heart begins to beat wildly, mirroring his breathing.

"Will you just shut up for once?" he grunts out with a sullen glare. The complete opposite to the calm demeanor he showed only moments ago.

I exhale as if his threats don't affect me, challenging him because he hasn't changed one bit. Still, a stubborn know-it-all who thinks he's king. Rule the world and everyone around him must bow down.

"Yeah? Well... make me," I say in defiance, holding my arms out so we stare face-to-face.

Something in the way his eyes bore into me, warns me

again that Logan never plays fair. He always takes things to the next level. His hand slides down my back and over my ass. My dress is floating, and with one move, his palm is against my bare cheek after he scrunches my panties aside in his hand. It doesn't help my reflexes are slow. With my hands ready to push him away, the jolt of my body from his fingers brushing against the entrance of my pussy startles me—the moan barely at bay as he repeats the movement again.

Is this happening?

You're dreaming...

This is some sort of nightmare that you'll wake up from soon... like now... or now... or now.

Wake up!

My mouth falls open, pressing against his ear from the pressure of him drawing our bodies close together. And just when I think my imagination has played wild and crazy tricks on me, his lips move to my collarbone, biting down on my skin.

"Logan," I whisper, strained and holding back the pain from his bite. "What are you doing?"

Not answering my question, he buries his head in my neck and grips harder. I have no idea what's going on and feel helpless because I'm unable to stop it.

This is wrong.

This is weird.

Why am I not fighting back?

His fingers dance around my entrance, and in one quick move, he shifts my panties to one side and they glide effortlessly inside causing me to suck a breath in and arch back while my body melts into him. His pace quickens and my blood begins to heat, my skin steaming in the cold water.

My body begins to act on instinct, succumbing to the

fire in my belly which is rising slowly and clouding any rational thoughts. With small but quick moans, my arms wrap around his back tighter, desperate to avoid eye contact while he continues to slide in and out.

The waves of the water allow my hips to sway freely, in sync with every thrust.

My stomach begins to flutter—the fire is beyond control —and is followed by a swirl which builds up and makes my whole body react. I'm sensitive to every touch and movement. Biting down on the tip of his shoulder, I lose control. My teeth dig into his skin as the ache mixed with fire ignites on every surface of my body and barrels through me in one explosive orgasm.

With my eyes closed, I ride the contractions which wrap around his finger and immerse myself in the pleasurable sensations overcoming me. The rise and fall of my chest evens out, reality setting in as to what I've done.

What *we* have done.

I don't have any words. I'm speechless. Incoherent.

Basking in an intense orgasm from just *one* finger.

The finger which belongs to the one man you vowed never to touch. And he vowed never to touch you.

So now what?

"I n-need to g-go," I stutter nervously, embarrassed and looking for an escape.

"Emmy," he calls softly, gripping me tightly in his embrace.

Squirming my way out of his grip, I muster every ounce of strength in my body and swim away as fast as I can, desperate to escape what's just happened.

The water becomes shallow as I stand to run away, but I'm completely soaked with water and one other thing.

Guilt.

FIVE

*"**Reality is a cold hard bitch.**"*
~ *Emerson Chase*

Bang. Bang.
Thump. Thump.
The vocals are loud, piercing my eardrums while my eyes stare directly at the ceiling. The sun is peeking through the blinds, reminding me of another beautiful spring day. With summer just around the corner, the air has become warmer removing the morning chill.

It's unusually warm this morning, my large bed socks becoming overbearingly hot. That, coupled with the constant pain in my head, leaves me frustrated and increasingly hostile.

After all these years, Dad hasn't changed one bit. He prides himself on being an early bird, the kind of person who wakes at 5:00 a.m., and has done more in the first two hours than I could achieve in one whole day.

When we were kids, he would blast music through the house at 6:00 a.m. forcing us all up.

Today's no different.

Mom used to complain, being a night owl like me. Yet, years of being married—to the most stubborn man ever—has her changing her ways. She hates to admit it, but she told me she gets more writing done first thing in the morning than she does at any other time of day.

I have to admit I've changed over the years, finding myself waking up early to get in a run or hang out at the local coffee shop before the swarms of paparazzi find me.

Great when you're on the West Coast.

The East Coast time difference totally kicks my butt.

I love Bon Jovi. I aced *Livin' on a Prayer* singing karaoke at pub crawls back in the college years. However, I don't enjoy it when I'm nursing the biggest hangover, *ever*.

Turning my body sideways, I snuggle on my side glancing at the pile of clothes I left on my bathroom floor.

Wet clothes.

From the lake.

The lake where Logan...

Don't say it!

You've forgotten all about it.

Okay, I'm calling bullshit on myself. You haven't forgotten about it. You slept. You slept because you cried yourself to sleep due to life being so fucked up and you have no clue what the hell happened last night.

Wesley Rich cheated on your gullible ass—that's what happened.

And, you hate yourself for enjoying what Logan gave you.

The soft pillow is perfect to bury my face into and try to

block out the images which haunt me as last night replays over in my mind.

I'm angry—livid. To the point where nothing makes sense.

One could assume my state of mind is bordering insanity, and I'm one step away from swatting the imaginary flies away from my face.

Thinking about the moment I saw the image of Wesley and how terribly sick to the stomach I felt, and how all I could think about was every promise we made to each other and how easily he'd forgotten them.

I bite on the pillow and let out a frustrated scream, knowing no one in the house can hear me with the loud music playing. The second I do, I regret it instantly as sharp pain ricochets straight through my temple causing me to wince and let out a muffled cry.

I begin to open my eyes again—forced to face reality.

My phone sits on top of my nightstand, dead and unable to turn on. *Your own fault.*

Leaning over the side of the bed with great difficulty, I remove my iPad from my bag. Dragging it up and onto my lap, I shuffle into a sitting position and tap on my inbox to start reading an email.

Emerson,
I know you're angry and not taking any calls. You know I don't like to take sides, I work for both you and Wesley.
But, he's an idiot.
I've negotiated a deal with a photographer, and have our lawyers drawing up contracts now. 2 mill and he's gone. It's our only way out of this.
Talk when you're back home.

Cheers,

Nina

P.S. I spoke to Wesley this morning. He's been trying to call you.

The temptation to chuck my iPad across the room crossed my mind. But I'm done throwing my expensive electronics because of what he's done.

Two million dollars?

Fuck! Money we worked hard for, down the fucking drain. I don't even want to think about how that affects our investments, it's the last thing on my mind right now.

I can tell by Nina's tone she hasn't slept. Probably the biggest scandal to rock her portfolio since one of her clients impregnated some illegal immigrant who babysat his kids.

My head falls back on the headboard. I have two choices here—one, I work with Nina and fix this fucking mess or two, bury my head in the sand like an ostrich.

There were so many things to think about, but my head's aching and my stomach begins to growl. To be honest, I'm surprised I even have an appetite given the amount of alcohol pumping through my bloodstream.

I climb out of bed knowing there's no way I can continue to sit here and do nothing. If I sneak downstairs now, I can possibly avoid Logan. I didn't even ask where he, Ash, or Alessandra were staying because I was too caught up in my own mess to think about any of it. I assume they're staying here and the thought makes me want to retreat back to bed.

There's no chance in hell I can look at Logan again. We can also kiss our friendship goodbye. Last night was many things, and regret is one of them.

As I step into the bathroom, I strip down to nothing and

stare at myself in the mirror. The reflection shows my pale skin, a few scratches on my leg from the random creature who attacked it. I run my fingers along my collarbone and notice a small bite mark on the top of my shoulder. The tips of my fingers run over the minor groove and my senses heighten. His teeth had bitten so hard it's left a small, purplish mark against my pale skin.

Closing my eyes, I focus on the throb between my legs which is persistent and ravenous. How did I let this happen? Was this a pity fuck? It wasn't even a fuck, merely a finger fuck for God's sake.

Opening my eyes quickly, I twist my body and turn the faucet allowing only cold water. I need to wash this away. The hurt, guilt, and desire for someone who should never ever be in my thoughts.

Logan Carrington? *What the fuck were you thinking!*

I linger in the cold shower blissfully unaware of my surroundings until I hear the lawnmower outside.

Dad's really pulling out all the stops.

Quickly getting out, I dry myself and dress in my denim shorts and a white tank with a unicorn on the front. I purposely wear my bikini underneath, hoping to catch some rays later when everyone's gone.

When Logan is gone... that's what you mean.

My hair is wet and tangled, which I manage to brush and tie up into a bun. I had it cut recently to the length of my collarbone, something Wes hates because he loves long hair.

Before I leave the bathroom, I pick up my damp and reeking of lake water clothes from last night. Throwing them into the basin, I run the water allowing the dress to soak before handwashing out the grime. *Poor kitties.* Their faces look sad and riddled with guilt.

Taking a deep breath, I walk to the door and place my hand on the handle. I haven't thought about what I'll say if I see him. It's only 7:05 a.m. and the boys train every morning for two hours. They won't be home until eight. That gives me forty-five minutes to grab breakfast then find somewhere to hide. *So much for not being an ostrich.*

I make my way to the kitchen. Only Mom is inside, sipping coffee and reading some book with a shirtless man on the cover called The Billionaire's Dirty Maid.

"Thinking of switching professions?" I tease, sitting on the stool facing her. When my ass touches the hard wood I'm quick to flinch, uncomfortable and sore.

Don't go there. Not in front of Mom.

What if she can hear your thoughts? She will forever judge you for what you've allowed him to do.

Mom places the book on the table, careful to keep her bookmark in place. She's dressed in a light blue buttoned shirt and white tennis shorts, her hair is swept back into a tight ponytail.

"Good morning." She smiles, sliding the box of cereal my way and follows with a cup of black coffee just the way I like it. "You got home late last night. I'm guessing you crawled home considering the dark circles around your eyes?"

I nod, lips pursed with my hands wrapped around the warm mug.

"I see nothing much has changed with the three of you. Instead of staying out and sneaking in candy, you've swapped it for rounds of alcohol."

I nod again, choosing my words carefully. "Except, now we have a fourth member."

Mom's eyes fall to her cup, and only now I notice she has dark circles too. They're not as prominent as mine, but enough to notice she probably spent most of the night crying. I feel terrible for not being a better daughter and supporting her.

"Mom, I'm guessing you didn't have a great night either?"

She shakes her head, lips pursed just like mine. Sometimes it's like looking in the mirror. Even the way her hands wrap around the mug exactly the way mine do. To top it off, she enjoys a strong, black coffee much like myself.

"Your only son comes home and tells you he's married some girl after knowing her for around one minute. There goes your life-long dream of watching him get married, dressing up in some fancy suit and giving him away in front of family and friends. I don't ask for much as a parent, Emmy, but promise me you won't hide something that big from me."

"I won't, Mom," I reassure her, hiding the guilt which riddles me.

What happened with Logan will *never* ever happen again, and as far as I'm concerned I wouldn't class it as something big anyway. It's a mere teeny tiny speck in our drama-filled lives.

Her eyes begin to tear up, so I quickly offer to change the subject to something more light-hearted.

"So, tell me, what's your latest book about?"

The expression on her face immediately changes. When Mom's asked about her writing or books, you can see the passion light up her face.

"It's a messy love square. I know I might get some backlash from readers, but I can't help but adore a good love square. Triangles are so done."

"Fun to read not fun to be in." I smile.

Mom begins to open her mouth when the back door

bangs against the wall and the sound of Ash and Logan filter through the kitchen. I look up at the clock on the wall, it's 7:30 a.m.

No!

There's no time to escape.

So I stare at my bowl of cereal nervously swirling the Froot Loops around the bowl and dunking them in the milk.

"If it isn't my overly opinionated sister. Ready to apologize yet?"

Thirty minutes ago, I was all about grabbing life by the balls. But when the guy who you've practically known your whole life—and is considered as family—is standing in the same room boring his eyes into you because he gave you an amazing orgasm, those balls have shriveled up and climbed into your asshole for shelter.

"Of course, not. Stubborn as usual." Ash laughs, grabbing a slice of bread and shoving it in his mouth with nothing on it.

My eyes are heavy, refusing to make eye contact. I raise them slowly hopeful Logan's not looking my way. As every inch of my gaze passes, my stare traces over his muscular body, analyzing it like I've never seen it before. By the time our eyes meet, his wicked smirk irks me as I shift my gaze once again.

Asshole.

"Geez Emmy, you can't even look at me. Yeah, I get it. I got married and didn't tell you. Would you just give Sandy a chance?"

"Sandy?" I throw at him in amusement. "You nicknamed her Sandy? That's so crass. Who are you? Danny Zuko?"

"Who the hell is Danny Zuko?"

I roll my eyes at my brother. Thank God stupidity isn't contagious.

"Sounds like quite a night," Mom interrupts. "How about we slow down on the drinking?"

"We were celebrating," Ash claims. "At least, until Emmy ran off like a child and Logan had to save her. What the fuck were you thinking jumping into the lake? Have you not heard of all the shit lurking in those waters? Jesus Christ, Emmy!"

I swallow the giant lump in my throat. There's no way Logan would have told Ash anything despite them being best friends. If Ash knew, he would have said something by now and Logan would be in the firing line.

Scrap that... Logan would be *dead*.

"I agree with your brother, silly move. Look at this bite on your neck?" Mom runs her finger across the mark that Logan left. I can feel my skin blushing, almost breaking out into hives as Mom scans her eyes over it.

I won't look at him. Instead, I continue to stare at my colorful bowl of cereal and pretend each loop is a buoy. One I can jump into and save me from the mess I've allowed to happen.

"I think I got bitten, too," Logan pipes up.

He removes his training shirt, showing off his sculpted abs and defined muscles. He's covered in sweat, but it only makes his torso look extra sexy.

You didn't just use that word.

While he continues to stand there half-naked, my body is battling with the unusual desire to lick the sweat from in between his abs, and the guilt reminds me I'm no better than Wes.

"Holy shit, bro? Something got you real good," Ash

comments loudly. "You better thank Logan for saving your sorry ass, Emmy."

"Thanks, Logan, for saving my sorry ass," I say dryly, pretending this conversation bores me when all I want to do is leave the room because there's this dark hole I'm sinking into and it is calling my name.

"It's okay, your sorry ass is probably grateful," he responds without emotion, matching my game.

I stand up, then push the stool under the counter, needing to clear my head. This is not how I intend to spend my time at home.

"Come hang with us today, Emmy. Sandy's out running but she'll be back soon. We're flying out at midnight, so we need to be outta here by eight."

Perfect. All I have to do is avoid them for the next thirteen hours and then I won't be seeing Logan for a very, long time. Maybe never.

"I'd love to, but I promised a friend I'd visit her today."

"What friend?" Ash questions, arms folded as if he's called my bluff. "The hot one, Audrey-or-something, the one with the perky rack?"

Logan's reaction to the 'perky rack' comment says it all. With his grin fixed and eyes dancing with excitement, it's easy to see he's moved past last night. *I'm just another notch on his belt.*

"No," I reply with haste. "None of your business."

Leaving the kitchen, I quickly make my way down the hall and up the stairs toward my room. Turning the corner, and just a few feet from my door, I feel my body being held back and the grip on my arm tight and rigid. "You can't avoid me forever."

I keep my back toward him, not wanting to deal with this right now.

"I'm not another notch. It was a mistake, okay? Just a poor reaction to some bad news."

"Excuse me?" He turns me around to face him.

Thank God his shirt's back on. My focus moves to the picture hanging in the background. It's my entire family including Logan and Aunty Reese. They have been in our lives forever. Even Logan's older sister, Laura, is standing beside me holding my hand because that's what she always did. A protector who looked out for me until she left to study in Japan with her grandparents.

In just one picture, you can see how tight our bond is. We are family—irrelevant of the blood flowing through our veins.

And then we both do this. It's wrong. So very wrong.

"What notch?" Logan growls, keeping his voice and temper unheard by the rest of the house.

"Notch on your belt. I was upset last night. You were there. Kinda like lover's revenge."

The minute I said it his expression changed. His heaving chest from his angered state remains oddly calm. His mouths opens as if he's about to speak yet, no words come out.

I take one last look at him, ready to terminate this conversation and walk away.

"Thankfully, I've got a long belt. Another notch ain't nothing to me," he brags, winking at me with an air of arrogance. With just one step, his back is to me and he quickly disappears around the hall. The quick footsteps echo against the dark chocolate floorboards until they completely fade.

Suddenly, the door to my sister's room opens, and she's standing against the frame in a pair of oversized sweats and a T-shirt that's matched in size. Sitting on top of her head is a messy bun with two pencils placed like a cross, it must be the latest fad or something.

"Ouch," she adds with a sympathetic smile before losing attention and directing it to the phone which sits in her hand.

"Please don't say anything," I beg. "It was a mistake." *Yeah. A big fucking mistake.*

"I won't," she promises. "But only if you don't tell Mom about this." She pulls her sweats down and reveals a tattoo of a rose that takes up most of her upper thigh. It's quite pretty—shaded in the colors of pink and blue.

"Oh. You're dead meat." I whistle.

"Not as much as you'll be if she finds out about you being a notch on Logan's very long belt."

I ignore her comment and enter her room. There's a white, plush sofa near the window where I throw myself and think of my next move.

Tayla's room is very bright. Decorated with purple wall-paper and black and white photos scattered all over the walls. She really enjoys photography, it's one of her passions next to texting.

"Can I borrow your phone?" I ask, hopping up into a sitting position.

"Yeah." She quickly scrolls on the phone then hands it to me. "Where's yours?"

"Long story."

I send a text to Nina, telling her I'm coming home tonight. She replies instantly and tells me to sit tight while she organizes flights and bodyguards to escort me at LAX—an extra precaution given I'm alone. I don't see the big deal and wait for fifteen minutes for the flight details to arrive.

"I have to go back home," I tell Tayla without mentioning anymore about Logan.

"Mom will be sad."

"I know, but I have to take care of something."

"Okay." She shrugs, losing interest.

"Tayla," I hesitate, sitting on the edge of the sofa with my feet flat on the ground. "I'm sorry if I haven't been around much."

Swiveling to face me, she crosses her legs. "You're busy. I'm busy. Ash's busy. It's cool."

"It's not cool. I should be here for you. As a big sister."

Looking around her room, I realize I have no idea who she is anymore. Almost like she's changed overnight. Tayla's entrance to our family came with mixed emotions. It had been Ash and me for so long then all of a sudden a baby was thrown into our lives. By the time she began to walk and talk, we were hitting puberty and busying ourselves with all the cool things teenagers do.

Since I began the show, my life has changed forever. Back-to-back filming plus, commercials, photo shoots, interviews, and then I ventured into my own business which Wes joined me soon after.

Our fitness line is something I feel passionate about—comfortable and affordable for the everyday consumer. I added my sparkle by throwing colors and patterns, instead of your boring black workout pants. Given my popularity on the show, the demands for the clothing exceeded our expectations and made us a fortune.

From there, we branched out further. Purchasing our apartment then a small cottage in the hills which we rent out. Wes does a ton of endorsements, and I was offered many which I declined at the time due to my hectic lifestyle. Add in there the social events including red carpets, award shows, and premieres and we have little time for anything else.

Wes doesn't like me coming home without him, and he's only visited once in three years.

That will change now.

It's all about to change.

I simply need to get on a plane and find a way to end the show.

And breaking up with Wes will do just that.

SIX

"The key to moving on is denial.
That, and eating cake." ~ Emerson Chase

I fell asleep on Tayla's couch, only to wake up soon after to the sound of a horn honking out the front of the house. My vision is blurred and worsens as I rub my eyes, exhausted and drained from all the worry and stress.

Hiding out in her room seemed logical, but with my stomach growling and my mouth parched, I know I'll have to make my way to the kitchen again eventually. And most importantly, I have to tell Mom I'm heading home early. I need a distraction. Something to occupy my mind and push away the pain even if only for a few moments.

"Can I borrow your computer?" I ask, mindful she has 'Property of Tayla Chase' stickered all over her electronics.

"Sure," she replies, moving off the bed and to me. She

leans over and types in the password quickly like I'm spying.

I thank her kindly with a trace of sarcasm, then proceed to log into my account and check my unread emails. Nina's sent another long email. Apparently, she's in full damage control mode and the network execs are beyond pissed. Wesley's being flown back to the States for an emergency meeting. They request I be there to discuss the future of the show also. It seems unnatural to sit in a boardroom and discuss how to fix our relationship. The thought of being in the same room with Wes makes my skin crawl. To think he could do that and expect me to carry on like nothing's happened makes me question my sanity.

Yet, once again, without any warning, my heart sinks as the love I feel for this man cannot easily be erased. With a quiet sniff, I hold back the tears, tired of crying over something I have no control over.

The damage is done—he's broken us.

Exiting out of the email, I run the mouse along the other highlighted items. I go by an alias name of Jane Smith. The plainest name one can think of. Using my real name's not an option with all the hackers who stalk the Internet.

There's a lot of junk including emails from retailers with their latest offerings, a grant to inherit money from dying widows in Africa if I click and provide my credit card details.

My eyes immediately stop scrolling when I notice a new email from John Smith.

Jane,
Avoidance can only get you so far.
John

I check my contact list to remind myself who John Smith is then it clicks—Logan.

Jane, John, and Joe—the three Smiths.

We did this so we could communicate with each other and keep our lives private, but we've been using text messages more recently. Ash sends me links to stupid videos of animals doing crazy things, and occasionally he sends an article worth reading. Logan rarely emails me anything unless we're in a group email.

My fingers rest on the keyboard, not sure how to respond.

Tayla's busying herself watching some hair tutorial on YouTube while I stare at the screen. Slowly, at less than a snail's pace, my fingers begin to move on their own accord.

John,
Same with cockiness. Don't you have another notch
to grove into your ever-growing belt?
Jane

I contemplate shutting down my email, but something makes me keep it open. It's almost as if I'm waiting to see how he can possibly respond to that. I swivel around on my chair and see Tayla smiling at something on her screen. "What's so funny?"

She looks up, unaware I've been watching her. "Oh, just a comment this guy left."

"Oh..." I acknowledge with a grin. "A guy?"

She nods, still smiling. "Yeah, we're not dating. He has a girlfriend..." she pauses, her eyes going up like she's in deep thought and then she continues, "... I think. He leaves comments here and there and they're just funny."

"Young love... I remember those days. Except, we didn't have phones so it was all about passing a note."

"A note? That's so old school."

"You're telling me. It would have been so much fun messaging a boy rather than passing a note down the class-room hoping that the gossip queen, Rosie Peach, won't sneak a look at it."

The sound of a faint ding catches my attention. Turning around to face the screen, I see another email from John Smith. Anxiously, I open it, not realizing I'm holding my breath.

Jane,
I think I might retire the belt for a while. A wise
woman once told me I was just like the rest of them.
I'm out to prove her wrong.
John

My eyes dart over the email, and for some reason, I can't hold back my smile. *My words have sunk in.* I try to think of a witty response, only I come up with nothing but lame replies, so I log out of my email and turn around.

"Should we talk about what happened in the hall?" I raise the topic wanting to clear the air and ease the guilt plaguing me.

"I think it's pretty self-explanatory. You screwed Logan. Ash... Mom and Dad will kill you."

"I... I didn't screw him," I stammer.

"Potato, potahto."

Is this a potato, potahto situation, though?

My crazy brain is justifying what happened as a slip of a finger. Maybe it accidentally made its way around the groove and just got lost. Okay, your brain is stupid and on some sort of crack. Accidental 'slips' don't result in such an intense orgasm.

"I really don't want to delve into the semantics but it was a mistake. Can we move on? I've had a shitty twenty-four hours."

Raising her perfectly sculpted eyebrows, she's quick to remind me, "Sure. But you brought it up you know?"

"I know," I say lightly, desperate to switch topics and blaming myself for bringing it up in the first place. "Do you want to go for swim?"

"Yeah, why not." Tayla hops off the bed, disappearing into her wardrobe. I tell her I'll be back, sneaking out of her room and bolting to mine like a fugitive on the run.

"We rarely get to do the girl thing anymore."

Mom is dressed in a white caftan and oversized sun hat, she's applying lotion as Tayla lays beside her drenched in oil. Mom hands the bottle to her, motioning for Tayla to put some on or out will come the story of Uncle Larry and his mystery mole that developed into skin cancer.

"We should do a girls' trip. No men or boys. No phones," Mom suggests, getting comfortable on the large cabana lounge.

"You lost me at no phones," Tayla mumbles with closed eyes.

"I'm in. But it'll have to be between filming..." I trail off, almost revealing my doubts about the show even continuing. I'm grateful Logan hasn't said anything. At least, if he had, I know Mom would have been quick to mention it.

The sun is out in full glory with the hot rays piercing my pale skin. I grab some lotion and rub it all over my body before closing my eyes underneath my sunglasses. Lasting only a few minutes, the heat becomes unbearable so I dive into the pool for a quick splash. The water's freezing against my hot skin, and with my entire body wet I climb onto the sizeable pink flamingo which is floating on the surface and lay across it, attempting to relax my mind and body.

I drift in and out of thoughts as Tayla cranks up the latest Bruno Mars album. It doesn't seem to bother Mom with her porno book in hand and iced tea in the other. I contemplate getting out of the pool, but the serenity and company ease my apprehension. I feel confident that perhaps in an hour or so, I can find the strength to talk to Mom and tell her what Wes has done. I tell myself another five more minutes until the five minutes passes and I make another excuse. On my fourth five-minute pep talk, the sudden sound of a splash followed by cold water hitting my heated skin, startles me to the point I almost fall off the flamingo in shock.

Fuck. Ash and Logan.

If I ignore them, maybe I can float away.

I also hate the fact that Logan's right—avoidance can only get you so far.

Alessandra is courteous, she's taking slow steps into the pool, careful not to lose the skimpy gold bikini which barely covers her body parts. Tayla follows behind her, admiring her bikini and asking where it's from. They seem to bond instantly over fashion, and somewhere deep inside I curb the teeny, tiny jealousy which begins to form because Tayla never asks me what I'm wearing. Unless, of course, it's to tell me my outfit is 'so last year.'

With Ash, Alessandra, and Tayla swimming in the pool, Logan stands on the edge watching us with a sly expression. His black swimming shorts sit mid-thigh enhancing his toned legs. Surprisingly, he wears a tan despite living in a country which rarely sees sun. The self-absorbed bastard probably hits the tanning salon. His eyes dart back and forth until they're locked on mine, and reminiscent of when we were kids he winks before diving into the pool heading straight to me.

I don't have enough time to do anything, and within a second, I fall into the cold water. I'm barely able to catch my breath, swallowing a mouthful.

Asshole!

The water accidentally travels up my nose, and when I make it up for air I ignore the pain that shoots to my temple and unleash my thoughts with a mouthful of profanities.

"You jerk! What kind of asshole planet are you from to do that?"

"You looked hot," he points out, complacent, and keeping his jaw firm. "Plus, I want to lay on your pink flamingo."

Ash snorts, pathetically, trying to hide his laughter.

I let out a huff, swimming away from them, annoyed at their childish behavior.

The step of the pool is finally beneath my feet, and I turn around to sit down while catching my breath and controlling my erratic heartbeat.

Despite Mom being poolside, Ash is busy making Alessandra giggle. From where I sit, it looks inappropriate with his hands beneath the water doing something I'd rather not know.

Logan's leaning on my flamingo with his arms crossed and shades on. My eyes wander along the water dripping from his burly arms to the way his hands rest on the floatie.

The same hands which are connected to the fingers that entered me.

Fingers that made me weak in the knees.

Jesus, I need to stop staring.

It's like arm and hand porn at its finest.

And only a few minutes ago, you were hating on him so bad.

"All right, how about I make us some lunch? Daddy will be back soon, and you need to get to the airport, Emmy," Mom reminds me, standing up from the cabana and dusting the back of her caftan while adjusting her sunglasses.

"You're leaving already?" Logan questions, eyes hidden beneath his shades.

"I changed my flight. I have to attend to some stuff back home. Avoidance only gets you so far," I cite, purposely avoiding eye contact with him.

I know he understands, knowing no one else will.

Mom's shocked I'm leaving early, but doesn't pry as to why specifically or what needs to be taken care of, assuming the network needs me for filming. Which is not unusual, she's used to me having to leave at the drop of a hat. If the network calls, I answer.

"C'mon, Emmy," Ash complains shortly after. "We never get to hang out anymore."

Bowing my head, I apologize and climb out of the water, walking to the pool house. With Mom making her way to the kitchen, I welcome the quiet with the intention of showering and changing into something less revealing for lunch.

Outside—where they all remain—the laughter contin-ues. The noise is muffled as I close the door behind me and enter the bathroom looking for a spare towel. The pool house is small. It's made up of a sitting area with a corner white lounge facing a flat screen television, and off to the right is a bedroom with a queen-sized bed. Everything is decorated in white and teal with matching artwork on the walls.

A gush of wind graces my skin, followed by Logan calling my name. I exit the bathroom to find him standing in the entrance with the door shut behind him. I throw him my towel and grab another, hoping he uses it to cover his half-naked body.

I'm done avoiding the topic. Wanting to clear the air between us, so I open my mouth quickly. "Listen, thanks for not saying anything to Ash or Mom. I'm not ready to talk to them about what's happened with Wes."

Leaning down, he dries his legs with the large towel before throwing it over his shoulder.

Why does his body need to look so good wet?

"You need to tell them. Especially your mom. Abbi will be upset if she knows you've hidden that from her. You never hide anything from her."

He's right. Mom does need to know. I just don't want to tell her I've failed... *again.* Also, add the burden after she's already feeling like a bad mom because of what Ash did.

I was always that kid who felt people would judge my mistakes on how I was raised. It saddens me to think people can be quick to point blame on Mom and Dad—terrible parents who raised a woman who was cheated on by her fiancé. Of course, they had nothing to do with Wes being a dickhead, but society has a way of placing blame to those who are innocent.

"I know..." I pause, treading carefully on the giant elephant gracing the room. "About what happened, Logan... I don't know what came over me, and we need to take this to the grave. Yes, I tell Mom everything, but not this."

Bowing his head, his mouth widens with a grin as he

lets out a loose chuckle, clutching his stomach with his hand.

Oh, why does he have to go and do that—make me look at his damn abs.

"What's so funny?" I ask, avoiding the rush of excitement which comes from looking at the most simplest body part— his stomach.

"That you didn't know what *came* over you."

I can feel the heat rising beneath my skin, the embarrassment of him witnessing a very intimate moment I've only shared with a handful of men. I have two choices— spin through the door like the Tasmanian Devil or take the mickey out of the situation.

"I'm usually not so quick." The moment it left my mouth I smack my forehead as Logan laughs. "I mean... God, this is embarrassing."

"I get it," he blurts out mid-laugh. "You're usually not an early shooter."

"I'm not exactly shooting anything, I think. That's a guy thing."

"Women can shoot."

"What exactly are they shooting?" Curious, I cross my arms beneath my breasts, waiting on his response.

With his eyebrow raised, he rubs his chin, delighted at the choice of topic. "You want the medical explanation?"

"You know what?" I shake my head unable to hide my grin. "Never mind. I'm sure if the questions persist I'll find my answer on Google along with a hundred disturbing sexual facts I didn't know existed."

"I'm happy to explain. Perhaps, educate you if needed." The corner of his mouth curves upward, wickedly teasing and coaxing me to say yes. Yet, I realize from years of experience, Logan Carrington knows how to manipulate me. Whether it be for the good or bad.

"I'm set." I laugh. "So, we're good?"

"We're good."

I contemplate hugging it out, but with my bikini on and his bare chest, I decide against it.

Saying goodbye, I leave him standing alone in the pool house with the intention of going home and forgetting our moment in the lake. I'm not sure if it was the shooting talk or our pact to forget what happened, but either way, the guilt's no longer there.

Our secret will remain *our* secret.

SEVEN

"I don't ask for much except my freedom."
~ *Emerson Chase*

The flight from home was turbulent and *long*.
After several delays, due to some bad weather, the plane was diverted and landed in Burbank.

I'm glad to get off—my stomach's queasy from the bumpy flight.

I barely made the flight to begin with being caught up at the repair store who replaced the battery in my phone. Apparently, all it needs is a charge and then it will be good to go. Thank God, because I feel naked without it.

Jimmy, my occasional driver-bodyguard, greets me at the terminal. Jimmy is six-foot-two, built like a soldier and could probably beat the shit out of anyone. Nina schedules him for events or times when she's worried about my safety.

I only notice a few paparazzi in the terminal all dressed

in their usual attire and snapping pictures hoping for some scandal. I'm not sure why she's worried but nevertheless, I greet him and we walk alongside to the black SUV which is parked curb-side.

We drive straight into traffic—a sea of tail lights which seem never-ending. As I lay back into the leather seats, attempting to cure my stiff neck from the awkward position I fell asleep in on the plane, the constant vibration of my phone disrupts my struggle to get comfortable.

I close my eyes, which lasts a minute before my hand moves on its own accord and I'm reading a text from Nina.

Nina: *Meeting scheduled with the board tomorrow morning. I'm confident we can fight to have you end your contract. Don't stress Emerson—I've got this.*

Finally, something going my way. I have faith in Nina to follow through with what I requested—terminating my contract so I don't have to work with Wes. I've had many hours to think about what I will say to Wes when I see him, yet a few blocks from home I'm left with nothing to say. Instead, my focus has been on Logan and the way we left things, amicable and friendly.

We agreed to remain friends, and with friendship comes the expectation I can text him. Quickly typing a message, I hit send before changing my mind.

Me: *This guy on the plane smelled like weed. Remember the time I smoked it and you gave me a lecture about how it would stunt my growth? Such a lie. What did you do with the bag you stole off me?*

I don't expect him to respond, knowing they're on a plane to England and probably out of phone service. With the apartment only a block away, I throw my phone into my purse and straighten my posture, staring out the window at the familiar houses lining the street.

Jimmy enters the code for our garage, parking his SUV in the same spot near the stairwell. The apartment block has four units and they all overlook the Pacific Ocean. Ours is located on the top level beside an entrepreneur, who divides her time between LA and Boston.

Jimmy takes my luggage upstairs, and with my feet dragging, I follow until we're inside the living room. He places the suitcase to the floor and quietly exits the apartment, leaving me alone with Wes who's sitting on the sofa.

This apartment used to be home only a few days ago. A place we both purchased and made ours. I remember the moment we got the keys, Wes carried me through the door and into an empty apartment. We both screamed with joy before making love on the cold tiles in the middle of the living room floor. Our bodies covered in sweat, clothes surrounding us as he cradled me in his arms while we stared at the ocean, talking for hours about our childhood.

It feels like a lifetime ago now, not the reality that's sitting on the sofa in gray sweats with a black Nike jumper. In front of him is his phone, a bottle of rum and a pack of cigarettes. I don't allow anyone to smoke in our apartment, and when I go to open my mouth and tell him my thoughts, the sounds of a tiny bell with soft pitter-patters distract me until George is rubbing his face against my leg.

"George!" I pick up his fat little body, cradling him in my arms. The smell of his doggy fur brings me so much joy and knowing he's alive and well, because the housekeeper didn't kill him from overfeeding him her exotic dishes from the Philippines.

After smothering him and kissing his little pug face, I put him down to brave the inevitable.

"You look good," Wes comments dryly, lighting up a cigarette and blowing the smoke into the clean air.

"You look like shit."

"Nice, Emerson." He lays back on the sofa, his eyes dark and surrounded by deep lines. Wesley hates growing any facial hair, so his mustache and beard come as a complete surprise. It adds ten years onto his baby face. He looks like utter shit and I reap some sort of joy from that.

"I'm sorry." Crossing my arms, I try to control the anger which has brewed—to the point of steaming—inside. "Am I supposed to feel sorry for you?"

"Em... please, don't. I'm just so—"

"Let me guess? You're sorry. You don't know how it happened? It was a mistake and you'll never do it again?" I finish, placing the words in his mouth.

The room falls silent, the only sounds are the sea crashing against the shore outside. Even George has left the room preparing for the shitstorm ahead.

Wes moves his body and sits on the edge of the sofa. His fingers tapping against his knee rapidly with nervous energy bouncing off him. He's probably high, and the thought alone angers me even more.

"Are you high now?" I yell, the sound of my voice echoing through the room.

"No."

My eyes move away, desperate to erase the image before me. This isn't him. This isn't the guy I fell in love with. And to make matters worse, I don't know how we got here. What's troubling him so much he ended up taking this road? Why was sniffing that deadly shit even a thought?

"I can't even look at you."

The built-up emotions hit me like a wrecking ball. Hard, fast, and knocking the wind out of my stomach making it difficult to breathe. The lack of remorse, the pathetic apology, the disregard for my feelings.

All of it has come to this moment.

The moment I need to tell him what I want.

"I want you to leave," I tell him in a stern voice, sucking in my breath to control the bile lingering around my throat.

Instantly, his expression changes—eyes full with his cheeks flushed, shading the pale white he reflected only moments ago.

"Emerson, please, don't. I fucked up. I'm sorry. I'll make it better. Please! We can move past this. Just give it time. I promise you, I *will* make it up to you." He doesn't move from the sofa, no attempt to get down on his knees and beg for forgiveness. Not that it will help. Stroke my ego, perhaps. But I'm beyond the need for ego-stroking.

I shake my head with a sardonic laugh. "If it was me being fucked by two guys, would you like me to make it up to you?" The minute I say the words, the pang of guilt stabs me as I so easily forget about what happened with Logan.

But this isn't the moment to think about it.

Logan and I made a pact—keep it a secret.

It wasn't a big deal. We had some drinks and were frustrated with Ash.

And what Wesley's done is far worse.

Yet, even as my mind tries to rationalize, the guilt lingers and allows me long enough to hear Wesley out.

"I know I screwed up. Things were just, too... you know... safe between us."

"Safe? Wesley, I can't even think right now. Do you know what I was more concerned about?" I pause for effect and then continue, "George... and what would happen to him rather than to us? Maybe that's saying a lot about our relationship." I storm past him with my suitcase in hand, straight to our bedroom. Shutting the door behind me, I lean back and close my eyes trying to calm my racing heart. George's yelp startles me, and with my eyes wide open, I scan the room to see him sprawled across the shaggy white rug that sits near the window. My body falls to the ground, limp and weak with the stream of tears staining my tired face. George senses something's wrong, stretching his stubby legs, he walks across to me where he lays his head on my knee.

"Tell me I'm doing the right thing," I whisper into George's face, holding him close and seeking the comfort of his warm body. "Tell me that somewhere out there, someone better is waiting for me."

George closes his eyes, resting peacefully as my phone vibrates in my bag. I wipe my nose with the back of my hand then reach over to grab it, welcoming the distraction.

Logan: *I sold your weed and bought those expensive soccer boots you said looked like they belonged to a drag queen. Better I look like a drag queen than you stunt your growth.*

I smile through my tears, placing my phone down and laying on the floor with George cuddled into my side. Logan has this way of making me laugh, although at times, I'm more annoyed than humored.

But for today, it's exactly what I need. That one text is enough to ease my troubles.

Within minutes, I fall asleep to the sound of George's grumbling snore.

"This is not how we expected to start the third season."

Jeffrey Marsh is the executive president of the network. A short, balding man, with a ruthless attitude and known as a shark in the industry. Surrounding him is his team who are all nervous and writing down notes as he speaks.

I sit beside Nina and across the table from Wesley. We've spent the last hour hearing Jeffrey crucify Wesley for his actions. You could feel sorry for the guy—if you weren't his fiancée who's been screwed over.

"I don't know what the fuck you were thinking, Rich? Do you know how damaging this is for the network? Drugs... really?" Jeffrey continues to pace the boardroom, up and down, repeating the same things over and over again.

I hate this.

No couple should have to sit in a boardroom and have their relationship dissected by money-hungry executives. Another reminder of why I want out.

"It's not going to work with Wes and me. We're not together anymore. I think it's best if I leave the show," I raise my voice, making myself heard and my demands perfectly clear.

Jeffrey sits in his chair, swinging back and forth while staring at the door. He finally speaks, filling the silence. "I understand your predicament, Emerson. But we're only a few shows into filming the third season. We're rating number one in our timeslot. The fans are obsessed with watching the both of you as a couple. Even if I said it's okay to leave, it's not just the network who suffers. It's all our sponsorships. They'll withdraw and it will affect the future of the show." He swivels his chair to face me. "Everyone who works on the show's future may be in jeopardy. Do you really want to be responsible for that?" He poses the question so lightly like he's asking me if I wanted fries with that.

Nina looks just as confused, after promising me it wouldn't be a huge issue given the circumstances.

Across the table, Wes stares at me. I swear he's smirking, but he's quick to change his expression when I make eye contact with him. I want to grab the glass of water in front of me and throw it in his face. *This is all his fault.*

"What are you trying to say?" I ask, heated.

"You're contractually obliged to film for another two seasons. Remember? You signed the contract last year while negotiating more money per episode." Jeffrey slides the contract toward me. "So, to answer your question... you're going to film, and you're going to stay with Wesley for at least this season. Now, toward the end of the season, I'm happy to show the cracks in the relationship. It will make for a good cliff-hanger for season four."

"You're joking, right?" I laugh nervously while looking around the room, but I'm met with blank faces. Blank because no one's standing up for what I want.

"I'm not joking, Chase. In fact, read your terms and conditions."

I don't listen to Jeffrey, begging Wes with my eyes to say something. He doesn't seem to follow, gazing at me oddly while remaining silent.

"Okay, I think we're done here." Jeffrey leaves the room followed by his shark posse.

Nina's quick to open her mouth the moment the three

of us are remaining. "Emerson. I'm sorry. I don't know what happened."

"It's not your fault," I respond, still in shock. "I guess I should go home." So, I mumble goodbye and ignore the rest of the staff as I exit the room and wait for the elevator. Wes follows quickly and enters the lift with only the two of us occupying it. I watch the numbers count down, keeping silent until the doors open into the lobby. Walking outside, swarms of paparazzi are on standby. Suddenly, warmth graces my hand. I look down and see Wes' fingers intertwined with mine.

"What are you doing?"

"What I've been asked to do. Make everything look normal. You're still my fiancée as far as the network is concerned," he responds eagerly, holding tight and pulling me along. "C'mon, let's go home."

"Wesley. Stop!" I pull my hand away, the both of us standing in the middle of the lobby. His body is stiff, his jaw tight and eyes impatiently waiting for me to talk.

As I'm about to tell him, no, the automatic doors open and the noise of the paparazzi, together with the non-stop flashing halts my original plan. They're watching, taking photos of this moment.

This is precisely what I want to avoid—looking like a fool to the world.

I stare at them one more time, then to Wes. His crooked smile soon follows, taking a step forward, wrapping his arm around my waist. With the bright lights hurting my eyes like they have always done, Wes leans in and plants a kiss on the side of my neck. "You're still my fiancée, whether you like it or not." The change of tone, grit in his voice, leaves me feeling unsettled.

I tried my best to walk away but was told I have no choice.

I'm forced to live with a man I no longer respect.

A man who's broken me.

A man who's made it his mission to make me as miserable as possible.

And the icing on the fucked-up cake? The whole world will be watching him do just that.

EIGHT

"It's the little things which make you happy.
Sometimes those little things can turn into
something greater." ~ *Emerson Chase*

S everal weeks have passed since that meeting.
A day which cemented the truth in my mind—
my life does not belong to me.

I had no option but to keep myself busy—photoshoots, interviews, and drinking whenever we were out at social gatherings.

Twitter's buzzing with some story calling me an alcoholic train wreck. It happens to be a coincidence that every photograph snapped of me is with a glass of wine in hand.

After the story broke loose, I made a mental note to stay clear of drinking in public. The network executives don't want my squeaky-clean image to be destroyed and ruin the show.

Yet, Wes could fuck two hookers. Go figure.

There's one thing I've made perfectly clear to Wesley—we *are* over.

The betrayal doesn't erase because we've been told to continue the show. When the cameras are on, we act as if nothing's happened, but as soon as they leave he sleeps in the spare room and he knows not to come anywhere near me.

I have to give it to him, he's tried his best to apologize through romantic dinners and roses being delivered. I'm just not interested. At least, in my eyes, the love has diminished to the point where I don't see any kind of future with him.

I've isolated myself from everyone. I'm glad everyone else's lives are so busy that it's convenient for me. Mom's wrapped up her book and has gone into stress mode as she always does when it sits in the hands of her editor. Her coping mechanism is baking, which is great if you're in the same house. Instead, she sends me pictures of the yummieness which only depresses me even further.

Ash and Logan are back to training in England preparing for the semi-finals in a few weeks. I know not to bother either of them. When in game mode, nothing else matters.

I do, however, find friendship with Alessandra. We talk regularly about life, work, and the downfall of living with Ash. He was and still is, a slob.

I've spent the day shooting an interview for our new workout clothing line when Cliff calls asking Wesley and me to film in the apartment tonight. They have done some edits but need more footage of us discussing our wedding. I dread filming this, it's a topic I want to stay clear of considering I have no intention of ever marrying him.

A couple of hours later our makeup artist, Reba, hovers

over me with her brush, touching up just under my eyes. Our regular camera crew, Karl and Josie, stand in position as we sit on the white sofa.

"I can't wait to make you my wife." Wes grins, tracing the tip of my ring which still sits on my finger burning my skin.

"I guess we should start planning the wedding?" I manage to say with a smile, but I'm mentally aware my body language needs to be relaxed and not tense.

"I'm thinking Paris. Winter. Just like when I proposed."

"That sounds beautiful."

"You're beautiful." Wesley tilts his head and moves his body in, placing his lips on mine. He knows it's the only way to touch me, and so I allow it. Kissing him back as if I want him, as if he's good and pure, never breaking my heart.

Every time we filmed over the past few weeks, he touched me as much as possible. I know very well he wants more and he isn't shy in telling me so.

I just can't do it. It's almost feels like I'd be letting my inner woman down.

There had been one occasion where I almost caved—he looked handsome that night and said the right words. What stopped me was the way his eye wandered mid-conversation to another woman walking past in a tight red dress.

I may not have had any sexual activity since the night in the lake, but the game is over, loser.

"I'm so lucky to have you. Don't you think it's fate? Us being on this show and falling in love?" He waits for my response, and because this conversation is scripted and not reality, I try to remember my lines as best as I can.

"I do think it's fate. And one day our kids will watch this show and see how we fell in love." I bite my tongue immediately after, tasting the nasty metallic tang of blood in my mouth.

Before the conversation can continue, my phone dances across the coffee table. Karl motions for me to pick it up, continuing to roll the camera.

"Hey, sis!" Ash's loud cheer barrels through the speaker, and I couldn't be happier to see his face even if we are being filmed. Cliff always prefers video calls rather than regular calls. Apparently, the audience responds well to them.

"Good news?"

"We won the game today!"

"Congratulations." I beam with joy. "Dad must be so happy."

"He's here with us. Actually, he and Coach are downstairs talking about something."

It's not uncommon for the cameras to film private conversations. If Ash consents to this conversation being on the show, Cliff may use this footage. Most of the time, unless the topic is interesting, it ends up on the cutting-room floor.

"And Logan? He must be just as pumped as you."

Ash laughs, chasing down a blue Powerade before responding, "So pumped that he's on the balcony surrounded by his girl posse. Did I tell you Alessandra wants to move out? I think she's over the random girls dropping by."

I keep my smile fixed, trying to ignore the ache in my stomach. The feeling is odd and unsettling. It's the same feeling I got when Mom and Dad took Ash to Disneyland one year, and I was forced to stay with my grandparents because I had projectile-vomited all over the hotel room.

The matter of fact is, we had a fling. It wasn't even a

fling. It was a moment of insanity. That moment of insanity should not translate into any sort of jealously—full stop.

"Tell him I said congrats, and give my love to Dad."

"Will do." He appears distracted, talking to someone in the background. "Oh, and Alessandra and I have some news."

"You're pregnant?" I blurt out.

"No," he answers panicking, I can almost see him breaking into a sweat. "We're thinking about having a proper wedding, something low key. Once this season dies down."

"That'll be nice."

Wes takes the phone from my hands, saying hello to Ash. They talk for a couple minutes about the game even though Wes has no interest in sports unless it involves a ring, mud and two girls in bikinis.

"Great. We'll be there," Wes finishes, handing the phone back to me.

Dad and their coach enter the room forcing Ash to say goodbye. As soon as the call ends, Wes starts to talk to me about Ash's wedding despite my mind being elsewhere.

"You didn't tell me Ash got married?"

"Yeah, it was the reason I flew back home. Remember, *that* weekend?"

He barely holds a smile, annoyed I've even brought it up especially in front of the cameras. Karl knows this is a sore topic—spending almost every day with the both of us—but zooms the camera in to catch our conversation at a more intimate level.

"Oh, yeah... I totally forgot," he lies. Brushing it off like it means nothing, he lifts his legs and rests his feet on the coffee table. "Who else was there?"

"Just my family."

"Your family?"

"You know Mom, Dad, sister, brother..." I spell it out in plain English, not understanding the stupid question or where he's going with it.

"That's it?"

"And Logan. But he doesn't count. He's like a brother to me. Reiterate... *family*."

"Then you're lying," he states, arms crossed.

I turn to face him. "I'm not lying. You asked who was there and I've told you."

"He spends an awful lot of time with your family."

I want to stab Wesley Rich straight in the eye.

He knows I don't like to talk about my family in front of the camera.

It's a part of my life I try to keep private, despite Ash and Mom being known. Logan has always been a topic Wes avoids. They have never actually met. The only reason Wes did meet Ash was when he flew over for a couple of days last year without Logan.

"Yeah, he does. He's part of *my* family. That's what family does, they stick together. Not get married to some billionaire and run off leaving their kids to fend for themselves in boarding school." I get off the sofa, grab my phone and move past the cameras, demanding Karl and Josie stop filming.

"Emerson," Karl shouts across the room. "I need more footage."

I wave my hand in the air, ignoring his plea, and head straight to my bedroom. Shutting the door behind me with a loud bang I know it will only be a matter of time before someone will find me and try to talk me back into living room.

But I'm pissed off.

At Wesley for disrespecting my wishes.

And as much as I hate to admit it, at Logan for being such a sleaze.

The anger rages and I don't know why I feel compelled to tell Logan my thoughts given we haven't spoken for weeks.

Me: *Filled up your belt, yet? I hear you've been busy.*

The second I hit send, I want to retract the message. Why the hell is there no recall button? Did Apple not understand during heated moments, one can so easily mouth-off based on unstable emotions?

Logan: *Nice to see you online. Your hair looks good in purple. But then again, I watched last week's episode, and I would compare my full belt to your engagement. When's the lucky day?*

I can feel the heat rushing to my cheeks. What does that mean? Comparing his belt to my engagement?

This isn't a contest.

And if it was, what the hell would be the prize at the end? Who became the most miserable because they lived a life they didn't want? Yeah, I'd win in a heartbeat.

Me: *You're still the same, Carrington. An asshole.*

Frustrated at myself for feeling this way, I look up and see George walk out of my closet. He has a guilty face. The same face he wears when he's been chewing on something pricey. My feet move forward to the closet where I see my vintage Chanel purse Mom gave me a few years back—nibbled at the sides.

"George," I cry, falling to the floor and picking up the remnants of the bag. He's really gotten into the beading, tearing it apart with his canine teeth.

I storm out of the closet, searching for him around the room. He's sitting in the corner, already in timeout with his head down and eyes conveniently avoiding me.

"Are you kidding me? George Puggington! How dare you eat my vintage Chanel? Go for Wes' shit, not mine!"

He knows he's in trouble, and with my day already going bad I fall onto the bed accidentally knocking my phone beside me. I hold it up in front of face as I lie on my back reading the text from Logan.

Logan: *A beautiful asshole, right?*

His cockiness makes me smile, and without overthinking, I type the first thing that comes to mind.

Me: *You do know how weird that sounds, right? I'm literally visualizing assholes and I think I'm a little scared. Women aren't programmed like men. You're all about the tits and ass. Ass being assholes.*

I know that will challenge him but I only stated the truth. We don't care about cocks as much as men are obsessed with the female anatomy and big juicy asses they can slap.

Logan: *And what is Emerson Chase all about?*

I read his question carefully and it gets me thinking about what I want. *Do I even know what I want?* No, because I no longer think about myself. It doesn't matter anyway, at least, for this season of that damn show. Signing on the dotted line means I signed away the rights to my freedom. With that morbid thought, I do what I do best, act like a smartass to avoid reality.

Me: *I'm all about hot soccer players who appear in Sports Illustrated and OMG the abs... like literally can you even DEAL with such hotness???*

In the confinement of my room, I laugh to myself when I read the text back. Logan's a womanizer and women are drawn to him. He knows they know that, and I should have known as well. Damn, I do, stupid brain just forgot for a few minutes.

Logan: *I don't think a man like that exists. Maybe you need to bat for the same side. Now THAT would make for some great reality TV.*

Smartass. I can hear voices coming close to my bedroom, so I type fast before they find me in here grinning like a fool over a stupid conversation.

Me: *You wear a kitty dress once and it's all about the pussy with you. MAN. ALL MAN. I need a man not a woman. Take your lesbian fantasy elsewhere. That boat has no chance of docking at my wharf.*

My name is being called and Josie walks in with her

camera faced down and headphones resting on her neck. She's much older than me—a hopeless romantic who only ever sees the good in people despite what they have done. *God love her.*

"You okay, Emerson?"

"Sorry. Just having one of those days."

"Listen, we can cut that footage and re-shoot? I won't tell Cliff."

"I appreciate that." I smile. "Can you give me a minute and I'll be out?"

She nods, closing the door behind her.

I quickly read Logan's message before heading to the bathroom to fix my hair.

> **Logan:** *I've got this sudden urge to go sailing. I'm glad you need a man... and I'm sure you've got a line waiting to dock at your wharf. You can tell me more this weekend when I'm in town.*

He'll be in town? I press dial, suddenly wanting to speak to him before I head outside. I don't expect him to answer first ring.

"You're coming to LA?" I ask without greeting him.

"I don't even get a hello?" I can hear him teasing me with his smile. "Yes. For two days. We have a meeting with the US Soccer officials."

"We, as in you and Ash?"

"No, we as in me and my female posse." There's a quick pause before his laughter filters through. "Yes, me and Ash. He's leaving Alessandra behind. Thank God."

"Where are you staying?"

"Not sure. They've booked us somewhere."

I hear my name being called again. If I don't hang up

now, Wes could walk in and all hell will break loose. "Listen, I have to go. We're in the middle of filming. I kinda stormed off set. Then George ate my bag. Long story..." I roll my eyes even though Logan can't see me. "I guess I'll see you next week."

"Till then."

We hang up, and without realizing it, I pull my phone toward my chest and smile. Jumping off the bed, I skip outside with a brighter attitude and make myself comfortable on the sofa. Wes picks up on my improved mood and begins the same conversation we started earlier.

"So, a winter wedding. In Paris?"

Resting my hand on his knee, I smile back with my heart in a much better place. "Sounds beautiful."

NINE

*"It all begins with something small.
A trigger—warning us something dangerous lies
ahead."* ~ Logan Carrington

Flying with Ash is never easy. He fidgets constantly. Annoys you by beginning a conversation when you've just placed your headphones on, then forces you to remove them only to have him ask if he can eat your fucking pretzels.

He goes on and on about Alessandra. Complaining about how she makes him throw his dirty clothes into the hamper rather than leave them on the floor, or how she scolds him for dumping wet towels on the bed. Honestly, that's something I can't fault Alessandra on—Ash is a fucking slob and no woman has ever been successful in changing him, no matter how much pussy they give up.

We've flown first class to the States with the US Soccer officials wanting to meet to discuss the team they're putting together for the World Cup trials. Chris had a lengthy conversation with Coach and there was talk about Ash and I playing for the US team.

I couldn't believe the news. World Cup—a fucking dream.

Representing our country means everything to me, so I'm incredibly keen to get onto US soil and possibly get picked.

That, and there's one other thing—*Emerson.*

Weeks have gone past without any contact, and just like we said we would, we kept it our secret. It doesn't erase the constant reminder of that night, though. Fuck. I can't even think about it now sitting next to Ash. Removing my headphones, I excuse myself to use the restroom, leaving Ash to watch some movie with subtitles because the fucker thought it would be porn.

It's a short walk to the main restroom, passing the other passengers who sleep comfortably in their sleepers or are busy typing away on their laptops. The hostess greets me, offering me a beverage. I tell her I'll take a beer when I'm back at my chair.

Inside the tiny cubicle, I take a piss then wash my hands thoroughly. Goddamn germs are everywhere, and I hate sharing such a small space. The quiet, confined area gets me thinking about Emmy again and the way we left things...

It was never my intention to finger her fucking pussy in the lake. I was angry at her for being such a bitch and turning into one of those Hollywood divas, at Ash for marrying the first girl to suck his dick, and most importantly myself for letting Louisa go.

I wasn't thinking. Something about Emmy does that to

me. She always has done since we were kids. She riles me up until I burst into flames, and do something stupid just to prove a point. But we aren't kids anymore. We're adults.

I touched her to shut her up. To get back at Ash for being a hypocrite and making me choose between him and Louisa. I wasn't myself that night—the anger had been bottled up for a while and coincidently quadrupled when the tabloids announced Manchester's top player, Jared Carr, dating Louisa Hemmings.

My Louisa Hemmings.

Past. Fucking. Tense.

Louisa wanted a life with me—marriage, babies, the big fucking castle outside London where she'd make me drive past every weekend. It was a relationship I never expected to last that long, but instead, it lasted a whole two years. The majority of the time was spent hiding it from the media and with her traveling globally for work. Most of our relationship was through text messages and video chatting.

She was switched on—a career in marketing with her own firm set up in London. She thrived on schedules, routine, and planning. Everything had to be planned.

Ash hated her, voicing his opinion on more than one occasion.

"Does she plan when you fuck too?" he asked once when we were out drinking with the boys. "Monday... you get blown, Tuesday... she likes a tittie fuck and Friday night... you take her in the ass?" He knew I hated discussing my personal life and that 'joke' took it over the line. My fist almost smacking him in the face if it weren't for Jerry, a teammate who held me back.

We didn't talk for weeks. I crashed at Louisa's apartment until Coach pulled us in for a meeting. He warned the both of us that our three straight losses were not unfortunate, *rather a lack of teamwork. We had to choose what was more important—soccer or women.*

I thought long and hard about what Louisa meant to me and if it was worth the fight. That was until Ash gave me another ultimatum—him or her.

Ash had been my best friend since I could remember, he was my brother. Louisa was in my life for two years, I loved her but it wasn't enough to give up everything I'd worked so hard for, and thus I ended our relationship thinking it wouldn't be hard because I'd find someone else.

It was more difficult than I'd thought. I missed the sex and her companionship. Despite her need to plan everything, I felt lost without someone nagging and getting me off my ass when I felt like doing nothing. I never let it affect my game though, training harder during the day and partying well into the nights on the weekends.

I wasn't prepared the night I ran into Louisa at that party. Her body wrapped around another man. She tried to be polite, apologizing for bringing this stranger to a mutual friend's apartment. The manipulative bitch knew she'd gotten under my skin, and to pay her back I fucked her assistant against the brand-new Porsche Daddy had bought her.

It was the same night Ash changed everything between us.

"Bro, I gotta tell you something but you can't flip, okay?" Ashley Chase had said this to me only once in the entire time I'd known him—the time he'd accidentally ridden my BMX into the lake and couldn't retrieve it because it had sunk to the bottom. The important thing was that he survived.

"I know you'll be angry, but hear me out. That woman last night, the one with the long, dark brown hair... I... I married her."

There were no words left to say. He married her! He was forced to go back home to tell Chris and Abbi, and I tagged along to reap joy in the fact he'd be crucified.

Then Emmy...

Emerson Chase was never someone I'd considered jumping into bed with. I had my moments where I found myself infatuated with her, but then I'd become distracted by someone else. I enjoyed tormenting her, she was an easy target. Yet, this trip back home was different. She'd changed. Even before she told me what had happened, I could see she was troubled.

Pushing her buttons was easy, but she always gave it back. She hated losing. Claimed she wasn't competitive, but I'd never met a more competitive and stubborn woman.

And sexy, hot...

I can't rid my mind of the image of her buried into me while we floated in the water. The way her body moved and so quickly peaking from the simple touch of my finger gliding in and out of her tight pussy. I wanted to stick my cock in her, and give her a taste of what a real man was all about. But I didn't. Our ties were too strong and there was way too much at stake.

I blame it all on her. She dared me like she'd always done.

I wanted an escape just as much as she did, but I thought she'd have pushed me away by telling me how disgusting I am, and how dare I touch her.

Yet, she didn't.

She couldn't stop staring at me, even when we were standing in the kitchen her eyes trailing my body like a hungry beast.

It started something bad.

I just didn't know exactly what that was yet. I knew it

would be awkward, but only if we allowed it to be, and knowing the type of person Emmy is plus, the fact she has no interest in me whatsoever, I was happy to brush it off like nothing had happened between us. Take the memory of her and store it for times when I needed to jerk off and had no one sucking my cock.

Until I watched her show—for the first time.

We'd just flown back into London and I was eager to begin training again. It pissed me off that Ash busied himself fucking Alessandra every night, and so with a few minutes to spare I did what I promised myself I wouldn't do, I streamed the last episode of Generation Next - The Proposal episode.

I couldn't fault the show. As far as my eyes were concerned this shit looked real, not two people acting in love. It was almost too perfect, and I had known Emmy for as long as I'd known Ash, and not one boyfriend or guy had ever made her smile that way.

She fucking loved him, or should I say still loves him, and they're still living together.

The dick fucks two whores then he expects to marry Emmy? You're damn right it pissed me off.

It's the reason why I stopped contacting her. She enabled his poor behavior and in my eyes that made her weak.

That whole family fucked me off right now.

Chris was also on my back about training harder, continually pointing out my weaknesses and giving me a massive complex.

Abbi kept pushing me to call my mom. Why couldn't Mom call me? Was it that hard to pick up the phone and call your only son? She never cared when I was a kid so why would she start now?

I didn't need anyone. Just someone occasionally to suck

*me off and that wouldn't be Emmy. At least, I didn't think it
would be her.*

Until she texted me.

As much as I wanted to ignore her—I couldn't...

After heading back to my seat and sitting quietly for the rest
of the flight, we land just before midday. It doesn't go as
smooth as I would like after being spotted by some fans in
LAX where we are asked for some pics. Being that they're
girls, Ash laps it up and grabs the number of the blonde
with the bouncing tits.

Personally, all I want is to make a quick dash to the
hotel to shower, get the grime and grease off me, then meet
with the officials and definitely *not* think about pussy.

"You want the blonde's number?" Ash hands the paper
over in the limo.

"Nah, I'm good."

"What the fuck is wrong with you? Did you score a
blowey off any of the girls at the apartment last week?"

The girls who hang around our apartment are the same
old leeches who follow us at each game and hover around
the entrance of the locker rooms hoping to score some dick.
The older one, a Scandinavian woman, sucked me off once
with no happy ending. *I wasn't into it.* When I started to
chafe I politely asked her to leave. It was the oddest thing
ever. Typically I'd be pulling her hair tight and watching
her eyes bulge from my cock going down her throat.

"Yeah, I did," I say, to shut him up.

He doesn't press any further, busying himself with his
phone.

"Emmy is taking us out for a late lunch after the meeting. You got plans?"

It catches my attention, yet I'm quick to keep my smile hidden. "Nope, where at?"

"Hold on..." He types quickly and responds a couple of seconds later, "Some Indian place near Melrose."

I hide the grin trying to appear by grabbing my phone and typing a message to her.

Me: *Indian? You know what happens to Ash when he eats Indian? Burning assholes.*

I see the bubble bouncing before her response appears on the screen. Ash has taken the moment to call Alessandra, and already they've gotten into a fight over him being photographed with his arm around some woman at Heathrow.

Emerson: *Burning assholes. Great visual yet funny at the same time. I'll make sure I order him the vindaloo.*

I sit back in the chair and stare out the window. Emmy was never on my mind before our trip back home, I guess since she's announced her engagement on television I figured she'd forever be gone from our lives. We rarely see each other, and every time we do it stirs this weird emotion —like nostalgia. She was always around us as kids, annoying the fuck out of Ash and me. Third wheel as I liked to call her. It wasn't until we left to train for the league did I think, thank God, we've finally gotten rid of her.

"Fucking ball breaker. Did you see me fuck that woman in Heathrow? No. But Sandy seems to think so," he yells into the air as I purposely ignore him.

What the fuck's new anyway?

"Hey, lil' sis." Ash places his arm on her shoulder, pulling her in roughly for a hug.

"Little? We're twins. Granted, you came first but I slid out of Mom's vagina right after you did."

Ash scowls. "Oh... hey ... thanks for that visual."

Emmy is still in his arms, watching me with a smile planted on her face. She looks so goddamn cute in this tight black bodysuit and skinny blue jeans. It shows every curve. And when I say cute, I mean fuck. *I could just eat her.*

She plays with her hair, moving it to the side and exposing her skin. Untangling herself from his embrace, she moves closer to me and wraps her arms around my waist and places her head on my chest. The familiar scent—something sweet—tickles my senses leaving me holding on to her longer than I should. Remembering that Ash is standing next to us, I let her go and pretend as if that means nothing whatsoever. And that my dick doesn't stir at the feel of her tits being pushed up against my chest.

"Let's go inside. I've got a hankering for something spicy." Ash rubs his hands together with delight, abandoning us without waiting for a response.

With the two of us standing outside the restaurant, she scans our surroundings to see if anyone's watching. It's Friday afternoon the streets are busy with locals and tourists. From where I stand, I don't see anyone following her with cameras, but paparazzi have many tricks up their sleeves and it won't surprise me if they're hidden in the bushes or in the apartment block across the street.

"Hey." She smiles nervously, a slight blush against her delicate skin.

"Hey, that's all I get? No, nice to see you, Logan. You

look so hot I can't stop thinking about your body in *Sports Illustrated* magazine."

"You are such a jerk." She tilts her head with a smirk, keeping her gaze lifted. "Let's go burn Ash's asshole."

I follow her lead, purposely walking a step behind so I can watch her ass sway.

Fuck, why do I torture myself? Because you remember how damn good her ass feels in your hands.

The restaurant is small and intimate—decorated in maroon and gold. It appears to be rundown with old weathered paintings. Only a few people sit inside, keeping to themselves in the dark corners. Emmy chose this place because she knows it's not a crowd-drawer, therefore, won't attract the paparazzi. The staff are very accommodating, offering the menu and serving the dishes with jugs of cold water.

"Fuck, this is spicy." Ash wipes his forehead with his napkin, taking a long gulp of the water and immediately refilling the glass.

"Hot? Is it?" Emmy questions, her eyes wide with an innocent pout.

"You don't think so?"

"I eat here all the time. Got a stomach made of steel," she says, patting her belly and pretending she didn't tell the waiter to add more curry powder to his dish.

"I just never..." he stops mid-burp, "... eaten anything so *hot*."

"Seems fine to me," I chime in, hiding my smile behind the fork strategically placed to my mouth.

Ash takes a break from eating, his uncomfortable stance making this moment too comical. Leaning back into his chair while breathing in and out at a steady pace, he motions the waiter and requests another jug of water.

"How was the meeting? You didn't tell me what happened."

"They've asked us to represent the States in the World Cup trials. Do you even know what this means, Emmy?" Ash bellows with excitement.

"That you'll play for the World Cup?" she answers looking back and forth between Ash and me.

"It's what we want but ultimately, the decision comes down to Coach Bennett and our commitment to the Royal Kings. It's not as clear-cut as we would like it to be, but Dad's handling all that. The problem is we've only just negotiated new contracts, so I don't know..." he trails off with worry but quickly smiles again. "If we play trials we'll get to move back home for a while. I'll fucking love that. I miss this place."

There's a mixed look of concern on Emmy's face. "Uh... that's great, I guess. When do you find out, and where will you move to?"

"Here," I tell her, face blank watching her reaction.

"Wow... that's so close." She hides her gulp behind her glass of water.

"What? You don't want Ash and me around?"

"You're both kinda annoying."

"We're not cool enough for her, eh bro?" Ash picks his up his fork, scooping another piece of chicken and smothering it in sauce. "We don't know for sure yet. We find out in a few months or something. Anyway, what are you up to tonight?"

Emmy lifts the napkin to her mouth, wiping her chin. My gaze instinctively shifts to her pout—full, soft, and inviting—covered in a glistening red shade of lipstick. Despite them being twins, she looks nothing like Ash. He looks like a dork with his crew cut and semi-broken nose.

She is gorgeous. Pale skin with a few freckles scattered on the bridge of her nose. Her eyes are blue, this bright blue which makes it difficult to concentrate if you stare into them. She's always had long lashes and was teased in school for them being fake. I remember she wanted to prove the bullies wrong and plucked them out in front of them. They brushed it off like it was nothing until she flipped her eyelids inside out and terrified the older boys. They called her the spawn of the devil and she lapped it up using it as her weapon against them from that moment on.

"There's a party on tonight. One of my friends is hosting it... Scarlett Winters? You might have heard of her."

Ash and I simultaneously turn our heads to look at each other. Is she fucking kidding me? *Scarlett fucking Winters.* Ash had repeatedly told me he jerked off to her tits every night. He dreamt that one day he would motorboat them and it would end with his cum all over her face. Crude but so very Ash.

"You never told me you're friends," Ash quickly repri-mands her.

"Yeah, and I never told you that Logan was the one who told Mom you screwed the older lady down the street when you were eighteen."

I kick her under the table until she jumps. "Way to throw me under the bus."

She points her fork at me deadpan. "You're a tattletale."

I place my glass down, leaning my elbows on the edge of the table. "I'm a tattletale? I don't think so."

"You told him I slept with the guy from the burger joint."

I exhale. "Ash was adamant he'd hocked loogies in his burger. I did that simply to prove him wrong."

Ash shakes his head disapprovingly. "Honestly Emmy, that guy was a geek."

"You told Ash I was the one who spiked his drink with drowsy cough syrup because I didn't want him to chaperone me to that party."

Again, I exhale but much longer this time. "I wanted to go to that party too, but knew you wouldn't listen to me when the fucking bottle came out. Who plays spin the bottle anymore? Dumbest game ever."

"Dumb?" She laughs. "Oh, that's rich coming from you. Your first kiss was at sixteen playing that game with that Debbie something-or-other. I can't believe you were sixteen when you got your first kiss. Talk about frigid."

Raising my eyebrows, I question her casually pretending it's not true. "Why would you say that? That's not true."

Ash clears his throat, avoiding eye contact. The little fucker had to open his big fucking mouth. When I was younger I was terrified of girls. I only kissed Debbie because of peer pressure and everyone calling me gay.

"Did you know Ash fucked your best friend Riley on your bed during one of your sleepovers?"

Her face pulls back in utter shock. "What? Where the hell was I?"

"You were in the basement with me. I needed waffles and you were trying to find the waffle maker then we got distracted with the fake spider I planted on top of the waffle maker."

"I nearly died," she whispers to herself. "And it explains why Riley complained all night that the room was hot in the middle of winter."

"You didn't almost die." I roll my eyes in frustration. "It

was fake. And what's the worst thing a spider can do to you?"

"Kill you," Emmy and Ash say in unison.

The both of them are petrified of spiders. A reason why Ash hates the thought of traveling to Australia to play the summer games.

"So, this party tonight? Can we come?" I switch the subject, knowing the spider talk doesn't ease their anxiety.

"I don't think so," she answers instantly.

"Why not?" I question, the same time Ash puts on his whiney face.

"I don't know because it's a Hollywood party and the cameras are following me around tonight. Trust me, it can get rather annoying."

What a stupid response. The cameras follow us all the time when we play. The games are all televised being shown nationally and internationally. They film everything down to every move, including when I'd been caught out many times in a heated argument with the referee and sent off for mouthing off.

And then it clicks.

If the cameras are following her, Wesley Rich will be there.

I've never met him. I know he comes with a silver spoon in his mouth from the many husbands his mother has screwed and then walked down the aisle with. Of his behavior I've seen on television, he's a fucking jerkoff. Something about his attitude gets under my skin.

When Ash told me Wesley and Emmy were dating, I was surprised she'd stoop that low. He enjoyed his women and was known to toss them out when he was done.

Apparently, she tamed him.

"Will Wesley be there?"

She keeps her head down, swirling the food on her plate. "Yes."

"Who cares, Emmy! I'm bored. Plus, I need some head to relieve the tension," Ash whines.

It catches her attention with a reactive response. "Uhuh... you're married. Don't go screwing things up. We don't need any more scandal in our lives."

"What are you talking about? There's no scandal," he corrects not knowing about Wesley's indiscretions. I hadn't said anything to him, keeping my promise to her intact. "And a hand-job doesn't count. It's not cheating."

I try to keep a straight face but let out a laugh. We've had this conversation numerous times and I agreed it doesn't count.

"It counts. Believe me. Seriously, you're an idiot," she tells him without emotion. "You can come... on one condition."

I shake my head glancing at Ash. "Here we go. What?"

"You don't touch any women and they don't touch you."

"Fine," Ash agrees, wincing and letting out another loud belch. "Excuse me. I need to use the restroom." He bolts off to the restroom leaving the two of us alone at the table. The remaining patrons have vacated the premises, leaving only the two of us and the waiter in the room.

"So, does that rule count for me? Or am I free to do whoever I please?"

She glances up from her plate, her blue eyes wild and staring at me with curiosity. "You're free to do whoever you please. You're not tied to anyone."

"I'm not," I say freely, keeping my gaze fixed. "So, what's the deal with you and Wesley?"

"No deal. We're just filming."

"As a couple?"

"For the sake of the network. Yes."

"But you live together?"

"Technically, yes."

I remain quiet, unsure of why my heart rate spikes and why my fist is clenched on the table while she stares blankly. The unanswered questions swirling in my mind drive me to the brink of insanity, but I have no right to put her on the spot because she has her life and I have mine.

"Go on. Ask the question. You want to know if we're still sleeping in the same bed or if I'm fucking him. Right?" She waits for my response, irritated we're even talking about this. "The answer is no, Logan. I don't fuck him."

"I never asked."

"I can see it burning on the tip of your tongue. He cheated on me. He was the one who broke our relationship," she reminds me.

"Interesting. Were you not the one who just told Ash that hand-jobs are classed as cheating?"

"Yeah, so?" She shrugs.

I lean in closer, purposely making her uncomfortable. "So, me fingering that tight little pussy of yours is *not* cheating?"

I expect her to blush, squirm in her seat, and make this moment awkward. But of course, Emerson Chase has to have the last word, the only woman to *never* back down. "In my mind we were already broken up. So, get off your high horse because you getting me off meant nothing more than that."

Fuck. Me.

Ash thunders back complaining that his ass will be burning for days, and now he knows what it feels like when women complained his dick's too big.

It's enough for Emmy to almost throw up on the table.

We call for the check before making our way outside. There's two men wearing baseball caps standing on the opposite side of the road. They keep to themselves though look in our direction every few seconds. LA is swarming with paparazzi, it's one of the reasons why I hate visiting the place.

We chat briefly about tonight with Emmy agreeing to pick us up at eight. The network's organized a limo expecting a huge viewership of this episode. She told us she'll need to let them know we're riding, and if the footage is to air it will require our consent as well.

Ash hurries the conversation, climbing into the car, rushing to get back to the hotel in case his ass explodes again. We take off and with Ash's erratic driving, I should offer to take the wheel considering this is a rental. He seems to know his way around, ignoring the GPS and cussing at drivers who are observing the actual speed limit.

Emmy's been the only girl to ever challenge me. She knows how to get to me and her comment in the restaurant doesn't leave me so easily. I know I'm competitive, but my desire to make her squirm overtakes any rational thoughts I once had about Emerson Chase.

Me: *Tell me something, Emerson Chase. Would me fucking you also be classed as nothing more?*

That will put her in her place. I really wish there's some sort of visual contact so I can see her face turn bright red.

Emerson: *I don't know Logan Carrington. Give it a try and see how you go.*

I stare at my phone, almost gulping as I read the

message. It's not like it took her minutes to respond where she had time to think about it—that reply was instantaneously.

My fingers can't type because I'm confused and unsure of how to respond. All I can think about is *thrusting my cock inside her. Placing my lips on her clit and tasting her sweet pussy once I've blown inside her.* All the things you shouldn't be thinking about because the man beside you is your best friend, her brother.

I place my phone in my pocket avoiding any further contact for now, at the same time Ash swerves into a gas station and runs for his life, leaving me alone in the car.

The temptation's too high.

And so, I type...

Me: *You're asking me to do something dangerous, Emerson. If you know me, you know I never back down from a challenge.*

The bubble lingers for what feels like minutes. Ash walks out of the restroom with a relieved look on his face. He climbs into the car and gives me a rundown about how dirty it was inside, and how his ass is literally burning, and he doesn't think he can go out tonight. I'm half paying attention to him until her message appears on my screen.

Emerson: *Ditto.*

"Can you believe Emmy telling me not to score tonight?"

Yes, I can. Emmy has always believed that if you commit to something you have to stick it through. Relationships are no different. And despite her telling us the ins and outs of cheating, she knows very well what she'd done with me was wrong.

It was nothing more than a lover's revenge.

Driven by anger, hurt, and wanting to make Wesley Rich feel as small as she was feeling.

I should walk away. Remove myself from this tangled web.

But I want in.

All in.

I want her revenge and everything that comes with it.

TEN

*"One of the deadliest combinations is
butterflies and jealousy.
Then, you know your heart's in real trouble."*
~ Emerson Chase

Logan's last message renders me speechless. I know
him well enough not to back down. Play the game
and you won't look like the fool who got jealous
when you threw in that comment of him fucking all of
Hollywood.

I'm standing in my wardrobe wearing my black-laced
bra and matching panties, wondering what I should wear
tonight. I really don't want Ash and Logan to come, but I
felt like I was backed into a corner. It's not that I don't enjoy
their company. I just know Wes can be a dick and he's never
met Logan which means he will go out of his way to be an
even bigger dick.

The texts between us are fun, but I've left it at that.

Logan's never showed interest in me before the night at the lake, and these flirtatious conversations are merely a part of everyday life from a man with a *long* belt. At least that's what I continue to tell myself.

The black off-the-shoulder dress is calling my name, paired with some heels which lace all the way up my legs stopping just underneath my knees. I place the shoes on first, knowing it's a mission to get these laces tied up. As gorgeous as they are they're a massive pain in the ass to get on.

My phone is lying on the white carpet beneath my feet. Leaning down, I notice Mom's name flash on the screen.

"What's up, Mom? I'm literally knee-deep in this leather heel that's a blessing and curse."

"Are those the ones you wore to that award show where the rapper gave you his number, and you had to tell him he had food stuck in his grill?"

"Your attention to detail is priceless, Mom." I laugh. "And yes, they're the hooker heels."

"Must be a special occasion."

"Just a party at Scarlett's house. Did I tell you Ash and Logan are coming?"

I hear the pause, followed by the sound of the oven timer chiming in the background.

"Your brother will be the death of me. Did I tell you I had a lengthy conversation with Alessandra, or how he likes to call her, Sandy?"

"Was it over the wet towels on the bed?" I cringe because my brother's a slob. "Or how he cuts his toenails in bed?"

"It was over them having an argument when he left. It seems she doesn't understand his lifestyle. The traveling part. I tried to explain it without getting involved. The last thing I want to be known as is the nosey mother-in-law."

"How about the mother-in-law who writes about cowboys getting it on in the barn with the farmer's wife?"

"You laugh now, but that bestseller paid for your ballet lessons which you gave up after one recital," she points out.

"Yeah, yeah... thanks, Mom," I tease gently. "Listen, I have to go. Wish me luck."

"Luck?" she questions. "With what, kid?"

Dammit. I haven't been honest with Mom about what happened with Wesley. Every time she brings him up, I quickly answer then steer the conversation to a different subject. I don't know why I struggle with it. Usually, I tell her everything. A part of me honestly believes if I told her the truth, it will make it harder to live a lie in front of the cameras.

"Things have been difficult between Wesley and me. I hope tonight we can relax," I half admit.

"I figured that," she soothes over the phone. "I'm here, kid. No judgment. Okay?"

"I know, Mom."

We hang up the call and I feel a bit better about how I left things with us.

With my shoes now on, I slip into my dress when Wesley walks in. He knows better than to walk in unannounced but disregards my wishes, standing behind me wearing his designer jeans and a dark gray shirt with his sleeves rolled up.

I *hate* that a part of me still desires him. The part which remains confused and hurt by his actions.

If only his hands hadn't touched someone else.

If only he didn't think that destroying our relationship was okay.

Taking a deep breath in, I turn around while placing my earrings on.

"You look good," he says, adjusting his cuffs.

"Thank you. So do you, I guess."

"You guess?" He places his hand on his heart, making a pained face with a smile. "Ouch. Okay, I deserve that."

"You deserve a lot of things."

"And not you, right?"

"You know where I stand with our relationship."

Wes bows his head then lifts it again only for his eyes to meet mine and they're full of desperation.

"It's been weeks, Em, and the only time you've let me touch you is when we're filming. Don't you understand how sorry I am? I'd do anything to take it back, but I just can't, okay?"

"This isn't the time to talk about it. The limo should be downstairs waiting, and I forgot to tell you Ash and Logan are coming. We'll pick them up," I say quickly while grabbing my purse and checking my hair one more time, avoiding his apology.

It's an awkward limo ride over to Scarlett's house. I finally introduce Wesley to Logan and almost instantly there's this weird tension. Thank God Ash talks about his restroom mayhem the entire ride over.

"Are you sure you didn't order a different curry to mine?"

"Positive."

"And you didn't go to the bathroom once?"

"Nope. Iron stomach."

"I just don't get it." He shakes his head.

"So, why are you both in town?" Wes places his hand on my knee, a gesture which generally wouldn't bother me but right now, it does.

There's a visible flush in Logan's cheeks. His eyes follow the movement of Wes' hand as they rest on top of my knee. With his mouth turned down he speaks through clenched teeth, "We're trying out for the US soccer team."

"Nice."

I want to strangle Wes for being a stuck-up, arrogant jerk.

We carry on with some small talk about the latest movies and who'll be at the party. Ash keeps the conversation rolling, talking non-stop so the tumbling tumbleweed won't roll past us. I know how he feels about Wesley, but he's never one to keep his mouth shut.

Ash switches topics to the relief of Wesley who looks bored with the conversation. "So, I guess I forgot to say congratulations. You know, with the engagement."

Wesley keeps his smile fixed, not letting on we aren't together. He slides his hand above my knee until it's resting on my hemline. I wriggle to move it away, only for him to grip tight. "Thank you. Your sister is quite the catch."

"Just take care of her, or else you've got me and Logan to answer to," Ash warns in a serious tone.

"Right. Of course, I'd never do anything to hurt her."

Wesley places his arm around me, moving my hair to the side and kissing the crook of my neck. Across from where we sit, Logan looks at me with deep curiosity. No other emotion on his face aside from that. His muscles are flexed underneath the navy, short-sleeved shirt he's wearing, his fingers tapping impatiently on the headrest beside him. His expression turns to boredom then he stares out the window uninterested.

"We're here," I announce with some relief.

Scarlett's mansion is a large, modern home hidden behind many trees to keep the property private. In the last few years, any movie she's starred in has become a blockbuster hit. The tabloids are forever in a frenzy over her love life. She apparently dates actors and funnily enough, our friendship began when she was rumored to be dating Wes.

Stories like that never faze me, so when I ran into her during a red-carpet event, we had a good old laugh and ended the rumor mill right there.

Scarlett's the most wanted woman in the industry. She's barely in town, but when she has some downtime, we usually catch up for dinner or drinks. I admire her ability to juggle it all and I often seek guidance about how to cope with this demanding lifestyle we call showbiz.

There's a small booth at the bottom of the driveway with two security guards checking the guests' names off on a list. Our limo drives through and up the steep hill until we stop out the front of the house. I can't be more grateful. There's way too much testosterone in the car and I'm desperate to escape.

Our regular camera crew are already positioned out front. Scarlett has given permission for the network to use footage for our show providing she approves the final edit. She told them they can only film in the foyer, living room, and outdoor area, where most of the guests are congregated.

"Okay guys, we need you to walk into the house. We'll film you entering from here." Josie points to the statue that sits out front. "Then Karl will come in from the right."

Ash waves goodbye, heading into the house with Logan beside him. I wait for Logan to turn around but he doesn't. He's looking too eager to join Ash and the loud music streaming from the house.

I take a deep breath while waiting for Josie to hook me up with the mic. She clips it on and tucks the rest of the unit into the back of my dress then does the same to Wes. I try to keep my shoulders poised as Wes holds my hand while walking into the foyer.

"Emerson," Scarlett yells from the top of the stairs. She steps down, wearing nine-inch gold heels looking absolutely stunning in a white jumpsuit. Taking each step slow, she finally hits the bottom level and greets me with a double air kiss before leaning over to Wes and doing the same, careful not to smudge her signature red lipstick. "I'm glad you guys made it." She walks us outside, linking her arms between ours. "Drinks are over there, make yourself comfortable, and please excuse the hoard of Playboy Bunnies that somehow got invited to the party."

Its not difficult to find them. You only have to look at every man and where their eyes are directed to spot them huddled in the corner—fake boobies in tow. Wesley laughs, making some joke about 'how many blondes does it take to change a light bulb.' I'm not listening to his answer. Instead, my eyes move around the room until I find the only male not staring at them, but rather they're staring at me—Logan.

I want to go and talk to him, but Wesley pulls me in the direction of the bar. He orders some drinks then becomes distracted talking to some friends of his. Thankfully, Scarlett's beside me and ushers me to the table sitting by the pool.

"Okay, so we want you to talk about what's been happening in your lives." Josie lowers the camera, adjusting the lens and zooming in to where we sit, the boom mic held firmly above our heads and out of shot. "Scarlett, can you please move a little bit back?"

Scarlett adjusts her position as per Josie's direction.

Josie turns the camera on while I pretend she's not there, jumping straight into conversation. "So, I've been offered a deal to expand the fitness line to Europe," I tell her, proudly.

"Em! That's great news. Does that mean you'll be spending time there?"

"Umm... not too much time. I'd be lonely, my family's back here."

"Speaking of family... Ash and Logan are quite something." She grins.

"Something, as in talented?"

"Logan Carrington," she mouths slowly with a smirk. "Mister *Sports Illustrated*."

I don't know how we got onto this topic so quickly, and I hate being filmed while talking about Logan.

"And Ash modeling those sports boxers for *Adidas*... how do you sleep at night?"

"Well," I say with a mouthful of champagne. "Usually great, but maybe not so much tonight since you brought up my brother in underwear."

"Oh, I get it. But Em... your brother is sexy."

I scrunch my nose, disgusted by her comment. I've heard many women talking about Ash like a sex object and it gets grosser every time.

"Okay, sorry." She raises her hand laughing. "And Logan? Is he seeing anyone?"

I shake my head instantly. "I don't know. You'd have to ask him that question. Soccer players talk about one thing only... the game."

I'm well aware of the pang of jealousy which hits me. For all I know, he could be dating someone and all these flirtatious back-and-forths are merely to fill in his time. I scan my brain to find another topic to talk about, quick to change the subject to her latest movie. "I can't believe you're filming in Australia next month. I'd love to go visit."

"I'm excited. We're filming for three months in Sydney. I need to find me an Aussie husband." She sighs.

"Oooh... that would be nice." I smile.

"I love their accents."

"And the way they call everyone mate."

"So easy-going," she says dreamily. "Like 'hey, there's a spider! No worries, mate.'"

"You lost me at spider," I tell her, with a shake in my voice. "I'll take my American boy."

"Your American boy, of course. Wesley Rich."

Josie stops filming, telling the both of us to relax while she joins Karl for a short break. As soon as she leaves the area, I finally chill with some more champagne and a few other actors who join us.

After my third round of drinks, my voice becomes louder as we fight to be heard over the music. With a sudden urge to pee, I remove my mic and tell Scarlett I'll be back.

Somehow, I stumble my way to the bathroom, waiting in line and chatting with a few people.

When I finish, my vision becomes hazy and I forget which way I have to go.

"Jesus, can't take you anywhere."

I hear his voice but can't see him. When I turn around, he's standing right behind me.

"Oh... there you are Mr. Hussy," I tease, placing my hands on his chest for support. "Let me guess... you've screwed a Playboy Bunny already. Wait... maybe two."

"You're drunk."

"I'm right, right?"

"I don't like blondes or fake tits."

"That's not what your mom said."

"What?" he asks in confusion.

"I don't know," I mutter. "I had nothing to come back with."

"That's not exactly a mom joke," he chastises. "Stop drinking, okay? It's like you're nervous or something. In the limo you were all weird."

"No, you were all weird!"

"Wait." He pauses with a smile. "Another non-comeback?"

"Logan," I say in a soft voice, suddenly tired. "I just need an escape from reality. Three shots and I'm almost there."

He moves his head left then right, scanning the area then dragging me to a quieter section away from the bathroom. I notice his eyes appear slightly red like he's tired or maybe it's from the shots the Playboy Bunnies made him drink. "Are you drunk?"

"I had a few. Not as much as you, though. I thought you told Ash you were laying off the drink because the tabloids said you had a drinking problem?"

"Geez." I lean on the wall, rolling my eyes at him. "Does Ash tell you everything? Don't you have something better to talk about than me? What else does he tell you?"

"I don't know." He keeps his expression blank. "Are you hiding something?"

"Nope." I hold his gaze. "I've pretty much told you everything. Wesley screwed some hookers, we're pretending to be engaged for the sake of the show, and when I was eleven, I was the one who accidentally threw your ball over the school fence which got eaten by that psycho dog."

Logan stares back in astonishment. "That ball was signed by a soccer legend, and you threw it over the fence?"

I lean in, playing with the lapel of his shirt, and sweetening my tone. "Accidentally."

"How do you *accidentally* throw it over?"

With a pleasing smile, I alter my story to ease his pain. "My arm kinda slipped... over instead of under."

"You owe me," he threatens.

"Yeah, add it to the list, buddy."

"Buddy?" He raises his brow with a smirk. "I thought we had a deal."

Lowering my head to hide my grin, I cross my legs to ignore the delicious throb which began the moment he pulled me aside. Our petty arguments rile me up and now result in this—me wanting his tongue to run along the inside of my thigh.

You did not just say that out loud.

Shit!

No, wait... his face remains the same.

Stupid champagne.

During my internal argument with my brain, Logan's closed the gap between us.

"The cameras have been following you all night," Logan whispers courageously in my ear. "How will I get to prove my point?"

This is it.

There's no phone between us to filter out the raging hormones.

My body's betraying me, calling out like a desperate whore. My brain is slower to come to the party, chilling in a hot tub telling all the rational voices to sit down and have another drink.

"You know Karl? He's easily distracted by good-looking men. Closet gay. When a model walks past him, he'll forget I'm around. He chases dick like I chase chocolate."

Logan's amused, shaking his head at my comment. "So, what happens if you want dick and chocolate?"

"I've never been in that predicament," I answer smugly. "Why? You got chocolate on you?"

"Are you saying you want dick and chocolate, right now?"

"How did we even get onto this?" I scratch my head, ignoring his cocky remark.

"Nice segue, Chase," he says with a broad grin. "What about your other camerawoman?"

"Josie? She likes to talk... about her cats and her new boyfriend. He just moved in and told her he never expected to be around so many pussies." I laugh instantly, remembering the moment Josie had innocently told us he'd said that. I swear she's a virgin because the joke flew completely over her head.

Logan tries to keep a straight face until something changes and his smile becomes a frown. "And Wesley?"

"What does it matter?"

"He's your *fiancé*," he states, dragging out the word fiancé like it fucking means something.

"I told you. He isn't," I tell him for the millionth time. "You've got a choice, Carrington... prove your point or go run off with Ash and score some Hollywood bimbo looking to put an athlete on their resume."

He keeps his eye contact firm, then slowly, they move and trace my mouth. I can't help but bite my bottom lip, attempting to control whatever the hell is happening between us right now. I'm semi-aware anyone can find us, including Wesley. But deep down inside, the possibility only adds to the thrill.

"C'mon," I push him. "What's it gonna be?"

He places his finger on my lips, lingering, then runs it

slowly down my body, against my skin and between my breasts. I'm sure he can feel the thump of my heart as it almost bursts out of my chest from the nerves of being caught. He continues to move down until his finger has grazed between my legs causing me to suck in a breath.

"You," he whispers with fire in his eyes. "I choose you."

ELEVEN

"The thrill of getting caught
is a dangerous thing."
~ *Emerson Chase*

H e presses his finger hard against my clit, only the thin fabric between us. I'm still holding in a breath, scared if I let it go my legs will fail and I'll drop to my knees which happen to be at eye level with his crotch.

Maybe that's not such a bad thing?

"Emerson," I hear my name being called, and like a giant bucket of cold water being thrown at us, Logan retracts his hands and shoves them in his pocket.

Scarlett turns the corner, looking slightly flustered. "We need to talk." She realizes I'm standing with Logan and she's quick to notice no one else around. I can see her mind turning, wondering what's going on and why the both of us look suspicious.

"I'm sorry. Did I interrupt something?" She hides her smile, eyeing me with curiosity.

"Nope," I say casually. "Logan asked for a room so he can screw a Bunny."

"Talk about throwing me under the bus, Chase," he notes with dark amusement. "Excuse her. She's chasing dick and chocolate."

My shoulders move up and down while laughing at how ridiculous that sounds.

"Sounds like I've interrupted a fascinating conversation. Maybe I should leave you guys—"

Logan interrupts Scarlett, "I need another drink. The Bunnies have the stamina of a... well... a Bunny. I'll catch you around later, Emmy."

Asshole.

Scarlett ushers me into her bedroom through a hidden stairwell behind the kitchen. Guests aren't allowed upstairs, but she still closes the door behind us so we can talk in private.

I've never seen her bedroom and even in my intoxicated state, I can't help but utter the words "Wow!" a million times over. It's huge. All white with a large four-poster bed in the middle of the room. Even her bed sheets look fancy with an intricate gold trim.

A few pieces of abstract artwork hang on the walls which brings the room to life. I swear they're couples in compromising positions but I'm drunk and have sex on my brain, so what would I know.

"There's not many people I trust, but I know you're not like the rest of the fake people in Hollywood."

"Ah... thank you?"

"My um... brother-in-law is here."

"Okaaay," I drag, unsure of what that means.

She shakes her head, almost in a state of panic. "You don't understand."

"Of course, I don't. You just said your brother-in-law is here."

"I'm in love with him, Em."

She crosses her arms, pacing back and forth at the same time I mouth, "Oh."

"Yes, oh. They have a daughter. I've pretty much avoided him for the past few months, but my sister confided in me and told me they've separated. Things aren't working out, and they both needed a break from each other."

"I've heard kids can do that to you."

"You don't understand."

"I'm trying to, Scarlett, but I guess you haven't painted the whole picture for me," I tell her.

"I made a move on him. When he first came here. It's awkward between us and now he's here, and single."

"I wouldn't call him single. Is the separation final? People have breaks then realize they're in love with each other again."

She nods her head in agreeance then quickly shakes it. "Morgan, my sister, she has a complicated life. Noah is... not so patient. I mean... he worships the ground she walks on but ever since she had the baby they've simply grown apart."

"That's sad... for the daughter."

"I know." Scarlett lets out a frustrated groan. "Em, please tell me to get over this. I hate feeling this way. I avoid him at all costs, and when I'm forced to be around him I pretend like there's nothing's there. I'm embarrassed about what I did but... I don't know. I haven't even been with a man for so long because I just can't get him out of my damn mind."

"Maybe you need a distraction fuck?" I suggest. "Like someone to just knock your socks off so you can move on."

She laughs. "I'll cross Logan off my list."

I clear my throat. "Logan is single."

"You're an awful liar."

"That's the truth!"

"Uh-huh." She grins. "God, what do I do?"

"Look, just have some wine and relax. You're beautiful. Men love you. I mean, really, how good looking are we talking?"

She grabs my hand and drags me outside the room and to the top of the stairs, the void opens to the main foyer where partygoers stand around. She points to a man positioned in the corner, chatting with some other men. It doesn't matter which one he is because the three of them are as hot as fuck.

The lighter-haired one is tall with a handsome face and sharp jaw—it's like *jaw* porn. The darker-haired one is wearing glasses and is dressed in a plain white tee and jeans —totally *glasses* porn. The third one looks slightly older, dressed much smarter and looks like a model from a designer magazine—absolutely *model* porn.

We're standing a fair distance away, but even from here, I can see he has lighter eyes similar to those of Logan. Great, more *eye* porn.

This party just got interesting. Now I understand her predicament.

"Oh... you're so screwed," I say without thinking.

"I told you," she hisses. "What could be worse than this?"

"How about almost fucking your brother's best friend only to be interrupted by a friend who's hopelessly pining for her brother-in-law?"

She turns to face me, eyebrows raised, her eyes wide and full of shock. "I thought you guys were just flirting. You're engaged."

"Nope. Wes fucked two hookers while snorting crack and everything you see filmed is a lie."

We both fall silent, staring into the crowd with heavy shoulders.

"We're both screwed."

"Yep," I quip. "So, your brother-in-law?"

"Noah," she corrects me. "His nickname is Mr. Rebound. Before he met my sister he was known for preying on broken women."

"What's new? Wesley does that now and he's supposedly committed."

She bumps my shoulder, laughing then quickly apologizes. "We should probably head back. Your camera crew look pissed off."

"Will you be okay?"

"Yeah, I don't know. I guess I have to go say hello."

"I'll come with you," I offer. "You know, for moral support."

She chuckles. "C'mon."

We both step downstairs weaving in and out of the crowd until we're standing beside Noah and his friends. I can see the awkward exchange between Scarlett and Noah, but move on as she introduces me.

"Haden Cooper runs the publishing house who published my book," she says proudly of the man wearing the glasses. "Lex Edwards owns a few studios in town and his wife is also my lawyer."

The older guy has these very green eyes, almost an emerald shade. It's hard to concentrate and not be rude by staring at them.

"And Noah is my brother-in-law."

"Nice to meet you all. I'm Emerson."

Haden snickers. "Oh, we know who you are."

I smile politely, holding back the flirtatious eye-batting. "Is that a good or a bad thing?"

Lex bows his head, hiding his smirk while Noah stands there mirroring Haden.

"Good," Haden responds. "We'll leave it at that since your fiancé is over there."

I turn my head to look where Haden's pointing. Low and behold, Wes is surrounded by a group of people, mainly women, who are all desperate for his attention.

"Ignore him, please," I say bored. "Lord knows I do."

"So, Emerson's here with her brother, Ashley Chase and his friend Logan Carrington." Scarlett sways the conversation, detecting my annoyance.

"I'd love to meet them," Lex speaks up. His voice is so masculine yet smooth as silk. "I'm a huge Royal Kings fan."

"Sure, if you can pry them away from the Playboy Bunnies," I joke.

The three of them laugh. "Easier said than done, right?"

I continue to chat for a few more minutes before Josie finds me and requests that I head on outside to film some additional scenes with a few Hollywood big names who are at the party.

I quickly excuse myself, promising Lex I will find Ash and Logan and send them his way.

We set up outside where I clip on my mic, and film for another hour. Our discussion revolves around weddings and my relationship with Wesley. I honestly couldn't have thought of a more mundane topic, but Cliff gave the camera crew strict instructions to film me discussing my wedding plans. *Fictional wedding plans since we aren't actually getting married!*

I make sure I don't have any alcohol in hand while filming, but when a waiter walks past with a tray of drinks I reach out and grab a glass, downing it in one go when Josie uses the restroom.

This wedding talk does nothing to curb my anxiety. Every time I think about it, I resent Wes even more. I bet he's not being filmed talking about the wedding because he's a guy. *Fucking sexist bullshit.*

Karl's now joined Josie and asks me to walk through the house and find Wesley so we can finish up taping. I keep walking and stop just shy of the fire-pit where Logan's sitting next to some woman. He hands her a wine, and despite the bullshit he said earlier she's a fucking blonde.

In the corner of my eye, I see his gaze shift to meet mine. I quickly move on, ignoring the jealousy building up inside me. *You have no right to feel that way*—ignore, *ignore,* IGNORE.

Inside the house, Karl moves the camera around the room capturing what I'm witnessing. I continue walking, pretending Logan's behavior doesn't affect me whatsoever because it shouldn't, and I'm terrified the camera will pick up my irrational emotions.

Wesley's moved to the main living room cozied up in the middle of women only. There appears to be no men around him, and oddly, it bothers me more than it should. I still care about him, and I hate admitting that.

"Here's my baby," he slurs. "Come sit on my lap?"

I don't sit on his lap. Instead, ask the skank beside him to shove over.

"Did I tell you girls how much I love her? She's going to be my wife." He laughs, grabbing my neck with his hand

and pulling my lips toward his. I watch him pull back with mixed emotion written all over his face. "You smell different."

My instinct is to sniff my armpits, but the more he stills the more I become paranoid. I shouldn't smell of anyone... Logan hasn't been near me. *Stop being so paranoid.* "I've been mingling with everyone, hugging everyone..."

He continues to watch me then follows through with a laugh. "Oh, yeah." Sliding his hand up my thigh, he leans into my ear. "I don't care what you want. I'm going to fuck you tonight."

"Stop it!" I tell him, pushing his hand aside. "You're drunk."

He leans back in and I know the microphone can't pick up too well over the noise in the room, but Wes strategically removes his mic.

There's a commotion near the entrance, a fight has broken out between two men. Karl turns to face them and film.

Wes grabs my thigh, applying firm pressure. "You think someone else can touch you? Then think again. You're coming home with me and the second we walk through that door, I'm going to take back what's mine. I'm done waiting for you." His demand to take me without my consent angers me beyond belief. *How dare he!* Wes thinks I so easily will forget what he did? I know I'm not thinking straight. I know the champagne's not only expensive, but it is rather potent clouding any rational thoughts or any ability to remain civilized.

He doesn't own me.

No one fucking owns me!

"You're a jerk. I'm not coming home. So, do whatever the hell you want!" I storm off and start looking for Ash and

Logan. Searching everywhere, Karl tries to keep up with me, calling my name frantically. I notice Ash huddled in the corner with his head buried in some girl's neck. I stomp to them, quick to pull him away.

"What the fuck, Emmy?"

"We're going."

"I'm busy." He motions with his eyes to the girl next to him.

"He's married," I shout at her. "Did you know that? Or you don't care 'cause you just want to be known as a whore?"

The girl stands up on her platform heels, her skimpy dress pulled up past her knees. She has on way too much mascara, so much so you can barely see her eyes in between her thick lashes. "Who you calling a whore?"

"Uh... you?" I bark with a smile, crossing my arms firmly over my chest.

I can see a look of shock filter out across Karl's face.

He wants drama, he's damn well got drama. Emerson Chase has her gloves on ready to fight anyone who crosses her path.

The whore launches herself right at me. Ash attempts to hold her back, while I shout profanities that would make any sailor proud. This is all *his* fault—he can't keep his dick in check like every other man. I'm so sick of it, and perhaps the alcohol isn't helping but it's heightening my emotions to the point where I have no control anymore.

My body jerks back, a hand restraining me, removing me from the space where that ditsy whore tried to pull my hair. *She fights like a fucking girl.*

"C'mon, Emmy. Just leave them alone," Logan grits.

I pull away from him. "Because you condone that?"

Whore launches for me again, yelling, "You're nothing

but a reality-TV slut."

She shouldn't have said that!

Trying hard to wriggle my way out of Logan's grasp is near impossible with the grip he has on my arms. He's stronger than I anticipated.

"Ash. Control her," Logan warns him. "I'm taking Emmy home."

"I don't want to go home."

"Well, I'm taking you anywhere but here."

Logan drags me away with Karl struggling to follow. We're almost to the front door when Wes stops me, blocking the entrance.

Wes' eyes are wild with jealousy, his veins prominent and scattered all over his red face. "You're not taking her anywhere."

"Get out of the way." Logan raises his voice, keeping his grip tight.

"I said..." Wesley almost spits, "... you're not taking her anywhere."

"You know what? Fuck you! You don't own me, Wesley Rich," I yell into his face. "Go back to your sofa full of sluts." The adrenaline running through my veins gives me the strength to pull away from Logan and push past Wesley until the fresh air graces my boiling hot skin. Seeking some sort of escape, I spot our limo and slide in demanding the driver take me home.

Trying to still my heart to no avail, I bury my head into my legs. I hear the door open but ignore it. At this moment I just don't understand life, or why all the men in my life have this need to act the way they do.

I don't look up immediately but smell him instantly. *I hate that he smells so good.*

"You're not going home."

"I can handle my own decisions," I argue back, defeated, and on the verge of tears.

"Why are you angry at me?"

"Because you're all the same. Ash is no fucking different and you're his best friend."

"We're not the same, Emerson. And I will *not* allow you to go home."

"It's not like he's going to get his way."

"Excuse me?"

"Wesley," I mumble. "He said he was going to have his way with me and that I had no choice."

Logan lets out a sinister laugh. "No way you're going home then. It will be over my fucking dead body."

"What do you care anyway? It's not like you're my fiancé. Or even my boyfriend. You're my..." trailing off I stop talking not wanting to say anymore.

His body slumps, his eyebrows knit together in a frown. I'm sure he feels defeated the same as I am feeling right now.

"What are you trying to say, Emmy?"

"I'm not saying anything."

"I-I know you," he stutters. "You always have something to say."

"Not this time..." I pause, then retract that comment and voice my thoughts without any care in the world. "We agreed it was one time and that was it. I got off, maybe you got off. It was a great night. Three cheers for knowing how to get a girl off in less than three minutes."

Logan lifts his head, watching me with a steady yet pained gaze. *Why does he have to be so beautiful?* Of all the glamorous men attending the party tonight, why is Logan the one I can't get out of my head?

"I just want to go home, Logan. All I want is to lay

down and close my eyes."

"I won't take you home... not to him."

I shuffle a little closer, resting my head on his lap. When he begins to stroke my hair, I fight to hold back my tears but lose the battle quickly.

"Why are you crying?"

"Because I'm tired..." I cry openly, through thin strained sobs, "... of everything."

"Then don't be."

It takes a moment to compose myself then sit up and question him. "What do you mean?"

"You're tired of the responsibility. You're tired of being in front of the cameras. So am I, Emmy. I'm done with it, too. Let's live a little... just you and me. No one else has to know."

"I'm not following you."

"Let's throw all caution into the wind, have fun, just you and me and no Ash. He doesn't need to know."

"But the show?"

"They don't always follow you."

"What exactly will we do?"

"Whatever you want, Emmy. Whatever your fucking heart desires."

I smile, through my tears. "Whatever I want?"

He nods with a grin, staring at my mouth as he runs his finger against my bottom lip.

I push the button to extend the screen and speak into the speaker, "Ted? Take us to Hollywood Boulevard."

"Yes, ma'am."

"What exciting things are there to do on Hollywood Boulevard?" Logan asks, wiping the tears from my face with his thumb while waiting for an answer.

"Just you wait and see."

TWELVE

"Revenge is an ugly disease."
~ *Logan Carrington*

"You misled me when we pulled up at Costumes and Toys." A wicked smile flashes on her face as her bouncing body moves in through the automatic doors.

When we pulled up to the store, I thought, *Okay, she's kinky and maybe it's my lucky day. How wrong was I to think it had anything to do with sex?*

I watch Emmy make her way to the wall displaying the wigs, ignoring the urge to grab her body and tell her how fucking sexy she looks in her tight black dress and the shoes. *Yeah, don't get me started.*

"C'mon." She gestures, calling me over. "Pick a wig."

"A wig? When I said let's have fun, what part of that screamed wig shopping?"

She shoves a brown, shaggy piece into my chest. "If you wanna play, you gotta keep it a secret."

Placing a blonde wig over her head she turns to face me, seeking my approval. I shake my head instantly—I don't want to be seen with *Florence Henderson*.

She searches the wall again and grabs a wig styled in a bob.

"It's pink," I say.

"Well, duh! What do you think?"

"The paparazzi will find you in a heartbeat," I tell her.

I scan the wall and notice a subtle black wig. Removing it from the hook I place it over her hair, carefully tucking in the loose strands underneath. Her deep blue eyes stare back at me oddly. With just this one gaze, I'm taken back to a time when life wasn't complicated. When the biggest hurdle was making it home before Mom, so I could cover the gashes on my leg from when I fell over jumping off the tree to prove I could fly.

And I got this—all from this one stare.

"That's better." I smile.

"Now you."

"Do I have to?"

"Yes," she says firmly. "Now stop being a baby and pick a wig."

Considering I've never worn a wig in my life, the choice seems overwhelming. I settle for a dark blond wig that makes me look like Justin Timberlake from his NSYNC days. It's either that or a poorly cut piece that will made me a dead ringer for Ozzy Osbourne.

"Great! Now you need facial hair."

I point to my chin. "I have facial hair."

"Hmm... yeah, but you're not hairy enough. You need to look like a man enjoying a Saturday night in Hollywood.

Not like Logan Carrington, soccer extraordinaire, taking Emerson Chase out on some wild sex ride."

I can't hide the smirk. "We're going on a wild sex ride?"

"Does it look like I'm dressed for a wild sex ride?" She pauses. "You know what? Don't answer that."

I can see the blush, yet she's quick to busy herself, picking up a mustache that will make me look like an aging porn star. "Is this absolutely necessary?" I ask for the final time.

Ignoring my question completely she finds a hideous-looking pair of reading glasses, thrown into a clearance bin. She also pulls out a bow tie.

"We're set," she beams, deliriously happy for someone who looks like she should teleport back to the seventies with her glasses.

"I've never looked more ridiculous."

"I'll argue that. Remember that Christmas jumper you used to wear? The one our neighbor knitted for all of us, but your snowmen looked like two giant dicks?"

She had to bring it up. That jumper still gives me the chills, yet my mom insists on keeping the photos of me posing in front of our barely decorated tree. The snowmen did look like two giant dicks. The neighbor absolutely had dick on her mind when she was knitting that piece of shit.

"Point taken. Where to now?"

"It's a surprise... you'll love it."

The bar's full of people, but it's expected for Saturday night in LA. There are groups who have empty glasses littering their tables, laughing heavily as their waiter brings a fresh round. There are a few couples who are keeping quiet but engaging in conversation. The music's loud and streaming through the giant speakers—an R&B remix with some 'Country Grammar' to start it off.

There's one small table available in the middle. We maneuver our way through the crowd, quickly securing the table which remains dirty with used glasses. The bar stools are high, giving us an advantage and bringing us to eye level with those dancing.

Aside from the dirty glasses, there's a menu in the middle of the table. I'm starving and can't wait to order then I realize it's a menu of songs—karaoke songs.

You've got to be fucking kidding me.

"Oh, no you don't." I pull the song list out of her hands, demanding she think of something else to do.

"We need more booze. Loosen your panties mister because karaoke is fun. It's something I never get to do. Look at all these people," she lowers her voice while leaning in, "They have no clue who we are. We can do anything we want."

Emmy has a point, not one person has recognized us so far. Everywhere you turn, someone has a phone out taking selfies or photographs of their friends.

"But it involves singing," I complain.

"Please?" Pouting her lips, and with eyes wide begging without shame, I finally give in.

"Fine. But stop giving me the puppy-dog look. Order a round of drinks so I can gear myself up, and don't pull any girly shit out like Abba or something."

She whistles for the bartender, looking terribly pleased with herself when he comes over quickly. I can't hear what she's ordering but it doesn't matter. I'll drink whatever to lessen the embarrassing performance which is about to happen.

"All right..." she raises her cocktail and presents her toast, "... to fun times. Let's go wild and live life to the fullest, if only for tonight."

We clink glasses, the both of us drinking it in one hit.

"Damn, woman..." I almost choke back the burn, "... you could drink me under the table."

"I could also fuck you under the table," she suggests with a straight face. "Or both."

I fucking love her boldness. Never wanting to admit to her that her smart mouth challenges me like no other woman has. When Emerson Chase comes out to play, you better have your A-game on because she never, *ever,* backs down.

I lean forward, bringing my face close to hers. "You're a fucking tease. Always have been."

"Whatever." She grins, pushing another glass in front of me. *Does she want me to be legless tomorrow?* I can hold a decent amount of alcohol but I've started to feel the effects. "You never look at me that way."

"That's not true."

"Oh, yeah... like when?"

"Graduation day," I tell her. "You wore this pink dress underneath your gown. When the strap of your shoe came undone you leaned forward to fix it. I saw your white lace panties peeking through."

She laughs, her beautiful smile unable to hide. "So, you caught a peek at my panties? You really were deprived."

"You were bare."

"Was I? I don't remember."

"I do." Raising my glass to my mouth, I hide my smirk. "I wanted to fucking eat it."

Her laughter slows down, becoming serious with heavy pants. Mirroring my moves, she hides behind her glass while gazing at me longingly. I want to kiss her mouth, tease her lips with my tongue and fucking taste her. Beneath my shorts my dick rages hard because all it wants is her.

"Is it hot in here?" She fans herself with a napkin, breaking my gaze.

"You tell me." I graze her arm with my fingers. "How wet are you?"

Her foot travels up my leg, resting in between on my crotch. She pushes against my cock, hard. My body jerks forward at how sensitive it is to her touch. When I see her bite down on her lip, I'm ready to throw her over my shoulder and fuck her senseless in the restroom.

"Jane Smith..." The name is called, Emerson pulls away reluctantly.

"Okay, I'm up next. Wish me luck."

"Good luck." I force a smile, not being too sure this is the greatest plan in the world.

For one—I can't sing.

And two—I hate singing.

Karaoke bars are for the brave. Those willing to make an absolute fool out of themselves and continue to go back for more. That, and everyone will be able see my cock standing proud because I have no chance of taming this wild boy.

She happily makes her way onto the small stage. With microphone in hand, she sways slightly, unable to contain her energy. "This performance is dedicated to all the women in the room that just want to be free. Screw men... we don't need them."

There's a loud cheer from the crowd—mainly women, of course. Some of whom turn to look at me wondering why she'd say that if I'm her boyfriend, or they've spotted the fake mustache which isn't hard to do. I find myself sinking into the seat, taking the remaining glasses with me and downing them in one go.

The music begins and I don't recognize the song until the fourth line. *"Don't tell me what to do,"* she sings loudly, drawing the crowd in. *"And don't tell me what to say..."*

The fire in her tune makes her belt out the song in a pleasant voice. I didn't think she could sing this well. Why haven't I noticed before? It makes me feel like there are so many things about Emmy I've never noticed before or, at least, ignored because I didn't think of her in any way besides being Ash's annoying twin sister.

Things like, how she twists the ends of her hair when she's telling a story, or how when she laughs her eyes light up and you find yourself smiling even if the story isn't funny. How she crosses her legs and tucks her foot behind her leg, and how when she leans forward the view of her tits is fucking magical.

The song wraps up and she receives a standing ovation. People yell "Girl Power," and fist-pump the air. On her way back to the table women stop her and give her a hug—an odd sentiment from a stranger. She lingers and gets caught in conversation enjoying her newfound freedom as a nobody.

I stand up, clapping my hands as she walks back while I notice the sweat glistening against her pale skin. Fanning her face again with a napkin, she can't hide the smile while trying to catch her breath.

"You were amazing. Too amazing. I think they all think I'm the douche you need to dump. Who needs dick? Girl power all the way."

She clutches her stomach, laughing. "That was so..." I wait for her to finish, realizing her smile begins to disappear and worry lines cloud her beautiful face. "I felt free."

I pull on her hand, motioning for her to sit down. This mood shift annoys the fuck out of me. One minute she's Miss Confident and the next she's controlled by that fucking moron, Wesley Rich. I saw it in the limo the way he manipulates her, and she justifies it by saying it's all for the cameras. Their relationship is nothing like mine and Louisa's.

Fuck, don't even think about her now.

You can't compare Emmy and Louisa.

"Why do you constantly remind yourself that you're trapped? What's a piece of paper, Emmy? A contract means nothing if you're unhappy. I don't fucking get it."

"Out of all people, Logan, you should understand. Your life revolves around your name signed on the dotted line. You're bound, legally, to the Royal Kings. Imagine if your coach started treating you like shit and you had no way of getting out?"

"He does treat me like shit. I just suck it up," I tell her, firmly. "The difference is, that I want to play. I wouldn't know how to exist without my name on the dotted line."

"Well, lucky you." Her sarcasm becomes bitter. "Why can't we all live like Logan Carrington?"

I remind her to keep her voice down, the mere mention of my name could alert people to our presence. The last thing we need is to be caught out.

"This is who I've become. I'm not like you and Ash, I don't have a passion that is my reason for living. I wake up every morning thinking what have I gotten myself into? The fame and money got to me."

"It did," I admit.

"I was like the popular kid in school except with a ton of money. Somehow I got caught up in being bigger than the rest of them."

"You are."

"Will you stop agreeing with me?" she complains, disappointed the glasses are empty when she checks each one.

"You want the cold, hard truth?"

"Maybe... I don't know."

"You have changed. You're not the same, and the fame did get to your head. But it's gotten to me, too, and to Ash. We're no longer kids from Green Meadows. People depend on us." I maintain my focus on her, trying to make some sense with what I'm attempting to get at. "If this isn't the life for you then move on. Tell the network you're done and move out of your apartment. Why you're still with him is beyond me."

My last comment only riles me up further. My blood is pumping furiously as I'm reminded how after tonight we'll go our separate ways and her direction is toward someone else's dick. Maybe it's an unfair assumption, but it still fucking pisses me off that she goes home to him despite what excuse she lays on me.

"I don't want to talk about this anymore. We're supposed to be having fun."

"Yeah," I drag, leaning back on my chair.

"I'm sorry, Logan." She straightens her posture. "How about you get up and sing now?"

"About that..." I attempt to think of a valid excuse. "How about we mark this as an IOU?"

"That never works," she huffs. "You used to do that in Monopoly until you were so broke you had nothing left, and still forced us to play because you thought you could make a comeback."

I smile, purposely playing with my mustache to annoy her. "Would a man with a mustache make false promises?"

She laughs, tossing her hair to the side and leaning

forward. "A man with a mustache is a sign of false promises, but I'll believe you... on one condition."

"What's that?"

"We ditch this place and find something else fun to do."

I smile. "Deal."

On the corner of Hollywood Boulevard and Highland Avenue, we cross the lights and follow the stars embedded in the pavement. I've visited this place a few times but don't see the big deal. The street's full of tourists who are snapping away as they capture this once-in-a-lifetime moment. They're rowdy and loud for being so late at night. Aside from taking pictures, a few homeless people walk up and down the pavement talking to themselves, and a few begging for money. I reach out of my wallet and pull out a few bills, handing it to an older lady with a shopping cart and a half-knitted hat.

"You know she'll probably spend that on a bottle of Jack?" Emmy tells me.

"Well, so be it. If it makes her happy then let her live for one night."

In front of the Chinese Theatre, we both notice a few paparazzi lingering near the street post. Emmy pulls my arm, looking left and right before crossing the street and dragging me with her. When our feet hit the footpath, she turns to me with fire in her eyes and asks, "What name suits a man with a mustache?"

"Huh?"

"Burt," she says confusing me even further.

Her hand is buried in mine—the touch of her skin electrifying me though I try to ignore the way it's igniting my whole body.

Emmy leads me to where the paparazzi stand and begins talking to them. "Hi. You look like you can take a great photo." She smiles innocently. "My husband Burt and I would love a photo just there in front of the Theatre. Would you mind taking one for us?"

He shrugs, barely speaking a word as he takes the phone from Emmy's hand. *What the fuck is she doing?* Has she seriously asked the paparazzi to snap a photo of us? Why the hell does she always want to play with fire?

We both walk to the spot she mentioned.

A few smiles and it's over—no biggie.

"Turn around, Burt," she whispers.

I spin around without thinking. The palms of her hands grace my cheeks, pulling them down until our lips are touching. *I should be shocked.* But instead, I move my tongue against hers as if I've waited a whole lifetime to kiss her. Even with the mustache in the way, the sensations which barrel through me are foreign. I've kissed many women in my lifetime, but none that make me question my entire life as much as this moment.

It could be seconds, yet it feels longer. Her tongue pressuring mine in a forceful wrestle that leaves my cock stirring inside my pants.

Fuck. We shouldn't be doing this.

I pull back, holding her arms at bay. "Emmy, we can't do this. Look around..." I motion my eyes to the paparazzi who begin walking toward us, phone in hand and looking equally annoyed for taking up his precious time.

She takes it from him, giving thanks before opening her mouth. "Just live a little, Burt. I bet all you do is play soccer then go home and watch porn, then wake up and play more soccer."

Confused by her mention of porn, I furrow my brows and purse my lips waiting on a further explanation which never eventuates.

"Yeah, I live and breathe soccer. I do watch porn on occasion but the real thing is much better."

"And, I bet you don't have time for relationships?" She stands tall, straightening her posture as if she has a hidden agenda.

"What's your point, Chase?" I ask, annoyed.

"We've always had fun together even when we hated each other, right?"

I nod, waiting for her to continue.

"So, let's have fun, Burt. No strings attached, I promise. I don't need strings... trust me. I just don't want to think about anything but the moment I'm living in, and if you happen to be there... well, then hip hip, hooray."

"You want to have fun without strings?" I repeat. "Is that what you're saying?"

This time, she smiles. "Yep."

In a lifetime full of propositions, I've never expected Emerson Chase to propose something like this. She's hurting, drunk on revenge, and out to make Wesley's life equally painful. I know that, I'm not stupid. I'm the pawn in her game and when she's done playing, I'll be on the sideline watching her live her life with someone else.

I need her. Regardless of her conditions.

Keep the emotions away, take what you want, and reap the benefits from the scorned.

"On one condition," I tell her, plotting it out so I get what I want. "You stop calling me Burt... and this mustache needs to go."

"Deal. But it stays on until we're back at your hotel."

"Hotel..." I repeat, caught off guard.

Running her hands along the front buttons of my shirt, she looks up at me with fire in her eyes. "Perhaps I didn't make myself clear enough, and maybe I underestimate your ability to read between the lines, Carrington..." She pauses, lowering her voice. "Sex. Fucking. That's what I'm talking about. Are you in?"

She wants me as much as I want her.

There are no more questions, no more rules, no more anything.

I'm in—*all in.*

THIRTEEN

"A fuck buddy. The best idea ever,
or a recipe for disaster?"
~ *Emerson Chase*

"About last night, Em..." Wesley corners me in the kitchen on my hunt for Advil. It's 7:15 a.m. and I'm running on two hours sleep.

When my alarm went off fifteen minutes ago, I'd completely forgotten about a photoshoot which was scheduled this morning at Venice Beach. I pride myself on being punctual and reliable, not wanting to let down the photoshoot crew. The old me would have been up at 4:00 a.m. doing sprints on the beach to get myself looking the best as I can for the shoot.

The new me wants to crawl into a hole and die.

"I'm sorry, Em. I was drinking and shouldn't have been so forceful. I know you're angry, I mean fuck, you didn't get home till after four," he says in desperation, pacing up and down the kitchen, stopping only to shove a bagel in his mouth.

I'm listening attentively allowing him to speak, but my head is pounding like a bitch and I'm ready to call quits on life and climb back into bed.

"I was angry," I tell him in a hoarse voice. "Not just at you."

"Your brother?"

I nod, keeping my words to a minimum. Talking hurts my brain.

He continues to speak but I'm only half listening.

Last night was... *I don't know.*

I was bold, brave, something I hadn't been in a long time. I took that bold me and pretty much offered to be Logan's fuck buddy.

What was I thinking? Like he needs a fuck buddy.

Logan pretty much fucks whoever and whenever he likes. There's no shortage of fucking. *Probably what happens when you're crowned the hottest athlete?* I hate to admit I've sold myself short, desperate for anything to make me wild and careless.

After we both admitted that spending a night together would be harmless fun, we jumped into a cab where we made out for the entire ride to the hotel. The cab driver warned us several times he charged extra to be a mobile sex vehicle. It was enough to break the ice, laughing for one moment and kissing heavily the next.

Kissing Logan is something else. I'm not the biggest fan of kissing. I mean, it's nice and everything, but I guess after years of being in a relationship you avoid the warmup and head straight for the main show. Yet, something about him is different. *It's intense.* Several times I found myself pulling back because he'd almost dry-humped me into an orgasm.

This coming from the guy who had zero appeal to me a few weeks ago, and now, I want him naked underneath me while I ride him like a cowgirl hitching a ride to town.

Stop thinking about riding him. You know he's well endowed. It practically poked your eye out in the cab.

"He's a guy, Em. Men are programmed differently than women."

I focus on Wesley, unsure of what we're talking about. Taking a punt, I comment, "Yeah, I know. But vows are vows regardless of how long you've known the person."

"You're right."

"You're agreeing with me?" I answer in shock, wishing I didn't stretch my eyebrows because the pain is unbearable.

"Yeah, marriage is sacred. People fuck up. Don't punish them for a lifetime because mistakes are just that... mistakes."

I can see he's still trying to justify his behavior in Amsterdam. If I had more energy, I would debate this topic and leave a very negative vibe in the room. But George walked in moments earlier, sniffing at his bowl and he's staring at me with pitiful eyes because I haven't put out his kibble. I know what he's thinking, *There they go again, fighting over the same thing. Why is Daddy such a douchebag?*

Opening the bottom cupboard, I take out the bag and pour a small amount into his bowl. Even then, George sniffs the bowl and holds back his need to snack on the dry food. George is a peculiar dog, he only eats food when everyone leaves the room, and even then, he waits a few minutes not wanting to be caught.

"He's your brother. That's family, Em. Just don't let it get to you."

Wesley was never 'pro' family. His mom is a well-known gold-digger who married some billionaire and moved from Bel-Air to the South of France. Her priorities are men and money. Although Wes hates talking about her, I can tell he doesn't approve of her lifestyle and wishes he had a mother less involved in herself. I've met her twice during our relationship, and each time I wondered how a woman could be so possessed by wealth. She's never shy in parading the fact that her son is a well-known star. Her only disappointment is Wes' sister—Clara. She lives in Utah on some ranch with her husband and two sons. A stay-at-home mom who couldn't care less about money.

Ash is something else, though. Sure, I was livid he could so easily disregard his marriage for a night of sex, but what I didn't expect was for him to be at the hotel, alone, later.

I think back to last night...

Logan pushes my body against the mirror which lined the elevator. Sliding his hand up my leg, he settled it on the back of my thigh. His kisses were fast, desperate, and left me breathless. He did this thing where he moaned every time I grinded against him. I fucking loved it, purposely doing it on repeat so I could hear his frustration come out each time.

The elevator pinged and I pushed him away with force to the other side of the elevator, bowing my head as the doors opened to Ash's voice.

"There you guys are. I was beginning to worry." He paused, and it gave me a chance to look up. "What's going on? Wait, did you guys get into a fight again? I swear I can't fucking take you two anywhere. Just move on, will you?"

"Actually..." I cleared my throat, "... there was this crazed homeless guy around the corner and he started chasing us, so we ran, hence why we're out of breath."

"Yeah," Logan follows. "I think he had a knife."

"A knife?" Ash stared at the both of us like we were crazy.

We nodded.

"It doesn't explain the wig and mustache."

"Funny story..." I laughed, trying to ease the nerves, "... our cab driver took a wrong turn and we didn't want to head home so we went to this bar, and there happened to be a costume shop. We thought why not have some fun, you know?"

We stepped out of the elevator, Ash standing with his arms folded and brow raised. "Why didn't you call me?" Ash proceeded to whine. "I would have been all for dressing up like an aging porn star."

Logan chuckled, ripping his mustache off with a pained face and removing his wig. His hair was a wild mess, and I found myself gawking at it like a fool.

"Maybe next time."

Ash foiled our plan to get naked and join the friends-with-benefits club. It wasn't such a bad thing. Logan and I were crazy together. It's like he brings out this other person in me who seems to lay dormant and wants to throw all caution to the wind not realizing the amount of trouble we can and probably will get into.

I'm distracted by my phone. The vibration causing it to sound against the marble top.

Logan: *We need to talk. Meet me at my hotel in an hour. My plane leaves at noon.*

Why does everyone want to talk this morning? I read

the text and quickly erase it, not wanting Wes to see. I pop two Advil in my mouth and accompany it with a tall glass of water.

"I have to go."

"Where?" Wes questions raising his eyebrow.

"I have a fitness shoot this morning, and have to pick up a couple of things."

"Right... what things do you have to pick up?"

"Feminine products."

He instantly backs off, turned off by the prospect of shopping for tampons. The lie pays off as he leaves the room allowing me to finally get some peace and quiet.

Inside the confinement of my room, I quickly respond.

Me: *I'll be there in thirty minutes.*

I sort out my bag and pack my things. The shoot is at 11:00 a.m. and if the traffic isn't too awful, I will have enough time to see Logan then quickly dash to the shoot for hair and makeup. I'm already dressed in my yoga pants and tank, adding a cap to cover my face from the sun.

Wesley is sprawled on the sofa, wearing only a pair of shorts as he aimlessly channel-surfs. He usually visits the gym early but lately, he's been hanging around doing nothing. Even though we aren't together, I've noticed his behavior and how he has lost the motivation he once had. A part of me feels guilty, knowing my constant cold shoulder makes it impossible for either of us to be happy. Then I remember how it all started, and I'm back to sporting the shoulder.

"I'm going. I'll be back after lunch when Karl and Josie arrive."

"What?" His mood shifts, tone agitated. "We're fucking filming again today?"

I'm surprised at his outburst. "You wanted to continue filming, Wesley. Poppy's coming over, so make sure the apartment is clean."

"We're both contracted to film..." he softens his voice, "... it's no fun anymore with you being so—"

"So what?" I cut him off.

"So distant."

"Maybe I have been distant..." I say in haste, "... but it's not without reason. Like I said, I'll be back." I walk off making a conscious effort not to slam the door. I'm tired, irritable, and want this day over with. If it wasn't for meeting Logan, I would have brought George with me. Instead, I've left him with a cranky father and an unappetizing bowl of kibble.

So with my cap down and shades on, I make my way to the hotel. No one notices me in the lobby, then I enter the elevator with two teenage girls who have just been in the pool. They're wearing almost matching bikinis which barely hide their assets.

"Oh my God, Livvy, did you know Logan Carrington's staying at this hotel? Maddie said she saw him in the lobby yesterday."

"Are you kidding?" She places her hand on her heart, chewing gum at a fast pace. "O.M.G. that means he's probably with Ashley Chase. I swear I would blow him in a heartbeat."

I'm secretly dying in the corner. The elevator is ridiculously slow and hearing about your brother being blown is enough to hurl.

"They are so hot," she squeals. "We should go find them."

"I think I saw them coming out of their room on level five," I tell them, keeping my face hidden.

In the corner of my eye, I see them look at each other.

"Are you trying to find them, too?"

"Me?" I laugh. "No. I'm not into celebrities at all, I think they're sell-outs."

The comment is enough to put the girls off surely, but no, they exit on level five on the hunt for their soccer stars. I exit on level twenty-two, taking a left and hoping I don't run into Ash. They're on the same floor but in different rooms— a request from Logan because Ash snores like a freight train.

The door to room 609 is in front of me. Knocking gently, I wait for any sounds of life before knocking a little harder. The door opens and Logan's standing in the entrance, wearing a towel around his waist with his hair dripping wet.

Don't look at his body.

Ignore the pack of abs screaming 'lick me.'

I smile politely then walk in holding my breath, letting it go when I scan the room. Logan's a complete neat freak, the total opposite of Ash. He's made his own bed and even hung the towels in the bathroom. The room is modern with the drapes open slightly to allow the morning sun.

I turn back around to face him.

"Did I miss the memo to work out?" he jokes.

I try to hide my smirk but it's impossible, especially as he stands there tempting me so badly.

"Did I miss the memo to join the Swedish hot-tub club?"

Logan chuckles, his wide grin accentuating his strong jawline. "I was taking a shower."

"How convenient of you?" I say, holding his gaze.

A look passes between us, and not to show how uncomfortable I am, I walk to the window and pretend to be looking at the view. I have to admit it is stunning. The Hollywood Hills in the distance and blue skies gracing us on this beautiful spring day.

As I look around, I notice a couple in the apartment block the next street over. They're inside what looks like a living room and the chick is on all fours as a guy eats her out from behind.

"Oh my God!" I gasp, covering my mouth instantly.

"What?" Logan stands behind me, a little too close. I can feel the towel touching my yoga pants.

"That couple." I point.

"Oh, yeah... them."

"Oh, yeah, them?" I repeat. "You've been here a day and you're talking about them like you're besties."

"They caught my eye yesterday. Although, he had his cock in her ass that time."

My eyes widen, the heat rising beneath my skin. Logan mentioning the word *cock* does something to me that needs to be restrained or I will jump him with that towel on. "Nice."

He laughs, placing his hands on my shoulders then massages them gently. "There're many words to describe being ass-fucked, but nice is probably not one of them."

"I wouldn't know," I admit, immediately regretting it. "Wow! Those palm trees are tall."

He turns me around, his stance intimidating me. "You don't go from telling me you've never had a dick in your ass to the height of palm trees."

"Uh... whatever." I roll my eyes. "I bet you've fucked a million girls that way, man-whore."

Logan continues to laugh irritating me further. "Believe

it or not, no. When I fuck, I want it over and done with and out of my apartment."

"Nice," I say again, with a fake smile.

"That's not nice, Emmy. I sense some jealousy in your voice."

"Me?" I point to my chest. "Jealous of what? I know what you're like, Logan. It's not a secret. I came here to talk because you wanted to talk. So talk." I fold my arms, keeping myself protected.

"You're hot when you're angry. Do you know that?"

"Yes, I do," I respond with sarcasm.

He rubs his chin, making it hard for me not to notice the playful grin he continues to maintain. "About last night..."

Of course, it's about last night. *What did I think it would be about?*

"Yeah?"

"I was going to fuck you," he states firmly.

"And? I was going to fuck you."

"Then we didn't."

"Well, Ash being a cockblocker is nothing new. Once, in high school, Mom and Dad were away and I brought this guy home. I swear Ash had his radar on because he clung to me like a bad smell."

Logan's grin disappears, his muscles tightening with a pinched expression. If I didn't know better, he appears jealous. I want to laugh. *How can he be jealous of something that happened in high school?*

"Wait... are you jealous? You know jealously looks nice on you," I tell him playfully.

"Stop with the word nice."

"Fine, but you're jealous? Just admit it." I poke at his chest, any excuse to touch him.

"I'm jealous that other men get to touch you, but I don't."

I stand perfectly still, my heart's racing followed by quick breaths. His stare is persistent, making it difficult for me to think straight. The green is his eyes make it problematic to notice anything else, but this hard stare makes me want to fall to the floor and beg him to have his way with me.

And then, I remember our pact—to have fun.

Our little secret.

"Then touch me," I whisper.

He raises his fingertip and traces my cheek. "We need to agree this is just for fun." He keeps his voice low. "Just between us."

I nod. I don't want anything else from him, but this escape.

"And fucking you won't just be *nice*," he accentuates. "If I fuck you, you're going to feel it."

Inside I've already descended into orgasm mode, but to keep my tough-girl persona, I think of a way to challenge him. I don't want him to believe he has the upper hand.

"You're on, Carrington." I tug on his towel, watching it fall to the floor. I'm taken aback by his cock standing hard. I've never been one to overanalyze with such detail but his cock seems absolutely perfect.

I fall to my knees, wrapping my hand around his length. His body instantly jerks. He moans as his hand wraps around my hair. I stroke it gently, his skin so soft yet rock hard beneath my grip. As I move my head in, I open my mouth and allow my lips to wrap around him, sliding into me as his whole body buckles forward.

"Fuck," he moans, pushing my head to him.

I take in as much as I can, his growl coercing me to go

deeper. His cock hits the back of my throat, but my reflexes push him back out in between my attempts to catch my breath. Beneath my yoga pants, my thin cotton panties are soaked, waiting for him to rip all my clothes off and fuck me hard like he's promised.

I pull his cock out of my mouth, and with barely any breath I tell him, "Fuck me like you promised."

His expression is pure torment, using all his strength to pull me up and toss me onto the bed, I lay there as he strips me leaving me bare in front of him.

Logan remains quiet, silently admiring the view in front of him. His eyes begin to wander, eating me up as they burn with fire when they land on the prize.

Spreading my legs with force, he positions himself in the middle, resting on his knees with his cock sitting at my entrance, gently caressing my clit. I close my eyes, moaning in delight as my back stretches against the white sheets.

He slides himself in, then waits, not moving but keeping himself buried. I open my eyes, maintaining an even breathing pattern to stop myself from coming straight away. His lack of movement leaves me wondering but now is not the time for questions.

"We were supposed to talk," he strains.

"You're buried inside me. I don't know how coherent our conversation will be."

He thrusts forward, catching me off guard and making me moan. "When I'm fucking you, it's just you and me," he commands, his tone powerful, posture straight while demanding I listen to him.

"It's just you and me," I repeat merely above a whisper. "But who else would it be? I'm not into threesomes, Logan."

His body falls onto mine, lips touching then he kisses me deeply. Moaning into his mouth, I place my hands on his back, scratching from top to bottom as he lays still again. I've never been slow-fucked before. Not realizing how intense everything can be in slow motion.

Lifting his head, he drops it again into the crook of my neck, tasting the sweat off my skin. The tip of his tongue dances against me until he's found my lobe, biting on it while using his hand to fondle my breast.

"I don't care what you do outside of this room. I don't care who you're with, engaged to, or claim not to sleep with... I care about only this, Emerson. All your focus is on me. Do you understand me?"

I nod, incoherently, wanting to tell him that his demands turn me on.

I yank his face away from my ear, holding his head in front of me so he understands that I feel the same way. "Logan, this stays between us. Whatever happens in this room stays between us."

He lowers his head, biting my lip and attempting to speak through strangled breaths. "You make me crazy. You make me think that nothing else in the world matters. Not soccer... nothing. I hate you for it."

Unable to hide the smile which appears, he pulls back watching me in amusement.

"I hate you for everything you've done to me since we were kids. I want nothing more than to fuck you hard right now so you're left with this moment torturing you for the rest of your life."

"Quite a challenge, Chase." His mouth widens with a grin, eyes watching the movements of my lips.

"Try me."

He pulls his body up, keeping his hand beneath my chin. Using only his hips, he thrusts himself hard, slamming his body against mine. My head tilts back, neck exposed as he does it again. I quietly beg for him to go harder, then in a slow excruciating pace, teasing me beyond my means. All that needs to happen is one more thrust and I'm all his.

"I don't play nice, or fair. I hate you as much as you hate me. And for everything you've done to me that's caused me pain... this is payback, baby."

Lifting my right leg above his shoulder, he spreads me wider exposing my clit, and without any further warning he lurches forward, slamming his cock in so deep it causes a ripple effect. My nipples stand on edge as the orgasmic sensations flood my entire body causing me to moan loudly until my throat runs dry.

Lost in this moment, barely able to open my eyes, I don't notice he's collapsed on top of me, panting heavily with our bodies drenched in sweat. His weight is heavy, but I don't want to say anything and luckily don't have to as he pulls himself out and lays beside me on his back.

We say nothing for a long time until the room no longer echoes our heavy breathing and falls completely silent.

"What time does your flight leave?"

"Just after noon."

"Logan, I'm on birth control."

He places his hands on his face, moaning underneath his palms. "Fuck, I don't know why I didn't ask."

I laugh. "Because you weren't thinking straight."

"No, I wasn't," he answers seriously, keeping his expression straight. "Now what?"

"You go to England, I stay here."

"Right."

I feel exposed having this conversation in the nude. My top sits beside me so I pull it to me, placing it on my chest to feel less exposed. "We said no strings attached. Fun, without strings. You have your career and I have mine.

Maybe when you're in town again we can get together and have more stringless fun."

"I'm still in town."

"Yes, you are," I agree.

He sits up on his knees and between my legs. Removing my top, he demands me naked in front of him. "I'm still in town for another twenty minutes. So, as far as I'm concerned, you've given me the green light to have more fun."

His cock is rock hard, again.

I swallow the lump trapped in my throat and smile back at him. "What ya got for me, Carrington?" I tease.

"Turn around, baby," he demands with a wicked grin. "You'll see."

FOURTEEN

"A man can always tell when another lion is sleeping in his den."
~ *Emerson Chase*

I haven't heard from Logan in weeks. Through conversations with Mom, I know they have a round of important games and their focus is on training. Without raising too much suspicion, I ask a few questions hoping to get some insight as to what else is going on.

"So, how're things with Ash and Alessandra?"

"Sandy, darling," Mom corrects me in a posh British accent. "They're okay, I guess. She's been looking for wedding venues. There are a couple of places on the east coast, but I'm not sure the boys can come back to the States for a while."

"Oh?" I hide my disappointment. "I thought there was a chance they may play for the US team?"

"I don't know if that's going to happen. Coach Bennett

is reluctant to let them go, and they're under a lot of pressure to win their season. Daddy flew over on Monday, so I guess we'll wait and see."

"Ash doesn't seem to care much about the wedding," I ramble on, pointing out the obvious. "He couldn't care less about anything besides soccer."

"That's your brother for you," she says plainly. "Wesley seems to be keen to walk down the aisle. I saw last night's episode, I didn't realize how sentimental he is."

I'm quick to shut her down, but still hold back what happened. "Oh, yeah. That episode about his grandmother? Load of shit, Mom, he didn't even know her."

"But he appeared so genuine?" I can hear the shock in her voice. "Emmy, what's going on? Between you and him?"

"We're just busy, Mom. The wedding's not on our minds."

The guilt eats away at me, so I give her only that small piece of information. Last night's episode featured our preliminary discussions about the wedding. Just a short conversation about Wesley's family and his relationship with his grandmother. Cliff wanted Wesley to have more of an appeal to our female viewers and his idea worked, many reaching out to Wesley after it aired about their family struggles with Alzheimer's. It painted Wesley in a different light—the sweet man with a heart of *fucking* gold.

The more successful the show's become, the more it becomes scripted. I never signed up for a soap opera, honestly thinking our lives would be documented in a positive way to help others in our generation.

"Take your time, kid, there's nothing wrong with staying engaged. I'm just glad to watch you get married, rather than hear about it over a cup of coffee." Her voice becomes muffled, and in the background I hear my sister's voice.

"Hey, Emmy."

"Hey, Tay-Tay," I cheer, happy to hear her voice.

"Ugh, don't call me that. Puh-lease."

"Sorry," I mumble. "What's happening?"

"Not much. Just school." Her tone remains uninterested and bored. "What about you? Anything interesting going on besides Wesley posting a photo of you in a bikini? By the way, nice hair. Totally love the purple."

"It's back to brown now." Knowing Mom's close by, I pray she doesn't say anything about Logan. "So, any chance of getting you to fly over for the summer? I'd love to spend some time with you once our filming schedule finishes."

"I'd love to, but me and the girls have planned a trip to Miami... if Dad lets me."

I laugh, rudely. "Yeah, good luck with that. Pigs will fly before Dad lets you hang out in Miami. He doesn't even let you go to the city."

"Thanks for bursting my bubble," she complains. "I got to go, I'll give the phone back to Mom."

There's a shuffle and more noise until Mom says she's back.

"Miami, huh?" I bring it up while scrolling through my phone looking for what Wesley posted.

"Maybe you can take her? Or maybe Ash and Logan?"

"Let the man-whores loose in man-whore city..." I keep my tone controlled, not wanting the spur of jealousy to be known.

"You're right. I love Ashley, but in a way, I'm glad Alessandra has tamed him. As for Logan..." there's a pause, and I wait with bated breath for her to continue, "... he's going to break someone's heart one day. I truly feel sorry for the woman."

I swallow the giant lump in my throat. "Why do you say that, Mom?"

"Because Logan's always struggled with stability. His behavior has been erratic and unpredictable. I love him like my own, but Reese leaving him did more harm than good."

"But Aunty Reese is your best friend. Why didn't you say something?"

"Why? Because she had her own battles. I just wished she would have worked them out and been there for him. At the end of the day, she's his mother, not me," she admits.

I don't know how we steered onto this topic. As much as I want more insight into the past, Mom is on point with Logan's behavior. He is like that, I know that. Everything we do together is erratic and irresponsible. But it's what I need, I'm sick of being the responsible one.

"Change of subject.... did I tell you George is in heat?"

Mom laughs through the receiver. "He's male. Can male dogs be in heat?"

"I didn't think so, but he's dry-humping everything in sight. In fact..." I look toward the window where I see him on the balcony dry-humping the outdoor furniture, "... he's going for it right now. He has a thing for the outdoors."

"I think I need to pay my grandson a visit."

"Yes," I cheer loudly. "Are you planning to fly over?"

"One of my fellow author friends has a ranch in the Hills and is planning a book launch in a few weeks. I'd love to support her plus, I don't want to cramp your apartment. Let me confirm the dates and we'll make something happen. I know you're a busy woman building your empire and all, but hopefully, you'll have time for your mommy."

"I always have time for you." I smile.

"Okay, kiddo. I gotta go. Meeting in the city with my publisher," she tells me in a rushed tone. "Do you think my red dress with the gold buttons makes me look like an aging whore?"

"You lost me at gold buttons, Mom."

We hang up with enough time to spare for me to get changed. I can hear Wesley shouting my name impatiently while waiting outside until he gives up and tells me he'll wait for me in the car. We have a lunch with fellow cast-mates at an upmarket restaurant near Laguna Beach. The drive alone will be long, and Cliff wants the cameras in Wes' car switched on to capture our conversations.

A part of me needs the distraction—my mind unsettled after the conversation with Mom.

Rushing around, I finally decide on what to wear and dash out to the car. Moments later we're on our way.

"So, who's at the lunch today?" Wes asks, switching lanes without using his indicator.

"Kyle and Kelly," I say. "Harley and Poppy. Oh... and Farrah."

Farrah is known as the Hollywood train wreck. Her father owns some oil company making them billionaires. She's a spoiled brat born with a silver spoon in her mouth. She's politically incorrect and goes out of her way to stir trouble—one of her favorite pastimes. Farrah is also a walking billboard for plastic surgery having done her lips, cheeks, breasts, and her latest being butt implants.

"Great, Farrah. I read on Twitter the other day that Daddy bought her a bigger set of tits," Wes comments with a sarcastic laugh.

"Really? Well, I guess we'll see them today. Maybe this is a coming-out party... for the double FFs or whatever cups she's sporting now."

Wesley takes the exit, driving toward Orange County as we both laugh at Farrah's ridiculous behavior.

"We shouldn't laugh. In all seriousness, Daddy's a game player. He'll probably buy this network and boot us off the show because we've made fun of her."

"Yeah, or he can offer to buy you a pair like last time."

I cringe, remembering the episode which was filmed at her parents' mansion where Daddy Dearest offered to buy me a pair of tits. The episode caused outrage on social media, but the ratings were high, and no one cared since high ratings equaled a bigger money pot. Most people took my side by blasting Farrah for supporting her dad's behavior. Others claimed I needed it, my tits being the center of attention for weeks until something else took over.

We continue to talk about Farrah, knowing Cliff encourages our bitchy rants to cause controversy. Aside from Farrah, the rest of us get along great. Kyle and Kelly entered the show as a couple. High-school sweethearts from a small town in Minnesota. When auditioning, the network thought the television show would break them which equaled drama. During our second season, they broke up for one week. No one slept with anyone else, but then Cliff wasn't happy with the boring outcome so he edited the scenes to make it look like they separated for the entire season, and slept with all of Hollywood. Neither of them minded knowing it was scripted and part of the whole acting gig.

Harley's the bad boy of the group. His real name is Troy Madden, born into a military family and moved from state to state growing up. He's nicknamed Harley because he has only one love in his life his Harley Davidson—Rosita.

Despite Harley being painted as the bad boy, constantly in trouble with the law, he's actually a big softy. He has your back and you know you're safe around him. Though the boys look up to him as a protector, it's Poppy who formed a unique friendship with him. The crazy British girl that came to the States to study fashion.

"We're here," Wesley announces, parking his car and handing the keys to the valet.

Stella's overlooks the Pacific Ocean and Laguna Beach. Owned by Stella Grace—heir to the Grace Hotel Chains—it's a known hot spot for the elite and celebrities. The restaurant is decorated in all white, with small splashes of azure blue on paintings hanging on the walls. Each table has been carefully arranged with large vases of freshly cut lilies sitting in the middle of each table with shining cutlery and fancy glasses.

We're ushered to a table outside where Kyle, Kelly, Harley, and Poppy are sitting. Saying hello and hugging each of them, we take a seat admiring the stunning view and perfect day while we wait for Farrah.

The waiter serves us some expensive wine, and we drink while having a light conversation until we're brutally interrupted by Farrah. Each of us has our own camera crew — Farrah's crew probably the worst of the bunch. I can't stand them. Two sleazy men—Rick and Marty—both of whom I can only assume have fucked by her which is why they do everything she says.

"O.M.G. you guys, it's been like forever!" She air-kisses us all, taking a seat at the end of table in her tight white dress that barely contains her confined double *FFs*. Her hair extensions touch the table, and she's quick to push them back, keeping the blonde tresses away as she drinks her wine demanding another glass. Another thing about Farrah she enjoys her wine and is rarely seen without a glass in hand.

Our food is served and we begin talking about our plans

for the summer. Majority of the conversation is non-scripted with the cameras recording the whole lunch.

Poppy's the first person to bring up our engagement. "How are the wedding plans going?" she asks in her English accent. "I'm so chuffed it's going to be a winter wedding."

Both Wes and I knew this would come up because Josie told us we have to talk about it. I also had a very heated conversation with my publicist, Nina, over when I can start talking about our relationship breakdown.

"Coming along nicely," I say with a smile. "We're scouting venues, and I'd love for you to come dress shopping with me."

Farrah laughs behind her fork, adding a sly comment, "You'd probably come out wearing some washed-up old rag."

"Funny, Farrah." I place my fork down giving Cliff what he wants whenever he places the two of us in a room. "That's what most men think when they've been with you."

Everyone at the table snickers, all but Farrah. She's trying to control her rage, drinking her third glass of wine and still demanding a refill. The waiter might as well leave the bottle in front of her.

"It's interesting you mention the wedding.... I've heard you guys are on the rocks?" She poses the question with much pleasure.

Wes places his arm around me, bringing my hand to his lips and kissing my engagement ring. With the cameras all pointed at us, I nestle my head against his shoulder and allow him to defend our relationship. "You believe everything you read, Farrah? Em and I are walking down that aisle. She's my woman."

I want to roll my eyes at such a barbaric reference, but don't want Farrah to read anything into it. This conversation could quickly escalate into one of our well-known fights that results in us being physically held back by security.

Things haven't always been difficult between us. In season one, we got along and became friends. Despite her wealth, we had a lot in common and bonded over that. It was season two when everything fell apart. She made some bitchy comments about me to Kelly and Poppy during a girls' night out, and once I saw the footage I knew I had to protect my back. She had a knife and was ready to stab me with it.

The crew yell cut, so everyone can take a break and regroup. The makeup artists go straight for our faces, touching up the foundation and lipstick from the warm sea air.

Wesley announces his need to take a piss, disappearing into the restroom.

Poppy gives me a reassuring smile from across the table, stopping the waiter to ask what the meaty-looking thing on her plate is. When she hears the word 'heart,' her face pales as she quickly pushes the plate aside.

I follow everyone's lead and pull out my phone. I log into my Twitter page, posting some tweets to keep the fans engaged. Within seconds, the notifications blow up my screen and I take a few moments to answer some questions. The fans love the interaction, but on the flipside so do the trolls.

There are a dozen unread emails, mainly from our suppliers regarding the fitness line. I make a mental note to log in from home after lunch and get some work done. The demands are huge and while I have a great team, I enjoy being hands on.

I scroll through the other unread items when a text appears at the top of my screen.

Logan: *How you been, Chase?*

The message from Logan comes out of nowhere. Two weeks and he doesn't talk to me after fucking me twice in the hotel room. Part of me is angry, another part forces the Zen to spread because I have no right to be angry.

We aren't in a relationship.

I quickly respond knowing I have only minutes before we started filming again.

Me: *Hello stranger.*

The bubble bounces, and there's a quick response.

Logan: *That's all I get? C'mon, play with me.*

I scan the table, everyone's still busy minding their own business. Wesley hasn't returned and with him gone, I type extremely fast conscious of being caught.

Me: *Play with you? I got no toys to share. How exactly do you want me to play with you?*

"Let's roll, everyone," Cliff calls from the end of the table.

Wesley's back, settling himself in as I tuck my phone into my purse. We dive back into conversations about a potential trip to England to watch the Victoria Secret show that Farrah has front-row tickets for. The thought of traveling to England excites me even though I've been there only once with my parents, and have only poor memories of rain and grumpy hotel staff.

But Logan lives in England.

Poppy claps her hands excitedly, suggesting we visit her hometown while we're there. Obviously, Cliff planted this idea in Poppy and Farrah's heads making it look like a spur-of-the-moment decision. It's the first I've heard of it, but the more we speak, the more excited I become.

In season one we did a trip to New York City. It wasn't so special given that I'd been there many times before. Our second season had us vacationing in Maui, where we had the time of our lives.

England will be fantastic. Except for one thing—I'm going to be there with Wesley not Logan.

Farrah talks about all the things she has planned for us, and when the cameras focus on her and Poppy discussing the tube, I half pull out my phone and check the text from Logan.

Logan: *Wherever you are, there must be somewhere you can go and privately video playing with yourself. I dare you.*

I quickly re-read the text, not realizing I'm holding my breath and the cameras are rotating between us. I shove my phone into my purse again, distracting myself in conversation before excusing myself to use the restroom.

"Emerson, can't you wait?" Cliff asks, agitated.

"No, Cliff," I answer in annoyance. "Excuse me."

I remove the napkin from my lap, disappearing to the back of the restaurant where I trap myself in the corner cubicle while pulling out my phone with desperation.

Me: *Why must you dare me? You know I never back down.*

I've never done anything like this. The thrill of the unknown pushes me to act spontaneously. I slide my panties off shoving them in my purse as I raise my leg and rest it on the lid of the toilet seat. Lifting my dress above my thighs, I position my phone underneath my dress, hitting the record button. Playfully rubbing myself, I close my eyes and allow the excitement to make me come in less than a minute. In no way does it compare to the times Logan made me come, but still, it rocked my body until I stop recording with my hands shaking.

Catching my breath, I hit send with the caption...

Me: *You wanted to play. Here you go. Have fun.*

The video takes a while to send, so I remove my panties from my bag, place them on and straighten my dress. I exit the cubicle and pop my phone on the expensive vanity to wash my hands. Gazing into the mirror, my cheeks are flushed and emit a glow. Grabbing a washcloth, I quickly dampen it and try to cool myself down before anyone notices.

The vibration of my phone is loud, echoing through the small restroom.

Logan: *Shit. Now I feel like I owe you something in return. Have fun.*

A video comes through and shows it is fifteen seconds long. I'm about to watch it when the door swings open, making me jump. In her tall heels, which hammer on the marble floor, Farrah is dripping in gold strung around her neck. She positions herself next to me, pulling a compact out of her purse. She dabs her nose without any effort to disguise her fake smile.

"You're not fooling anyone by pretending you're together. I know Wesley hasn't been on his *best* behavior."

Her catty comment doesn't warrant a response, so I'm surprised when I open my mouth. "You and your games... worry about your own life instead of ours," I point out, throwing the towel into the basket.

She raises her perfectly shaped eyebrows, gliding her red lipstick on then pouts her lips while admiring herself in the mirror.

"I'm the real star of this show. Everyone knows that. Let's see if you make it to the next season," she threatens.

"If by star you mean whore... then yes. Title's all yours, Farrah." I move past her, closing the door behind me and stopping just down the hall. I mute the sound on my phone, clicking play on the video. Fifteen seconds of Logan pulling his cock until he explodes all over his palm.

Fuck.

He got me.

I quickly respond, wanting to delete any trace of our naughty afternoon.

Me: *We're even. Well played, Carrington. Hopefully, I'll get to see the LIVE version when you're in "town."*

I hit delete and hide my phone in the base of my purse hoping he doesn't respond. If Wes knew what went on he'd be livid. Despite our arrangement, he tries every day to make a move on me. I've just been lucky with being able to palm him off or make excuses.

Back outside, I sit down and get comfortable as dessert

is served. It looks scrumptious—some flan dish with a syrup substance lying on top. As I push my spoon into the bowl, Farrah returns and acts as if nothing happened between us. "So, girls, London? Shopping... British men... are we in?"

Kelly smiles, not pleasing Kyle.

Poppy claps her hands, excited to visit home and spend time with her family. "Count me in."

"I hope you meant for the shopping?" Wes asks seriously in front of everyone.

"What's wrong with a little harmless flirting with a tall British man?" I tease, knocking his shoulder playfully.

In a decidedly odd tone, he says, "My *woman* doesn't harmlessly flirt with anyone."

"Oh, Wes, baby," Poppy cries. "Stop being cheeky. She's not an object."

"Poppy," Wes grits. "You know I love you, but stay out of this."

One of the cameras zooms into Wes' face, irritating him even more.

"Wesley Rich... get off your high horse and treat the woman with respect. That's all I'm saying."

"Yeah, Wesley Rich," I say, not taking this argument seriously. "I have brains, too, you know. It's not *all* about the looks."

Everyone laughs, except Wesley. He sulks in his seat while we finish our conversation about London.

The cameras stop rolling and Cliff's quick to interject, "Your itineraries will be emailed across tomorrow. We've known about this for months but only received the all-clear yesterday. A week from today... we'll be leaving for five days."

A few of us ask some questions, but no one really says

anything else. We wrap up lunch by telling each other goodbye and making our own way home.

On the drive back, Wes is unusually quiet.

"Why did you take so long in the restroom?"

"You want a number?" I question, keeping the conversation light and my nerves at bay.

"Oh," he mutters.

"I also ran into Farrah... she said some words, I said some words."

"Right."

His one-word responses make for an uninteresting conversation, so I lay my head against the window and watch the scenery until we reach home and park the car.

We go our separate ways as we walk inside. I head straight for the bathroom where I shower and change into something more comfortable. With no plans tonight, I decide to ditch work and lay on the couch, catch up on some television while responding to some fans. I posted a pic Josie sent me of all of us posing at the table captioning the picture—*Filming lunch with the gang.*

As soon as I posted the pic, comments flooded shortly after.

"What are you doing?" Wes plonks himself on the sofa beside me wearing his sweats and no shirt. He did it on purpose, and as much as it irritates me, I'm still reminded of how attractive Wesley is.

I raise my phone showing him the pic. He smiles then grabs the remote.

"I thought you were going out for drinks?" I ask him, half paying attention as I respond to a fan who comments on my dress.

"Nah. Thought I'd stay home."

I keep my thoughts to myself, scrolling down until I see

Logan commented on my post. Most people would think nothing of him commenting since it's known we're family friends and that Ash is his best friend. The smartass, of course, has to have a final say. *Must have been a hot day in Cali. Your cheeks look flushed.*

With Wes beside me, I keep my smile hidden and refrain from commenting. I scroll through the other comments until my phone rings and Mom comes up on the screen.

"Hey, Mom. You're on speaker and Wes is here."

"Oh, hi honey!" Mom greets with an upbeat tone.

Wes leans forward, speaking into the phone. "Hey, Abbi, long time no speak."

"I know," she agrees. "I'll be there in three weeks. Did Emmy tell you?"

He looks at me, rolling his eyes. "No, she didn't."

"My fault, Mom. We just got back from lunch. But that's great news," I tell her. "We found out today we're heading to London next week for the Victoria Secret show."

"How fantastic," she cheers. "Are you going to visit Ash and Logan's place?"

I can see Wes' demeanor change instantly, watching me with cautious eyes.

"Hadn't thought about it. I might call Ash tonight and see if I can squeeze some time with him."

"Oh, kid, call him later. They're out on a double date. Alessandra set Logan up with a nurse from her work. Can you imagine that? I hate to admit, but I think those boys have a fetish for medical professionals."

Logan's on a date with a nurse?

My stomach hardens at the thought. I'm well aware Wesley's still watching me, so I quickly come up with something to say to suppress my jealousy. "All right, Mom, I'll give him a buzz tomorrow."

"Night, kiddo... night, Wes."

We say goodnight in unison before I hang up and throw my phone on the sofa beside me.

"What are we watching?" I ask, eyes fixed on the screen ignoring my head telling me that I have no right to be jealous. We agreed that whatever went on outside that hotel room doesn't matter. Who we saw, what we did.

"Game of Thrones?"

"Sure, why not."

He pauses the screen and turns to face me. "Em, I'm trying here. I *fucking* miss you," he strains.

"I know," I say quietly, turning to face him.

His stubble covers his square jaw, and with his eyes serious and begging for forgiveness, I find myself softening under his gaze.

Placing his hands on my cheek, I rest my face in his palm allowing myself to revisit the feelings of being in love with Wesley Rich. He's warm, and only a small part of me wishes things were the same. The other part of me is raging with jealousy that Logan's fucking some slut.

I allow him to kiss me—without the cameras present.

It's soft, sweet, and nothing like the ravenous Wesley who would practically maul me each time we kiss. When I retract, he tugs on the string of my tank and pulls it down, exposing my shoulder. He kisses my skin, and when my eyes close all I see is Logan.

This isn't fair. I feel guilty no matter which way I look at it.

Moving his hand against my stomach, he moves upward until he's cupping my breasts, growling into my neck and applying pressure with his body weight. The passion builds, but the mere thought of screwing Wes again is outweighed by the guilt of what I've done.

"Stop," I murmur, laying my hands on his chest and pushing him back.

"Emerson, please don't. I need you," he begs.

"I need more time."

His expression changes, eyes wild and full of anger. "You can't fucking do this," he yells. "Walking around and teasing me, telling me now when I know you need to be fucked. It's been over a month, Emerson. If you don't need to be fucked then you're fucking someone else."

"I'm not fucking anyone else," I lie so easily.

"Then prove it. Fuck me. That's all I ask of you."

"No, Wesley, give me time to forgive you."

"You've had time," he pushes, disrespecting my wishes.

"Two months is not enough time to get over the hurt of you fucking two hookers," I argue back. "We were supposed to get married. You threw that out the window, for what?" With my heart racing, scared he will call me out on what Logan and I have done, we both remain as silent as possible, the vibration of my phone distracting me. I quickly pick it up wanting to diffuse the argument.

There are two notifications on my screen. One from Farrah tagging Wesley and me in a picture. I forgot she'd even taken it. Wes has his arm around me and I'm smiling. The caption reads—*Even when the cameras stop rolling, these two can't keep their hands off each other. #SoontobeMr&MrsRich*

I don't know why she would post something like that, but I show Wes the picture calming his curiosity. I can see his shoulders relax, the breath of air he's holding in releasing slowly.

The second is a text from Ash.

Ash: *Mom just told me you're coming to London.*
I'll call you tomorrow. Trying to find somewhere else
to crash tonight because Logan took his date home
and told me he's fucking her till the sun is up.
Night sis.

I don't know why I showed the text to Wes, maybe because I wanted him to see that Logan and I have nothing going on. That, and my heart's pumping so hard, emitting a burning sensation in my chest. Placing the phone down, I sit against the couch pretending my silence is driven by our argument and not by the hurt and jealousy over a man who means nothing to me.

"How long do you need?" Wes breaks the silence.

I answer with haste, "For what? To repair a broken heart?"

"I said I was fucking sorry!" He raises his voice again, running his hands through his hair.

My stress levels peak, on a night when I want to lay here and do nothing. I don't understand why Logan has to be such a prick. Demanding me to come play then running off with someone else. Mom's right, he will destroy any woman who falls in love with him.

Not that I'm in love with him.

"How many times do I need to tell you? You can't erase the past so easily. And by the way..." I add, bringing up his stupid comment during lunch, "... your barbaric persona at lunch today was not well received."

"Neither was your comment on fucking British men," he shoots back.

"I never said I was going to *fuck* British men." I shake my head, laughing at the way he twists my words and makes me out to be the bad guy.

"That's right. You won't. Nor will you fuck any other man." He puts his arm around me, flipping me beneath him and pinning me on the sofa. He stares me down, keeping his body upright on both his arms. With a supremely threatening gesture, he bellows over me, "I'm no longer taking no for answer." Tugging my top down, he exposes my breasts, reacting with wild eyes.

I battle with his touch, missing the parts of him that still feel the same. I fight the jealousy reminding me that at this moment, Logan's buried in some other woman's body. My emotions run deep, tugging me in each direction without an answer in sight.

And so, I do what I need to do to remind myself that Logan isn't mine.

"Fine, Wes.... have your way."

FIFTEEN

*"It takes a moment of terror to realize
everything missing from your life."*
~ *Logan Carrington*

I can't get her out of my mind. I've done everything I
can to forget about her. Nonstop personal training
from the crack of dawn. Then team training at the
main fields. When training's over, I exert myself at the gym.
Then when night comes around, the exhaustion kills me.

And, repeat.

Day after day.

"I know you want to win, but don't you think you're
pushing yourself too far?" Ash worries, stretching his legs
before our game.

"I'm fine," I tell him, raising my arms above my head
and stretching my muscles.

"You haven't been the same since we got back from the
States. I think I know what your problem is."

I raise my brow, wondering if he knows how hard I fucked his sister and that's why I can't sleep at night. If he knew the image of her lying beneath me is so ingrained in my memory that nothing else matters right now.

"You're lonely. You haven't fucked some good pussy and you're on edge."

I shrug, bored of his interrogation. With the ball at my feet, I shoot for the top right corner.

Fuck. I missed it by barely an inch.

"You never miss." Ash panics under duress. "We're going out tonight."

"I'm not interested."

"Not even another nurse?" He winks, positioning the ball in front of him.

"Maybe..." I play the idea in my head. "No, actually, I'm busy."

He exhales, distracted by the whistle as Coach calls us in to begin our warm-ups.

We're a strong team, and *this close* to winning our quarter-finals. Where our team let us down, Coach is quick to point the finger. Coach is an angry man, dedicated but unforgiving when it comes to mistakes. He repeatedly warns the both of us to pick up our game and not allow our personal lives to affect it whatsoever.

Ash proved himself—Alessandra's not a distraction. *She's a nothing.* Although she lives with us, she's rarely home, and on occasions when they both are there they do separate things.

We finish on time and instead of hitting the gym, I stumble back home and lay in bed. Even when I try to relax, I think of her. The way her body melted underneath my touch and how her eyes begged me to fuck her hard. I couldn't stop staring at her body, from her nice round tits that pinched perfectly between my fingers, to the smell of her sweet pussy.

She's perfect in every fucking way.

And I hate that.

Yesterday had me weak. Coach drilled me for sloppy defending and even I knew something was off. I needed a release, and it began with an innocent text which ended up with her rubbing her clit and coming for me. I came three fucking times watching the video.

My dick's red, raw, and stinging like a motherfucker with how hard I rubbed it out. I've never seen such a beautiful sight—wet, bare, and perfectly pink.

I wanted to call her and hear her voice, but I held back, reminding myself that we're having fun. Playing this dangerous game of not wanting to be caught and standing on the ledge playing with fucking fire.

But all of it, everything, begins to eat away at me.

I couldn't curb my jealousy when I saw an image of her on Instagram with Wesley, posted by Farrah Beaumont referring to their lunch date and how happily *in love* they are. I recall the moment vividly—punching the lamp beside me and seeing it smash to the floor in a million pieces. I didn't expect to experience that type of jealousy, yet I did, and there's no cure but to forget she even exists.

Ash was pumped I agreed to go out on a double date. The nurse he set me up with was a friend of Alessandra's, a woman named Georgia. She was pretty, long legs and firm ass. Small tits but it didn't matter. I fucked her once with my red-raw dick and ended up having to pull out when the rubber got uncomfortable. I shouldn't have done it, but I needed someone else to make me forget about her. I've never been so preoccupied during sex. My mind wasn't in it, thinking about Emmy the entire time.

I'm tired of it.

I want my life back without Emmy in it.

Georgia became clingy, demanding a second round and wanting to stay the night. I told her I didn't do sleepovers so she left the apartment in a blind fit of rage while calling me every name under the sun. I didn't care, because I long for solitude.

Without Ash or Alessandra, I have too much time to think about all the things I shouldn't be thinking about.

Then, I caved.

Season One—Episode One.

I binge-watched the whole first season of *Generation Next* and finally saw the so-called 'moment' Wesley Rich fell in love with Emerson Chase.

I hated watching him gain her love.

I hated, even more, witnessing their first kiss and subtle walk to the bedroom. The way her smile changed after that, she was happy and content.

I detest he makes her feel that way.

I hate the fact he still controls her.

Actually, I hate everything about them.

Yet, the masochistic side of me continued watching until my eyes grew heavy and sleep was imminent. I've started a bad habit and it's one I don't know how to break.

We ramped up training due to the big game this Saturday against Manchester. I'm pumped and ready to go. They have had straight wins—no losses this season—and I want to break their luck and show them we're going to take this game to the next level.

Ash leaves training early to run some errands. I don't

ask, annoyed 'errands' are more important than the fucking game. With Chris watching on, I know he will control his son—I don't have to be the responsible one today.

Every limb, bone, part of my body is in deep pain. I can barely walk to the elevator, even pressing the button's a struggle. I don't ever remember training so hard and mentally killing myself on the field. I'm drenched in dirt and sweat but opt to shower at home peacefully rather than in the locker room with the boys so I head home.

As I open the apartment door, I plan on taking a shower but having only an hour to spare before heading out to the studio to join a panel to discuss this week's highlights.

The smell of Alessandra's strong coffee graces the apartment, along with a familiar laugh.

"Look who's here." Ash is sitting on the coffee table, facing the sofa, and I don't notice anyone until Emerson sits up and gazes straight at me.

My chest broadens, my muscles stiffening harder than I thought possible, as I'm shocked to see her sitting inside my apartment. The first thing I notice is her hair has changed again, it's a silver tone with light brown roots. She's dressed in a pale pink knitted sweater with dark blue jeans and knee-high boots.

Why does she have to look like that?

Casually sexy.

The worst type of sexy.

The sexy that reminds you why you're drawn to her.

Her smart mouth and alluring eyes make you want to fall to your knees and worship her like no other man has.

Fucking hell! Grow some balls. You're still angry at her.

The back of her hair is a mess from lying down, but she doesn't seem to notice or care.

"Hey." She waves, watching me cautiously with her deep blue stare.

I force a smile, scared to give any other reaction away other than my state of shock.

Alessandra has joined us, handing Emerson a cup of coffee.

"You're here?"

"She's filming for the next three days," Ash tells me animatedly. "We should go out to the pub or something."

"I'm on a tight schedule," she announces, moving her eyes away from where I'm standing.

"Then don't let us stop you." I carry my bag, walking straight past them. Inside my room, I throw my bag down, while leaning back on the door with my eyes closed.

She's here, and real.

No longer a figment of my imagination.

Opening my eyes, I try to get the image of the way she stared at me out of my head. Her blue eyes always do that to me. It's like putting me in some kind of trance that stops me from thinking straight or with some sort of reason.

Stripping down to nothing, I step inside my bathroom and take a long, hot shower, relaxing my tense muscles. The only muscle I can't relax is the one down below which is raging hard with no happy ending to cure the sadness it's currently facing.

I could rub one out, but choose not to—a way to avoid the torture of reliving our moment in the hotel. Something I've done on too many occasions which only makes everything worse.

I get dressed in my navy suit, white collared shirt, and matching navy tie. Splashing on some cologne, I finish with placing my watch on my wrist and then make my way to the living room to be greeted by only Ash.

Fixing my cuffs, I pretend to be uninterested asking, "Where she's gone."

"I think back to her hotel."

"Where's she staying?"

"Somewhere in London," he responds without giving me many details.

I hide my disappointment, wishing I hadn't acted like a dick because I'm pissed off she's still with Wesley, even though I have no reason to be since we both agreed to have fun without getting involved. Probably the most-stupidest idea I have ever had.

"I'm meeting her tonight for drinks if you want to tag along."

"We have a game tomorrow," I remind him.

"Yeah, yeah, I know. Just one drink. How often do I get to see my sister, huh?"

"Get changed, we only have ten minutes before the car arrives."

Ten minutes later he emerges fully dressed and looking presentable.

"It's like you're fucking Clark Kent," I joke, always amazed at his ability to get ready within the smallest amount of time.

"It's called... a wife... and an ironing board."

"You'd be caught dead saying that in front of her," I point out.

"Probably. She likes to suck my dick so I could save myself that way."

We both laugh, closing the door behind us as make our way down to the hire car and toward the studios.

～

The panel took four hours for a one-hour segment. I've done several of these and being in front of the camera's no biggie. On panels, like today, we engage in a healthy debate over club corruption and how it affects the players and coaches. The discussion lasted for most of the segment, and by the time we finished I needed a drink.

The car service drives us to the pub where Emmy and her crew are hanging out tonight. I dread seeing Wesley, knowing I have to restrain myself from punching him in the fucking face.

Then there's that part of me that wants to play dirty.

A challenge if you will, to make her squirm while under his watch.

The pub's located in the West End—small, quaint, with the usual drunken crowd that frequent these types of joints on a Friday night. When Ash and I moved here a few years ago, we hit all the pubs each weekend until it no longer became fun and the women were all the same.

Outside the pub, there's a hoard of paparazzi standing by with cameras in hand. A few attempt to take photographs through the glass, but appear disappointed when they look at their cameras.

Two of them spot us and ask for a picture, and whether we're ready for the game tomorrow. Ash talks their ears off, and I start to pull him along desperate to get inside.

Two bodyguards stand out front—tall, built like fucking tanks who watch anyone who enters.

"Oi..." the bearded one holds Ash back, "... what business you want in there?"

Ash bravely removes the man's hand from his chest. "My fucking sister, Emerson."

He lets us go while his facial expression remaining impassive.

Once inside we find they're sitting on stools in the corner—four of them to be exact. I recognize Harley, Poppy, and Kelly from the show. Emerson's sitting with them and there's no Wesley attached to her hip, for once.

Ash makes his way through the tight crowd, and I follow until we're standing behind them. The first thing I notice is the gray turtleneck skin-tight dress she's wearing that sits short and rides up as she crosses her legs. With the same knee-high boots she wore earlier, she's looking incredibly sexy. Her hair's messy and to the side with giant silver hooped earrings to accessorize her plain-colored dress. She looks fucking amazing. I quickly realize the redhead with the English accent is introducing herself while I've been staring at Emerson.

"Name's Poppy." She overly grins. "You must be Logan 'cause you sure don't look like Em's twin brother."

I smile confidently. "That's this guy over here. I'm definitely not her twin brother."

Ash takes over the introductions, throwing in some jokes and making everyone laugh because that's what he always does. We order a pint, and it isn't long before Wesley, Farrah Beaumont, and another guy turn up.

As soon as Wesley sees me his demeanor changes, barely saying hello he settles himself next to Emerson where he purposely places his arm around her as if he fucking owns her. I force myself not to stare by trying to avoid any eye contact with either of them, or hell will break loose and my fists will be out and his blood all over the floor.

"Big game tomorrow, boys?" Harley, one of her co-stars mentions.

"Sure is. Playing to get into the quarter-finals."

"What do you do to prep for a big game?" the other girl, Kelly, asks.

"We trained earlier today and should be in bed sleeping right now."

They all laugh, everyone but Emerson and Wesley.

"Is it true you can't have sex before a game?" Farrah teases, rubbing her hand along my suit jacket and trying to entice me with her fake tits and equally phony pout.

In the corner of my eye I notice Emmy's adopted a sullen look. Staring directly at the both of us, she's watching every move. If I didn't know better I'd swear she looks jealous.

Could it be?

Emerson Chase jealous because another woman has touched my fucking arm and asked me about my sex life.

"Ask Ash," I respond, smirking. "He's the married one. I'm single, so unless someone offers to jump in my bed tonight I wouldn't be able to tell you." I continue to keep my gaze fixed on my glass that sits in front of me, though I am desperate to see Emmy's reaction. Unlike her—falsely tied to Wesley for the purpose of the show—I am as single as you can get. I could fuck anyone I please and no one will say a goddamn thing.

Wesley raises his glass to his lips, keeping his persistent stare fixed on mine. "Just make sure the woman you take isn't spoken for," he warns with menace. "Or man... never actually seen you with a woman."

"Oh..." I mouth with confidence, "... the best type of pussy is the one which belongs to someone else."

Ash rests his hand on my shoulder, his laughter barreling through the conversation. "I don't think it's a big deal but Logan won't. Any chance of losing and he'll minimize that. He likes his testosterone wild and pumped."

Great. When did we switch to talking about my testosterone?

Yeah, it's fucking pumped all right and desperate to ravage the girl sitting across from me, the one with the jealous stare.

We're interrupted by a group of girls who recognize all of us and scream so loudly demanding a picture. We all huddle together and pose for her selfie which encourages other patrons to come forward and request the same photograph. After what feels like forever, the bodyguard steps in and tells everyone to back off.

"I'm over this," Wesley snaps, drinking his beer and checking his watch. "Let's get out of here. I'm bored. Wanna hit up a club, babe?"

Babe.

I wonder what broken glass might feel like against his pretty-boy face?

"I'm tired, and jetlagged. You go."

"I'm in," Farrah pipes up. "C'mon Wes, let's get out of here."

Wesley removes his arm from Emerson, who appears annoyed and frustrated. It's clear by her demeanor that the thought of him clubbing with Farrah Beaumont is not something she agrees with and the reaction alone leaves me bitter.

When he leaves, I'm quick to direct my passive aggression toward her. "How sad, your fiancé left you alone."

She smiles, but it's not a smile that's sweet and endearing. "Don't you have some nurse to fuck?" she bites back with wild eyes.

Bitch.

Why the fuck is she be angry about that?

I can't understand women and the way they think. Their minds are like puzzles which are impossible to figure out.

"Maybe. She was boring the first time so not sure why I'd go back for seconds."

She's unable to look at me, shaking her head and staring at the table with her glass in front of her.

Ash talks over us, yet I don't pay attention as I watch her type on her phone. Within seconds, my pocket vibrates.

Emerson: *You're a fucking asshole. Go ahead, fuck nurses and see if I care. I shouldn't, right? Since I fuck my fiancé every night.*

I can't even look at her. The heat rising underneath my jacket is red hot as the anger and hurt consume me. *Is she for fucking real?* I can't even deal with what she's admitting if it's true. Again, what fucking moron comes up with the brilliant idea to sleep with other people?

Me: *You're a fucking bitch. The nurse gave good head. I think I will go back for seconds.*

I watch her mouth open in shock. She's distracted for a moment as a bartender serves her a wine which she proceeds to down in one go, demanding another almost immediately. He lingers to talk to her, flirting with his young smile. I quickly type and hit send, catching her eye and she half looks down at the screen.

Me: *Why don't you go fuck the bartender too?*

"Bro, we need to head back. We seriously need rest," Ash yells over the noise.

As much as I want to stay and argue with Emerson, it's

an hour drive home and it's already close to 9:00 p.m. We always go to bed well before midnight for a training session which starts at 4:00 a.m. If our A-game isn't on, we could potentially lose a crucial game.

"You gonna be okay, Emmy?" Ash asks, throwing some bills on the table.

She slides them back to him, ignoring me while slipping her phone into her purse. "Don't worry about me. I'll be fine. And take your money... let the producers pick up the tab. Or, I can continue flirting with the bartender. Maybe even take him home."

What a fucking low blow.

We both stand when a man, short, maybe five-foot-six blocks our way. He's easily in his late forties, balding and wearing a brown jacket with some weird logo on it.

"Emerson Chase," he beams.

But something's not right. His forehead is dripping in sweat, and I don't like the way he licks his lips when he called her name.

She smiles politely, saying, "Hello."

"I love you. I mean... I honestly love you," he pants.

I look over at Ash, wondering if this guy's for real.

"It's nice to meet you." Again, her smile is fixed as she doesn't indulge his behavior.

"I have you on my wallpaper." He extends his hand, the wallpaper on his phone an image of her in a bikini drenched in water. Then, he continues to flick through his photos and every single one is of her.

What a fucking nutcase!

"I'm in love with you. I've been waiting for so long. Will you come back to my apartment for dinner?" He steps forward.

Without even thinking, I place my hand on his chest restraining him from going any further.

"I don't think so. Leave her alone," I grit.

The man seems shocked Emmy is not stopping me.

Ash quickly interjects, "You need to go now. And I don't want you near my sister *ever* again."

"But you don't understand..." he laughs nervously, wiping the sweat off his forehead with his sleeve, "... I'm in love with her. I've been following her since she landed. I even followed her to your apartment. We're soulmates. We're meant to be together."

Emmy begins to look panicked. I grab her hand, pulling her to me. My grip is tight, but I refuse to let her go and be with some maniac.

"Let's go," I whisper into her ear. "You're not staying here."

"But my friends?"

"Let's go, Emmy. I ain't leaving you here with this lunatic," Ash yells at her, the same time the man tries to push past Ash with a sense of desperation. He tries to swing a punch, but Ash's reflexes have always been on point, blocking him and urging him to the floor.

The bodyguards rush over to where we're standing, pinning him to the floor and yelling for backup.

The paparazzi have caught wind of the situation, snapping heavily and disregarding the instructions from the pub owner to get the fuck out of the venue.

Ash grabs her arm, forcing me to let go as we make our way out of the pub and onto the street. It's no better outside, our sight blinded by the sea of flashes trying to catch every move. With a sense of urgency we hop into the car, instructing the driver to take off at full speed.

Ash sits in the back with Emmy, attempting to calm her down. "Have you seen that guy before?"

She shakes her head, dazed. "No. But I don't come here, and he said he's from here. Back home, about a year ago, I had to file a restraining order against a man who tried to break in."

"You never told me that," Ash scolds her. "Did Mom and Dad know?"

"Yeah, they did. I didn't want to stress you out," she says softly.

We drive out of the city and onto a quieter road. My adrenaline is still pumping from the heated exchange, thinking what may have happened if we'd left her. I never realized how famous she is. I mean, I know the show's popular and that she has millions of fans, I just didn't expect it to be at this level of crazy. Every time we've been together, people usually leave her alone.

I'm starting to see what she was trying to explain to me.

"Why don't you have bodyguards all the time?" I question her, keeping my tone controlled.

"It depends on what we're doing or where we're going. We do a lot of the time, but mostly we can fend for ourselves."

"You're a woman," I seethe. "How do you expect to fend for yourself from a man that's been stalking you for God only knows how long?"

"I don't always need a man to protect me," she begins then stalls. "I'm doing fine on my own."

My eyes move to the rearview mirror where I can see Ash's expression of confusion. It's not long before he asks the question that Emerson has been dreading since the moment she found out about the dickhead screwing those hookers.

"But you're not on your own. You have Wesley. Though, I'll tell you again, Emmy... the guy's a dick."

"Ash..." she says, then goes on more confidently, "... we're not together. Something happened not long ago and I broke it off with him."

"But on TV—"

"It's all fake. We're contracted to finish filming and we have another six weeks to go. Don't always believe what you see."

That last comment's obviously directed at me. For that's what I'd done, assumed everything I saw was the truth. And even when she admitted they weren't together, it shouldn't have mattered because we both agreed to see other people.

I didn't want anyone touching her, looking at her, or damn well stalking her.

Fuck. Stop these thoughts.

She's here, and safe.

That's all that matters.

"You're staying here tonight until we sort out some round-the-clock bodyguard tomorrow. Trust me, the couch is comfy. I've been banished to sleeping on the couch several times," Ash reassures her with a smile.

Alessandra brings out the extra bedding and a set of PJs for Emmy to change into. She says thank you then disappears to the bathroom. Ash calls it a night pulling Alessandra into their room and shutting the door behind them.

I sit on the sofa and bury my face in my hands. Tonight's been too much. The panic like I've never felt in my entire life, and the anger toward a stranger because he wanted something that's mine.

Wait! Fuck. You didn't just use the word *mine*.

I need to sort out this mess with her if I have any hope of playing tomorrow. My mind's beyond fucked. I haven't even practiced the field moves in my head, something I always do before a big game.

The creak of the bathroom door followed by the click of the switch alerts me she's finished. Shifting my head sideways, her legs are beside me and it's a sight that does nothing to tame my hunger for her.

"We need to talk."

"Then talk, Logan."

"Not here," I tell her, standing up and walking to my bedroom.

I switch the light on and wait for her to enter, closing the door behind her. Her eyes wander across the room, from my perfectly made bed to the soccer medals displayed on my shelf. She walks over to the shelf in the pink shirt Alessandra lent her and thick, white socks. With her back to me, I take the opportunity to scan her body, desperate to throw her on my bed and make her mine.

There's that damn word again.

She turns to face me, crossing her arms underneath her breasts. "I hope you have an explanation for why you've been a prick."

"Do you have one for being a bitch?" I retaliate.

She shakes her head and follows with a sinister laugh. "Nice. I'm a bitch because I haven't spoken to you? Two-way street, buddy. You weren't exactly blowing up my phone with text messages."

"You're marrying him," I yell, then quickly lower my

voice hoping Ash doesn't hear. "And you're still fucking him."

"I told you I'm not with him. How many times do I need to say it? Believe whatever the hell you want. I was angry in the pub," she says, frustrated. "What does it matter anyway? We said no strings attached and as far as I'm concerned you fucking that nurse confirms it."

"You're right," I agree. "We said no strings attached, so none of that should have mattered."

With her eyes wide and brows furrowed, I can see she's hurt about my last comment.

"You know what?" I say softly. "You sleep here, I like the couch."

"No, it's your bed and you have an important game tomorrow. I don't want to be the reason you're tired."

I remove my tie and place it on my chair, unbuttoning my shirt and laying it on top. Considering we've seen each other naked, I find it amusing she can't look my way, purposely avoiding where I stand.

"Look, I'll let you get changed." She turns around and faces the shelf, looking at the gold medal that takes pride of place in the middle. "Was this the first premiership you won?"

"Yes." I smile, remembering the moment fondly. "I actually cried."

"I can imagine. It's such an achievement, and both of you have worked toward that your whole life. I don't think I ever remember a day when you haven't talked about soccer or even kick the ball around. It's in your blood."

Dropping my pants, I hang them over the chair and remove my socks, leaving me only in my black boxer shorts. "You can turn around now."

She spins around and keeps her eyes fixed on my face. I can see the struggle because it mirrors mine exactly.

"I don't want to sleep in your bed. Logan, this game is important."

"I know my body and my limits, it'll be fine." I pull the cover back motioning for her to hop in. She does so with reluctance and when she's settled in the middle, her gaze meets mine and lingers.

Does she know how sexy she looks in my bed?

How much I want to climb in beside her and hold her tight, to only let her go so I can watch her body unravel beneath my touch?

"Goodnight, Emmy."

I walk to the door and switch off the light. As I begin closing the door I hear her call my name, making me stop in my tracks. "Sleep in your bed... with me."

Letting out a sigh, my body turns around of its own accord. "Emmy, you don't know what you're asking," I whisper in the dark.

"Yes, I do..." She pauses with a hitched breath. "I'm asking you to stay with me."

"It's more than that."

"Maybe it is, Logan. I don't know anymore. But for now it's just this. Please stay with me."

I know if I climb in my bed—with her—I'm jeopardizing everything I've worked hard for in the past year.

And even with that thought weighing heavily on my mind, I close the door behind me and walk straight for my bed.

SIXTEEN

"How do you smile when your heart's
falling in love with the wrong man?"
~ *Emerson Chase*

The bed moves as he climbs in resting his warm body against mine.

"Logan," I whisper, desperately trying to ignore his lips which have already found their way to my skin. "You really do need sleep."

"I need you more."

Four simple words which crush any hope I have of keeping our arrangement platonic.

I came to London for the show despite Logan living here. With his mood swings and lack of communication, it was clear we had fun and the fun was over.

That night with Wes, on the couch, ended in disaster. It started off heated, and just before he slid himself in, I froze and remembered where he'd been and the trail of possible diseases that tagged along with him. It killed the moment and even frightened Wes. It wasn't just the possibility of him carrying something nasty, it was also the guilt of being with Logan.

Wesley doesn't deserve me as much as I don't deserve him.

That's the cold hard truth.

From the moment I saw Logan walk into his apartment, I knew everything between us had changed. My heart did something—a pitter-pat, a flurry of madness—signifying something dangerous.

It's invested in him.

It craves attention from only him.

All the things it shouldn't be feeling, and tonight has cemented that.

I don't want him looking at anyone else.

I don't want him touching anyone else.

And I don't know how to hide my feelings anymore.

Lying here with him, his body pressing against mine with his cock rock hard and grinding on my hip means one thing, and I know I don't have the strength to fight it. I want him buried inside me, thrusting hard and owning every inch of my body.

"You're not supposed to have sex before a game," I remind him.

"That's an old wives' tale."

"Somehow I don't think old wives were screwing soccer players. I'm sure there's a medical explanation as to why you shouldn't shoot your load into my vagina."

He pauses, withdrawing his kisses and raising his head. "How about I shoot my load into your mouth?"

I smack his chest, laughing simultaneously but quickly

becoming distracted by his hand sliding beneath my shirt, squeezing my breast. "No shooting of your load, anywhere."

"Damn." He nibbles on the sensitive spot of my lobe. "There's several places I'd love to shoot my load."

I'm unable to hide my grin, grateful for the darkness that lays between us. "Like where?"

I can hear the smile in his voice. The cocky bastard knows he has the upper hand right now.

"Let's see..." he keeps his head positioned near the base of my ear, trailing his finger along my chest, "... here."

Keeping a straight face is hard, holding back the giggles even harder. "Yeah, I guess so. If you like the whole pearl-necklace thing."

"Hmm..." He traces my collarbone then switches in the opposite direction, moving south until he stops on my thigh. "How about here?"

"For a soccer player, you have a shitty sense of direction. Maybe go northwest."

His teeth graze on my lobe, biting down with slight pain that pleasures me. The tip of his finger trails north, just like I directed him, then moves west and in between my thighs until it brushes with my clit. Then with a sudden thrust, it enters me causing my back to arch. I hold in the moan, biting down on my lip tasting blood.

"Sshh," he commands. "I haven't finished."

I weave my fingers through his hair, bringing his face to mine. "I don't know what else you could possibly show me. And I just bit my own lip to keep quiet so maybe we need to go to sleep now."

His lips crash onto mine, sucking on my lip where I tasted my own blood. My body feels at a loss when he removes his finger from me, bringing it up to make me taste myself on his finger. I suck, and a growl erupts from his chest which is barely contained in this quiet room.

"So, now I own all of you. I've even tasted your blood."

"If someone heard that, it could be taken the wrong way."

"Because vampires exist?"

"If they do, I'd sell my left kidney to screw Edward Cullen."

He lifts his body, and through the moonlight which barely peeks its way through the drapes, I can see his expressed has changed.

Does he know how unbelievably sexy he is? Especially when he plays the brooding lover.

"Why am I jealous of you wanting to screw a fictional vampire?"

"You tell me." I run the tip of my tongue along his jaw. "I can't quite work you out."

His hand grips onto my hip, positioning himself with his cock dancing around my entrance. With no words to say, he slides himself in much to my pleasure and waits for his breathing to stabilize.

"I can explain many things, Emmy, but right now I'll say this..." he trails off.

The rhythm of his body distracts him, and me, until I press on his chest and catch my breath begging him to finish his sentence. "What is it, Logan? Don't leave me hanging here."

"When I'm not around you, nothing makes sense. When I'm inside you, it all makes sense."

"But we promised to keep this just fun."

"I don't like other men touching you."

"Edward Cullen is not another man." I attempt to keep light of the situation.

"Don't do that," he notes with dark amusement. "Do you know what happens when you make me jealous?"

I shake my head.

"I will punish you."

Curiosity gets the better of me. "Like what? Spank me? I wouldn't mind that."

"I *won't* make you come."

It's my turn to laugh. "Yeah, right. You know what? That's just cruel and besides, we're back to the whole *you* are the one who's not supposed to come." Pushing my hands on his chest, I move him off me and use my body to straddle him. There's a sense of danger with Ash in the same apartment. Basically, he will literally kill us both if he walks in and sees us together.

I clear my throat in an effort to keep my voice low and unheard. "I'm making an executive decision here... you can't come, no shooting of loads anywhere. If you play bad it'll be on me," I command. "So, with that decided, I'll come."

He cups the back of my neck and draws me into him. "You're fucking crazy."

"Crazy... maybe." In a bold move, I lift my legs and raise my clit, positioning it in his mouth. Beneath me he moans, gripping onto my ass tight and sliding his hand around my asshole making me flinch with nerves. I've only tried it once, and with that one time, I practically died of pain. It was the worst experience of my life, and I don't want to revisit anything which results in something going inside my ass.

He continues to flick his tongue, mixing the movement with gentle sucks. My body moves up and down, using the headboard for support as I ride his mouth on the verge of combusting at any given moment. Keeping quiet is the hardest part, my moans trapped inside, and with nothing to bite but my own lips it only heightened the moment.

Logan moves his mouth catching his breath. "I want you to relax."

What does he mean by that? I'm beyond relaxed. I'm about to come until he stops me.

His finger moves around my ass, playing with my entrance.

Oh no. My body tenses, nerves settling at the fear of the unknown.

"Logan, I—"

"Relax," he repeats.

I breathe in and out, trying to focus on controlling my racing heart. With his spare hand, he brings it to his face, spreading my lips and running his tongue along the inside of my pussy. The sensation begins to build again causing me to rock slowly. I rub my clit along his mouth, lost in how my body is reacting—hair standing on end with goosebumps covering every inch of me.

I'm almost there, riding him hard until his finger pushes against my ass and slowly slides in stopping immediately.

My body stills.

My heart racing like a fucking maniac and all I can think about is Logan's finger is sitting in my ass. The pain subsides after only a few seconds while he continues to flick my clit, bringing back the pleasure once again.

I press harder, my body demanding he finish me off. Then, he slides his finger in deeper and stops. The pain, again, stopping my impending orgasm.

"I'm going to finger this tight ass of yours and you're going to come now," he murmurs beneath me.

I'm terrified. It'll hurt and I'll have to offend him and tell him to pull out. Then there'll be this awkward feeling between us and I'll feel like a failure for not being an ass girl.

His tongue circles my clit in the same motion. The more he spreads my lips, the more exposed my pussy is to his mouth. I begin to rock again, laying my palms flat on the wall as he eats me like I'm his last meal on earth.

The fire in my belly stirs, and when all of my skin ignites and there's no way to escape from him but to spiral out of control, he slides his finger in and out of my ass in sync with my body.

I don't expect the raw pleasure. My body continues on this high from him worshipping me this way. I want to scream at the top of my lungs, making the whole world see that this sexy man beneath me is the only one to have ever made my body react this way. I didn't want to stop, ever. I want all of him now, and for the rest of my life to take me however he wants.

I want him to own me.

I need his jealousy to drive him to the brink of insanity and take that out on me however he desires. I want to do all the things my body doesn't know it craves.

And I want only *him*.

My body loses all self-control, collapsing on top of him as I use the little energy I have left to lay beside him. The sound of my heart beating is obnoxiously loud and does nothing to control my breathing.

"You're beautiful when you come for me."

"How would you know?" I struggle to say. "I practically smothered you to death."

He props himself up on his elbow, sweeping my hair away from my face. Lowering his head, he kisses the tip of my nipple causing me to shiver in delight.

"You're not helping me right now," I beg him to stop because I'm greedy and hungry for more.

"I'm sorry," he responds playfully. "So, the deal is if I

win the game tomorrow, I get to do whatever I want to you?"

My chest begins to rise and fall, overcome by laughter. "When did I say that?"

"It was right before you came... something along the lines of you can do anything you want to me."

"I don't recall that."

"To be fair..." he says with concern, "... you weren't held to ransom. I could have easily stopped."

"You're a pain in the ass." I grin, messing his hair with my hand to annoy him.

Why does he have to be so beautiful, grinning back at me like a fool?

"I'd like to be a pain in *your* ass. You seem to enjoy it."

I pull the sheet to cover my body, despite the hot flashes from our current choice of topic. I shouldn't be embarrassed to talk about it, and maybe after that small trial run I could be open to more.

My hands move around the bed, searching for my shirt. I place it on along with my panties which magically disappeared. Despite my reluctance to leave I know he needs his sleep.

"I have to go. I don't want Ash waking up and finding me here. He can't know about us," I remind him.

"I know, Emmy." He sighs in agreement. "Go to the living room. I probably won't see you till the day after. If it goes our way tomorrow, we're out all night celebrating with the club. If it doesn't go our way... then we're screwed."

"I wish I could come to the game but we have a filming schedule I can't get out of."

"With Wesley..." It's a statement, not a question.

"Don't do this, Logan." I get out of bed standing beside

him. "Focus on your game and not on what either of us can't control."

"We can't control?" His eyes bore into me, a mixed look of confusion and denial. Sitting up in bed, his back against the headboard, he rests his hands on his lap waiting for me to respond.

"Our emotions, Logan."

There's silence, something which doesn't surprise me. Neither of us expected the situation to end up here—in bed discussing any sort of 'emotions.'

"Emmy..." he trails off, running his fingers through his messy sex hair, "... I can't discuss this now."

I sigh but keep my posture straight and confident not wanting to show him how much he affects me.

"Of course, you can't," I tell him with a smile "Go to sleep, Logan. There's always another time."

"Good night."

"Good night," I whisper, closing the door behind me and allowing my heart to feel the pain.

Wanting more terrifies me.

Not because I'm incapable of falling in love.

It's because I shouldn't be falling in love with Logan Carrington.

SEVENTEEN

*"Family means everything to me.
Those joined by blood, marriage,
and those who are destined to be in your life
no matter what."*
~ *Emerson Chase*

I couldn't sleep a wink. My body is still on West Coast time, I'm wide awake and staring at the ceiling. I lay in a room that divides two important people in my life — my brother and the man who consumes me. It would have been selfish for me to drag Logan into a conversation about us with his focus needing to be on tomorrow's game.

Yet, my brain refuses to shut down.

So many questions need answering.

There are many things which stand against us, and it's difficult for me to hold back the resentment toward everyone who will have a 'say' in our relationship. It's not just Logan and me. There's Wesley, Ash, Mom and Dad. Oh... and the *whole damn world.*

And that's to say Logan's head's in the same place as mine right now. I know him well. Understand how driven he can be, yet when it comes to matters of the heart, he thinks with his dick only.

And I have no idea if I'm any more than a notch on his belt. After all, he did screw that nurse.

How many other women has he been with while we're having our stringless fun?

The time on my phone tells me it's after midnight. So, I toss and turn, desperate to clear my head to no avail.

Me: *Do you think people would notice if I fell off the face of this Earth?*

I send the text to my sister knowing she will respond instantly since her phone is practically glued to her hand. I made a conscious decision to keep in regular contact with her after my trip back home.

Tayla: *Is this about Wesley and Farrah at that club?*

Huh? I remember they went to some hip club, but I made no effort to speak to him afterward. He has free rein to do whatever or whomever he pleases. Our 'almost' sexual encounter was a huge wake-up call for him. I think it's finally sunk in how stupid his night in Amsterdam was and everything he lost in his life for a moment of pleasure. It hasn't stopped him from acting like a jerk, and this season has been the toughest for me trying to keep up the charade. I'm ready to move on.

Me: *???*

Tayla sends me a screenshot of Farrah's Instagram post. It's nothing unlike what she would typically post, with Wesley's arm around her in the middle of the club with her ridiculous duck face.

Me: *The jerk can piss off with her duck face. I can't sleep. Why didn't you come to London with the parentals?*

She types ridiculously quick and the message appears.

Tayla: *Exams. A boy. London with the parentals would have been lame. Need I say more?*

I smile, easily forgetting she still has to answer to Mom and Dad. You'd think they would loosen the strings with Tayla having already gone through the teenage phase with Ash and me, but if anything they're stricter.

Me: *I'm guessing Gran's with you? Slip some brandy in her night tea and you're good to go for three hours till she wakes up to pee. I should get some sleep. Night sissy.*

She follows by sending me some random GIF making me giggle quietly beneath the soft covers. I put my phone away and will myself to sleep when my mind begins to unwind and the exhaustion takes over.

~

The boys left for training at the crack of dawn. I didn't hear them leave, falling asleep and waking up to the smell of coffee filtering through the apartment.

Alessandra has a shift at the hospital then plans to catch the end of the game when she's done.

She cooks me breakfast, gives me some clothes to wear and suggests I stay in case the stalker's watching me.

As much as I would love to stay, we have a schedule to adhere to so I call Cliff and explained what happened last night. He seems genuinely concerned, organizing a car service and bodyguard to pick me up.

Back at the hotel not long later, I quickly shower and change into something more relaxed. A pair of light blue boyfriend-cut jeans and a white T-shirt. I place my sneakers on, ready to join the rest of the crew at Poppy's parents' house. With my purse in hand and a jacket in case the weather cools down, I open my door to find Wes standing outside, blocking my way.

"Is it true?" His tone is sharp, almost demanding. There's dark circles around his eyes and his clothes appear rumpled and worn.

"Wesley, the car's waiting downstairs. Can whatever this is wait?"

"No, it can't wait, Emerson."

I shove my hands in my pockets. "What?"

"That a man is stalking you?"

I purse my lips, eyes wide while nodding my head.

"And you slept at Logan's?"

"Ash and Logan's," I correct him. "They live together. Ash took me home because I wasn't safe alone."

Wesley had no problem expressing his anger. His fist is resting against the door panel, curled into a ball with his knuckles white. "He could have brought you back here."

"You were with Farrah," I remind him. "Don't pull that shit with me."

He latches onto my arm with force. The pressure begins to hurt as I wriggle out of his grip refusing to let him intimidate me.

"Are you sleeping with him?"

I begin to panic under his firm grasp. *Why on earth would he think that?* Everything Logan and I have done is in private, there's no way for Wes to find out. But the guilt and question accelerate the beating of my heart until I'm sure it will explode at any moment.

"Who are you talking about?" I play dumb, keeping my gaze controlled.

"Don't give me that bullshit, Emerson! Logan Carrington. Are. You. Fucking him?"

"You know what..." I keep my voice low, mindful of people in the rooms surrounding us may hear, "... leave him and my brother alone. As for you and me, we're over, Wes. If I want to fuck someone, I believe I have the freedom to do so."

He slams his fist on the wall, damaging a painting that falls onto the ground. *Great.* Now we look like ungrateful celebrities that go around destroying property.

"Don't you fucking dare think for a second you have that freedom," he threatens, cornering me underneath his stance.

I've never seen Wesley react this way. Angry yes, but this is something else and it frightens me.

He's never been violent toward me, and I've always felt safe around him, but right now, I just want him away from me, terrified he'll do more than threaten me with his words.

There's a commotion in the hall. The familiar voices of Kyle and Kelly move toward us. Kelly picks up on the heated air between us, suggesting we head outside as she pulls me along quickly leaving the men behind.

The automatic doors open and the photographers begin snapping. I tell her to stop midway to the car and pose for pictures. Sometimes, it's best we do this rather than they get unauthorized shots that can easily be misconstrued as something else.

The men walk outside and toward us. I don't know why I call Wesley over, maybe because I begin to panic that Logan and me being anywhere together is raising red flags. I pull his arm to me and wrap my hand around his waist, placing my left hand on his chest to purposely show off the engagement ring.

The paparazzi click away in a frenzy, asking a dozen questions we don't answer.

The four of us tell them we're done, entering the limo waiting along the sidewalk.

As I climb in, Wes stops me and brushes his lips against my ear. "I can play nasty, Emerson. Remember that."

The smile on my face fades.

Reality kicking me like a force of nature.

Poppy's parents' place is cute and not at all how I imagined. It sits just outside of the small town they lived in—a quaint cottage built by Poppy's great-great-grandfather. Aside from her parents who reside in the house, her teenage brother also lives there.

Poppy's mom, Delia, is the loveliest lady I've ever met. A spitting image of Poppy but with orange curly hair that appears wild and unruly.

She offers us a cup of tea and some scones while we all settle in the cozy living room.

Cliff's standing beside the fireplace, directing everyone to sit down. He strategically places all the couples together, leaving Poppy and Harley separate. The only person not here is Farrah.

Aside from the fact that Farrah wouldn't be caught dead in this house—her words—Cliff purposely left her out to stir conflict between her and Poppy. A stupid idea since Poppy isn't the type of person to get riled up over something like this. She's breezy and enjoys her life without too much drama.

"Okay, Delia, you can tell everyone the story about Poppy losing her virginity to the milkman. The fans will love that."

"You lost your virginity to the milkman?" Wesley laughs.

Cliff stops him, annoyed. "Save it for when the cameras are rolling, will you?"

Poppy leans over and whispers to the group, "The milkman's son. He brought us fresh milk every day."

"We'll do a quick tour of the town, give the local businesses some exposure, then we'll come back here and watch the game." Cliffs shuts his folder, removing his glasses.

"What game?" Wesley questions him.

"The fucking game. Royal Kings versus Manchester." Cliff appears highly strung, more so than normal. "We spoke to the network and got approval to show footage. I think it'll be good if they win given Ashley and Logan make an appearance this season."

"They do?" It's my turn to ask the questions. "They agreed to that?"

When I signed my contract three years ago, I strictly

stated my family are not to be filmed. It surprised me that neither Ash nor Logan has mentioned their appearance to me.

"They did. So that's the plan. Karl..." Cliff yells across the room, "... turn the cameras on."

The cameras begin rolling and we take cue, conversing over Poppy's wild childhood. The scene takes about an hour and then we proceed to head into town. The town itself consists of four stores—bakery, grocer, post office, and gift shop. Poppy has a story to tell about each one, some funny and some nostalgic.

By the time we head back to the cottage, it's game time.

I've been nervous all day, praying that last night doesn't affect Logan's game.

Ninety minutes of angst about to start.

Logan scores the first goal but is soon trumped by the opposing team scoring their first goal. An hour later and it's still a tie with my head glued to the television.

"This is game is so boring." Wes yawns beside me.

"Will you shut up? You've said that three times already," I hiss.

With ten minutes to go, Ash bounces off Logan and with a bold kick, Ash shoots the winning goal. I jump up at the same time as Poppy, screaming at the television in excitement.

The crowd goes wild, the cameras zooming in on Ash as he falls to the ground elated. The coaches are jumping inside the commentary booths. The only people not celebrating are Manchester. This is a decider game and now they won't make it to the quarter-finals.

Even Cliff's happy—a rare moment of him cheering them on behind the cameras.

"Oh my gosh, Em, your brother is amazing," Kelly squeals. "You must be so proud of him."

"I am." I beam, shaking my head with pride. "I'm so happy they won."

"And Logan fucking killed it," Kyle says in awe.

I don't know what to say. Logan killed it because Logan always kills it. That's who he is and I can't exactly say he killed it because he has the biggest blue balls ever.

"Just like Ash, that's why they're best friends."

The game ends with the final score two-one. The Royal Kings make it to the quarter-finals. The on-field camera chases Logan down, interviewing him while he tries to catch his breath.

Through the screen, I stare at how amazingly beautiful this man is. His whole face is grinning, eyes bright with not a hint of exhaustion. He brings the water bottle to his lips and it's a perfect opportunity for me to study them and remember how soft they feel against my skin.

The sports journalist holds the mic up to him. "How did it feel to score that first goal?"

"Amazing," Logan strains, barely able to talk. "It was a tough game and they played well. Ash just cemented that final win."

"The two of you are unstoppable. Would you say that your friendship helps you play as a team?"

"He's my brother... it's more than just friendship."

"How are you going to celebrate this win?"

He drops his head, hiding the devilish smirk playing on his lips while running his hands through his hair. "With something big."

I hide the smile which tells the world celebrating this win means I get fucked harder than I've ever been fucked before. I should be scared, but down below, the excitement stirs at the unknown.

Wesley sits on the couch with his chin held high refusing to comment. His legs are restless, bouncing up and down, his expression tight with a reddened face.

"Is it time to go, yet?" He removes his phone from his pocket, distracting himself much to Cliff's disapproval.

"And that's a cut," Cliff shouts, switching positions and pointing to Wes. "Wesley, outside. *Now*."

We head into the dining room to finish off with dinner. I tell Poppy I need to use the bathroom but walk past the front door to find out why Cliff wanted to speak to Wes alone.

"I don't care what fucking chip you have on your shoulder, Rich. Get over it and fucking look like you love the girl," Cliff berates.

"I do love her," Wes answers softly. "I just can't seem to fix things. I don't want to lose her."

There's a short silence. "Then keep ya dick in ya pants. Why the fuck were you out with Farrah last night? That club was full. People would have seen you."

"Nothing happened. We danced. She wanted to go back to the hotel to suck me off. I said no. I don't want to lose Emerson."

I didn't expect my heart to race this fast—the guilt and shame weighing me down. I walk away not wanting to hear the rest of the conversation because it only makes everything worse. Perhaps I'm a monster. Two wrongs certainly don't make a right, but the thought of giving up Logan is something which hurts me more. And that alone terrifies me.

We finish at Poppy's with a lovely dinner her mother prepared for all of us.

By the time we hit the road, it's late and most of us are exhausted from a long day of filming.

Kyle and Kelly call it a night. Harley wants to go out and Wesley decides to join him. They ask me to go, but I kindly refuse hoping Logan will call.

"Why won't you come out with us?" Wesley stands solid, folding his arms with an arrogant stare. "You have somewhere better to be?"

Harley watches the both of us. "Listen, I can go if you guys want to talk."

"No, Harley," I tell him, frustrated to the point where I'm no longer thinking with my head. "No point keeping it a secret since our lives are open for public consumption. Wesley and I aren't together anymore."

Harley appears uncomfortable but attempts to maintain composure. He's a man of few words—dark, broody, your Charlie-Sheen-in-Ferris-Bueller's-day-off type.

"I kinda figured that." He rubs his hand on the back of his neck. "Not my place to comment. I just want to go for a drink and maybe pick up a British bird. That's what Pop told me to call them."

It's his attempt to break the ice. I make the effort to smile at his gesture, unlike Wesley who continues to stand guarded, ice-cold.

"Maybe I should do the same, huh? Score some British *bird* that wants to be around me. American women are so over-the-top."

"Well, don't let me stop you," I fire back, angry at his insensitive comment. "You go have your fun and I'll have mine."

The comment leaves him speechless, bearing down on his teeth with a clenched jaw. I walk away and head to my room, longing for peace and quiet. As I walk in the room is dead silent—the kind of silence I long for. Shifting to the bed, I lay flat on the mattress, my stomach against the fancy sheets and close my eyes.

When did my life become this drama-filled soap opera?

Like most couples, Wesley and I used to have a pretty normal relationship. A few fights, only a handful of massive blow-ups, but for the most part we got along.

Now, it's a giant mess. If the cameras filmed our actual *real* lives and not the ones we pretend to portray, the fans would go nuts. This is reality. Caught in this messy love triangle with two men who rival each other for different reasons.

Boredom finds me soon after, so I post some pictures online, reply to the thousands of comments that follow instantly. Pictures from our Victoria Secret show to our tour of London. It's been a busy couple of days with no end in sight.

Finally, I scroll through my phone and find an old picture of me, Ash, and Logan that Mom sent me recently. It was taken when we were eleven at a school carnival where the three of us were in charge of the cotton-candy stand. Mom snapped Ash with cotton candy all over his head from when Logan and me dared him to put his head inside the machine.

I type a comment beneath the photo, telling everyone how proud I am of these boys winning tonight's game. I hold onto my smile, remembering this time with happiness. These two boys are my life, and every part of me is terrified my relationship with Logan will break us if things don't work out.

I shut down my Instagram and call Mom. She texted me yesterday to say she would be flying in for a day to watch the game. As much as she would have loved to stay longer, she had a pressing deadline and Tayla back home.

"Hey, kid!" There's a considerable commotion in the background. I can barely hear her over the sound of Queen blaring through the speakers.

"Where are you, Mom?"

"I can't hear you. Hold on... okay?"

Waiting for the connection to become clearer, there's a muffled sound then her voice feeds over the speaker again. "Okay, I'm back... phew."

"What on Earth are you doing, Mother?"

"We're out at this pub celebrating the win. I forgot how much I love pub crawling."

"When did you ever pub crawl?"

"When I was a loose cannon and didn't have three kids busting my chops."

"I've never busted your chops." My smile turns into laughter while my body begins relaxing on the bed. "Are you with Ash and Logan?"

"Yeah, I think they're around here somewhere. I lost sight of things after the second pint," she follows with a hiccup.

"And Dad?"

"I think he's being tattooed by a Scotsman."

"Mom, shut up. Dad? The two of you shouldn't be allowed out."

"Come, join us! We're in the city."

I look at the time, it's only half-past ten, and even though I'm exhausted I want a chance to see Logan. Tell him how happy and proud I am of him.

Yeah right, your damn kitty is itching to get some.

"You know what, Mom? I'll be there soon."

I jot down the pub address she's currently at and hang

up immediately. I'm still in the same outfit as today but decide to change. I put on a black jumpsuit with long sleeves and a plunging neckline, pairing it with some high-waisted jeans and my knee-high boots. I ditch the coat and throw on a scarf to keep the cool air away.

I leave the room and spontaneously decide to knock on Poppy's door.

"Hey Em, you're dressed all fancy for bed."

Poppy's wearing her pink pajamas with unicorns patterned all over. On her feet are fluffy white slippers that looked like rabbits.

"Pop," I say with a smile. "Wanna go on a pub crawl?"

"A pub crawl?" Her face lights up. "Sure! I was about to order room service and watch *Titanic*."

"Okay, that's depressing."

"Let me get changed."

Poppy emerges wearing a black knitted top, tartan skirt, and bright red leggings. "Okay, I'm ready! How do I look?"

"Like Poppy." I laugh.

"Let's go, we just need to make one stop first."

We meet Mom and Dad a while later at a pub called Randy's. The place is full of Royal Kings fans dressed in their jerseys. Poppy made us stop at the concierge and had him hunt down a place which was still open that sold jerseys. We found the place not too far from the hotel and pulled them on over what we're wearing.

The atmosphere is buzzing. Drunken patrons all singing loud and proud, buying each other rounds of drinks. There's a mix of young, old, and any other person you can think of. I spot Mom at the back, where she has her arm around a toothless man singing to The Proclaimers.

"Emmy," she beams, stumbling over to greet me.

There are many things in life you witness, but watching your parents drunk is always a classic moment. Dad's at the next table over, doing rounds of shots with a bunch of young guys. It's equally disturbing that the drink is called a Juicy Pussy.

"Hey, Mom." I lean in and give her a hug. She reeks of beer and smoke. "Have you been smoking?"

"Oh, lighten up, kid. Who made you, Mom?" She chuckles loudly with the toothless man.

I take satisfaction in knowing tomorrow she'll be sporting the worst hangover and regretting her actions. Serves her right for partying so hard at forty-nine.

I introduce Poppy to Mom. They seem to hit it off straight away and bond over another pint.

"Where's Logan and Ash?" I ask, scanning the pub.

"They just left with the team for the next pub over."

We lasted five minutes in the pub until Dad announced, "It's time to pub crawl... *again.*"

Everyone cheers and we follow him out to the next pub, walking along the street like a drunken march.

The next pub is called Hudson's Corner. A bigger joint and even more crowded than the last.

"Emmy," Dad calls over the crowd.

I slide my way through, holding Poppy's hand so we don't separate. "Dad, ease up on the shots. You're not twenty-one anymore. Plus, it can't be good for your meds."

He laughs, kissing my cheek. "You see this, Alan? This here is my daughter, Emmy. Ash's twin."

"Twins?" Alan acts surprised. "Blimey! You're gonna break some hearts."

"She already has." The voice comes from behind me, and without turning around my smile is stuck. I twist my body and Logan's standing behind me dressed in a checked navy and white shirt, tucked into his navy slacks with tancolored shoes on his feet. His large watch is hanging off his wrist and hair is styled perfectly to the side.

He looks delicious. Like an Armani model from a magazine. Perfect in every way.

"Poppy, you remember Logan?"

"Yes." She beams with a crooked smile, them jumps up and hugs him, much to his shock. "Congratulations, you smashed it today."

When she lets go, he waits, searching our surroundings.

I lean in and hug him careful not to close my eyes.

"I'm so proud of you."

"I can't wait to be inside you," he whispers in my ear.

I pull back, careful not to raise suspicion and trying my best to control the heat throbbing between my legs. I'm wearing a black lacy thong, and it's doing nothing to curb the ache as the thin piece of string rubs against my clit making it ten times worse. "So anyway, where's Ash?"

The cocky bastard keeps his expression fixed, his luscious lips grinning with delight. He turns around for a moment, then spins back with his eyes directed at mine. Ash is standing in the middle of a crowd, jug in hand with bloodshot eyes, singing the team's anthem.

"Oh God, he's gone," I mutter.

"Your brother is a toot," Poppy says cheerily.

"Yeah. Where's Alessandra?"

Logan shrugs then leans in. "People are watching us. I'll meet you later."

Many people in the room spotted Poppy and me wanting selfies, so Logan walks away and begins chatting with some of his teammates, leaving us alone with the small group of fans who join us.

Ash spots us and runs straight to me, almost colliding with Poppy.

"Emmy!" He hugs me tight, suffocating me with his odor of sweat and beer.

I struggle to remove myself from his grip. "All right, you're kinda strangling me."

"Can you believe I scored that last goal? Especially, since I had a huge fight with Sandy and was *too* pissed to tell you."

Well, that explains why Alessandra seemed almost robotic that morning. I didn't think too much of it at the time, assuming she was stressed about the game like me.

"Where is she?"

"I don't know. Don't care. I'm so glad you're here." He suffocates me again, then stands on the table with a wobble, whistling loudly to the crowd. "I wanna do a speech."

The crowd cheers, a loud rumble with feet banging against the wooden floors.

"Firstly, to Coach... you fucking break my balls, dude, and now I know why."

Coach Bennett tips his hat, smiling like a drunken fool.

"To Mom and Dad... I fucking love you guys. You're the best parents ever."

Another loud rumble from the crowd. Mom's almost in tears, quick to wipe them away as she downs another beer. Dad looks equally emotional, rubbing his eyes with a dirty napkin from the table.

Those two are unbelievable.

"To Emmy... you're my sister for life. I wouldn't have wanted anyone else shooting out of Mom's vagina with me.

Vagina log ride for life!" He raises his glass as everyone laughs.

I scrunch up my face at the godawful speech. Mom's vagina did *not* need attention and it's not helping that she finds it equally hilarious.

"And to this guy..." He points at Logan with a proud smile, holding his glass to his chest. "My brother for fucking life. No one will ever come between us."

The crowd roars until Ash yells drinks on him. I don't think he's thinking straight. The pub's at full capacity and it'll cost him a fortune. I should say something, but choose to teach the moron a lesson by ordering a drink myself.

Poppy and I hang out with the fans who join us. They're a cool bunch, eager to chat, but not so eager it's creepy. We drink some rounds, talk about the show, sing along to the songs that scream over the speakers. We do a live Facebook video. Probably not the brightest idea but still a lot of fun.

We crawl to another pub and by the time we get there, we begin losing people to the copious amounts of alcohol entering their body.

"Kid, we're heading back to the hotel," Mom slurs while Dad's almost passed out at the table.

"Did you want me to take you?" I ask, a little worried that Dad looks legless. "No, you stay here. Join us for breakfast tomorrow before our flight leaves?"

I kiss her cheek and follow her to the street to call for a cab. Logan follows with his coach, Dad in between them as they carry him to where the cab waits.

"Are you sure we can't help you, Mom?"

She shakes her head. "Enjoy the night, kid. I love you."

"Love you, too, Mom."

The cab drives off and we're standing on the street

watching it drive away. Coach Bennett calls it a night, reminding Logan he needs to be at the studio by half-past ten tomorrow for a segment.

It's just after two in the morning. The streets are deserted with only a few drunken people stumbling around. The night air is crisp, prompting me to fold my arms to shield out the cold.

"I've got a room at the hotel the next block over. You cab it, I'll walk it." He slips something into the back pocket of my jeans. "And by the way, you look damn sexy in that jersey."

"I'll keep it on just for you," I tease. "But what about Ash and Poppy?"

The two of them are surrounded by a small crowd, laughing and telling awful jokes which everyone finds hilarious.

I tell Logan I need to say goodbye to Poppy, so I head inside to talk to her. "Pop, we need to talk for a sec."

Pulling her to the ladies' restroom, I check the stalls to make sure they're empty. "I need you to cover for me."

"Okay? Like a secret mission. Oh, how exciting!"

"Not really," I drag. "I'm staying at another hotel tonight."

"Oh, I understand. The housekeeping is tardy at our hotel." She nods agreeing. "Did you know that I found several pubic hairs on my pillow? I mean, why on the pillow? I'm not a princess but switching rooms seems like the best option."

"I'm sleeping with Logan," I blurt out.

There's a giant pause, her eyes wide in shock. "Um... right. Logan as in—"

"Logan, as in... Logan. I know what you're thinking, I'm a cheater because of Wesley."

"Honestly, Em?" She rests her hand on my shoulder, easing the tension. "I know things aren't great with you and Wes, and rumors are a rife about how he's treated you. No judgment from me."

"Oh, Pop..." I hug her tight, almost in tears. "It feels good to tell someone."

"So, are you like serious?"

"No... I don't know. We're having fun."

"He doesn't look at you like that."

"What do you mean?"

She opens the stall, placing the lid down and sitting on the toilet to rest her feet. "The moment he saw you, his face lit up. You make him happy. And trust me, Em, I'm great at reading faces. I can read anyone."

"Really? What does my face say?"

"You want to end this conversation 'cause you need to get laid."

I laugh softly. "Can't argue with that. And tell me what Wesley's face says?"

"He's a wild child. Always has been. You tamed him, but boys like him can only be tamed for so long."

"You're telling me," I huff. "And Farrah?"

"That I can't tell. The plastic gets in the way."

We both fall into a fit of laughter, our stomachs hurting until we manage to control ourselves again.

"Don't worry, Em, I got your back."

"Thanks, Pop." I hug her tight again, letting go and stroking her hair. "You're one of a kind, you know. You should have been my twin."

She clutches onto her stomach barely able to get her words out. "Vagina log ride. Your brother is something else."

"That he is," I respond, with the proudest smile on my face.

EIGHTEEN

*"There are no more questions.
She is mine."*
~ Logan Carrington

She's laying on the bed. I watch the way her body is waiting for me. Her eyes are wide in a curious yet frightened stare because she has no idea what I'll do to her. Her innocence radiates all around us with a part of her which remains untouched.

Emmy belongs to me, at least, in my eyes she does.

Despite my desperation to be inside her—taste her arousal all around me—I linger and savor the sight in front of me. Her eyes begin to wander, trailing down my torso and centering on my cock. The hunger consumes her. She licks her lips then bites her tongue, her chest moving up and down, the breaths hitching and barely audible.

"Are you done eye-fucking me?" she teases with a

straight face. "I thought you had this grand plan to take me however you wanted me?"

I've fantasized about this moment for a long time, despite my reluctance to admit it. Emerson's always been beautiful. She has this air of confidence that, for the most part, gets her into trouble. She also has a sweet side, a side not many people see because she keeps her circle tight.

She knows she has me. Lying in the hotel bed all sexy begging me to fuck her however I want. I need to do things to her. Explore my animalistic side because we both agreed to have fun and she wants this just as much as I do.

"You're a tease." Keeping my eyes fixed on hers, she moves her legs, spreading them to catch my attention. Her pussy's desperate for attention. "I must be *that* good if you're soaking wet just waiting for me."

Emmy spreads her legs wide, raising her knees to give me a more open look. Pouting her lips, she slides her hand between her legs and brushes against her clit.

Fuck. What the hell is she doing to me?

"You mean this?" Her fingers graze the wet arousal glistening around her entrance. In small, circular motions, she rubs it gently before lifting her fingers to her mouth and tasting her arousal.

I swallow the giant lump in my throat, covering up my need to blow on myself by just watching her. I continue to observe for a few more seconds before I'm on my hands and knees crawling toward her.

When my body's positioned over the top of her, she gasps when my cock flicks against her pussy.

"Logan," she breathes my name. "I'm scared."

Her short lived confidence is shattered as she murmurs those words.

I'll never hurt her. I just want to show her a different type of pleasure.

"I won't hurt you."

"Physically, I know."

There's something in her eyes, a look that passes between us. Unsure of what the lingering emotion means, I place my mouth on hers and kiss her deeply. As my cock begins to throb, threatening to give early, I break free from the kiss to control my urges.

"I will *never* hurt you."

"You've already hurt me. Once." She lifts her knee and shows me an old scar. I remember what it's from—the time when I pushed her off the zip-line because she was a scaredy cat and I'd never seen her scared before.

I tilt my head, lifting her knee to meet my lips. Kissing it gently, I reassure her, "I will never hurt you, *again.*"

"Do you promise me?"

"I promise you," I whisper, placing my body on top of hers, our intimate position making this moment more arousing.

"Then take me," she says confidently. "I'm yours."

Two words that ignite an already-burning flame into an uncontrollable fire. I ravage her with kisses, covering every inch of her body.

I fuck her tight pussy for what seems like forever, building the sweat between our bodies until we're both drenched. I taste her arousal, making her come multiple times and forcing her to keep going because I know her limit isn't reached. And when I get greedy, I watch her, on her knees, suck on my cock with her eyes desperate for more. The noise she makes from the excess saliva has me teetering on the edge until I have to back off for just a moment, cooling myself down and throwing her onto the sofa beside the bed where I make her spread her legs and demand she come... *again.*

She's insatiable. Wanting me to do things to her that I haven't done to anyone before.

When her body lay limp, exhausted from her blissful finish, I take the liberty to make her suck me off again, commanding she take me all in.

Then we switch it up again.

"Logan..." she hums with her eyes half closed. "I don't know how much longer I can go."

I'm pounding her hard, knowing she's on the verge again. Her body gives me the signs, her pussy clenching around my cock warning me she's close. "You said that three orgasms ago. I'm not done with you, yet."

She moans in delight, ignoring her exhaustion and begging me to make her come again.

I stop abruptly, her body reacting and eyes opening.

"Don't stop."

I grin wickedly. "Baby, this is just the beginning. Are you ready for your finale?"

She arches her head back with a laugh. "I'm ready."

"Get on all fours," I command.

I grab onto her hips and help her move, kissing the top of her shoulder to ease her nerves. The curves of her ass are beckoning me, delicious and fuckable. I run my hands along the curves, stopping just shy of her hole. Building up the saliva in my mouth I drop some onto her ass, spreading it nice and wide ready for me to enter. I slowly graze the tip of my cock, entering slowly as her body almost buckles. I stop, rub the small of her back, and wait for her to push back. When she does, I move in deeper until I'm all in.

Brushing against her ear, I whisper, "Are you okay?"

"Why do you have to have such a big cock?" she barely speaks.

I try not to laugh, taking it as a compliment. I grip onto her hips, using them as handles and guiding her through the pain. Her moans become deeper, and when her back buckles, I know she's almost there.

I lean forward, twisting her hair in my hands and pulling it back, so her face meets mine. "Come for me."

Her face turns bright red and when I demand she come again, she muffles her screams biting down on her lips. It's enough for me to finish, and when I deepen the strokes, it spirals through me ripping my entire body to shreds until we've both collapsed on the bed.

"I can't even... what's the... talk," she finally gets out.

A small laugh escapes, but it's filled with pain from my aching muscles. I've worked myself to almost death these past few weeks and it paid off. I don't know what excites me more—winning or having her lay naked beside me.

"Aren't you tired?"

"I could go again."

"I think my vagina is broken," she mumbles with a smile.

I turn my body around, making her do the same, so we're both laying sideways. Staring into her sleepy eyes, I think about what this day has meant to me. Yes, I worked hard and it paid off. Soccer isn't just a sport to me—it's my life. I don't exist without it. But the victory means nothing without her. I've never felt so alive than at this very moment although my body argues with me about that.

Emmy isn't like any of the women I've been with, and she sure as hell ain't Louisa.

She's Emerson Chase.

"Tell me what you're thinking," she says with her eyes closed.

I think about her question, running my fingers along her cheek. "You're here."

"Where else would I be?"

"I don't want to answer that."

There's a struggle to open her eyes. They're tired but still bright blue. "Logan, don't... we can't."

How do I tell her I want her exclusively?

With the pressure of our careers and lives, it will be damn near impossible to make it work. We don't even live on the same continent. The media won't allow us to have a relationship, and what about our family? Everything about us is difficult.

She shuffles her body closer to me, placing her lips on mine so we gently kiss. "You only have to know that I don't sleep with him anymore. Trust me, please."

"Your text said differently."

"You fucked that nurse," she rebuts. "Logan, we both did things out of anger and spite. I'm telling you the truth now... I don't sleep with him. Please accept that or we can't move on."

I grit my teeth, trying to remain calm although every part of me wants to tell her how I really feel. How last week I'd spent my time watching Season Two of Generation Next. How at night when I can't sleep, I find myself stalking the both of them online. It's a sick obsession, and one I can't shake no matter how much I try.

"Or anyone else?"

"I'm so tired I can't even think. No one else... just you..." Her gentle snores fall on my chest, and with her final words easing my anxious thoughts I hold onto her, wide awake til the sun comes up.

The clock on the bedside table marks 7:00 a.m. We're due to meet Abbi, Chris, and Ash for breakfast in forty-five minutes. I know Ash's staying in the same hotel, but have no idea where he ended up last night.

I didn't sleep a wink, thinking this would be our last night together for a very long time. Despite our win yesterday, Coach pegged me for an exclusive training camp in Spain that will begin after finals if we win. It'll be a grueling four-week camp with zero chance of seeing her.

The thought alone drives me insane. So, with her naked body lying beside me in the sunlight, I move on top and enter her slowly, fucking her until she begins to wake up.

The beautiful sight of her perky tits beg me to suck on them. Even her pussy feels raw, fucked beyond its means from our wild night. We last only a few moments before I blow inside, her body following closely behind.

We catch our breaths—her smile remaining on her tired face.

"Well, good morning to you, too."

"What can I say, I'm an early riser."

Her body lays flat and I wiggle myself out of her. "We have to leave soon."

"Already? Did you even sleep?"

I shake my head. "But you did. You're so cute... you still do that pouty sleep face from when you were a kid."

She sits up with a struggle, holding onto her head while wincing. "When did you ever watch me sleep?"

"A dozen times," I answer truthfully. "Whenever you fell asleep on the sofa, and that time we camped in the backyard."

"Oh yeah," she reminisces along with me. "You stayed

awake all night and pretended to be a clown with the freaky mask. Ash couldn't sleep for weeks after that."

I laugh, a fond memory that still haunts him to this day.

"I should shower." She yawns, stretching her arms then pulling them back wincing again.

"What's wrong?" I ask, worried.

"You've fucked me to the point of thoroughly fucked. I can't move." She stands up, hobbling to the bathroom and turning on the shower. The water runs for a while with steam filling the room and clouding the mirror. I hop in with her, noticing her skin looks red-raw and there's a few bruises.

"I'm sorry if I hurt you." I kiss her arm from where I gripped on so tightly.

"No, you're not." She laughs. "You loved every second of it. It doesn't hurt, I didn't feel a thing. I'm completely numb right now except for down there..." she points, "... where it kinda stings."

I grab the soap and bend down, washing her softly and noticing how sensitive her skin is. She relaxes enough to hold onto my shoulder, and when I finish, I kiss her lips.

"It's going to be awkward at breakfast."

"Maybe we should tell them," I say with a straight face.

"Tell them what? That we're fucking? Oh, that's going to go down real nice."

"Why not?" I joke lightly.

"Because they think we hate each other."

"Okay..." I challenge her, "... then we'll pretend to hate each other. Besides, the best sex is hate sex, right?"

She smirks, throwing a towel my way. "Game on, Carrington."

∾

"Dad, you look like shit," Emmy tells Chris while scarfing down her breakfast even though she complained her jaw hurt from all the deep-throating.

"I'm not twenty-one anymore." He grimaces at the rare sun gracing us this morning. "God, I don't remember how much your head can hurt after a big night."

Abbi sits quiet on her chair, sporting oversized glasses and a hat.

"Mom? What about you?"

She raises her finger motioning Emmy to be quiet.

"I think Mom and Dad partied too hard." Ash chuckles, unaffected by his beer consumption last night. "Where did you end up, Emmy?"

She shuffles nervously, crossing her legs. "I got a room. I was exhausted from the day out plus, I didn't want to travel back this morning."

"But isn't your hotel like ten minutes away?" I put her on the spot, watching her expression change to annoyance.

"Ten minutes in distance is doubled in London traffic."

"But there's no traffic," I point out. "Just seems odd that you'd stay in this hotel."

"I think it's odd you're a jerk," she argues back.

"Kids, keep it down, please. My ears hurt," Abbi complains.

We end the conversation and eat breakfast quietly, watching a re-run of the game on the big screen television. Seeing Ash score that final goal brings back joyous memories of that moment. *He fucking nailed it.*

"Has anyone seen Poppy?" Emmy asks. "We kind of went our separate ways at the pub, and the last time I saw her she was telling jokes at your table, Ash."

Ash bows his head, studying his plate before his eyes look up at me.

Oh fuck, *he fucked her*.

The look of guilt, I've seen it several times before. I can tell by the way he looks at me, warning me to not say anything out loud.

Jesus, I know his fight with Alessandra got to him but I didn't expect this to happen.

"I think I saw her leave the pub," he says blasé.

Emmy wipes her mouth with the napkin, leaning back on her chair. "I should probably call her. Just to make sure."

"You know what?" Ash interrupts, slightly panicked. "She's a big girl. I'm sure she got back okay."

"When did you leave the pub?" Ash switches the subject to me. *Fucking dick.*

"Don't remember. Was exhausted, so it's kind of a blur."

"Sorry, Mom and Dad," Ash warns before turning back to me. "You picked someone up, didn't you? Was it that blonde with the low-cut tank and short mini who asked where you were staying?"

"Which blonde?" I screw up my face, pretending to be uninterested.

"Oh, yeah," Emmy adds with much delight. She pushes her tongue against her cheek, watching me with a wide smirk. "The blonde who offered you her room key. She said she was kinky and wanted to tie you up. Sorry, Mom and Dad."

"I don't know what you're talking about."

"You *sooo* got laid," Emmy teases. "She would have fucked your little socks off."

Ash laughs, stealing the last sausage from the plate in the middle off the table. "Good. You need a good screw after your dry hump. Especially after your breakup with Louisa."

He continues to laugh at the same time Emmy's face

changes. It's a look of curiosity, and something else I can't quite figure out.

"Who's Louisa?" Emmy questions, clearing her throat.

"Remember I told you about her?" Abbi intervenes. "The love of Logan's life—"

I'm about to stop that statement until Ash interrupts, "You were about to marry her. Did I tell you I ran into her last week? I don't know why I forgot to tell you. She broke up with what's-his-face and asked about you."

If that had happened three months ago, I would have gladly called her and picked things up from where we left off. But I sit here, unaffected by what he's told me and more concerned by Emmy's quiet reaction. I hate the fact I can't read her, there's a total blank expression on her face.

"Honestly, bro. She's great," Ash continues. "Yeah, I know I dislike her, but you were happy with her. Looking back now, I've never seen you happy with anyone besides her."

"Second chances don't come often," Abbi says, placing her arm on mine.

"Abbi, leave the boy alone. He has time to worry about a relationship later. The next four weeks is training and games, and I don't want anyone distracting him," Chris says sharply.

Emerson refuses to look my way, removing the napkin from her lap. "I'm going to head back to the hotel, we have one final shoot today and then we fly out tomorrow."

Abbi and Chris stand up, hugging her before she turns to congratulate Ash then waves across the table to me—without any eye contact—and says congratulations.

Moving her chair in to the table, she turns around and hurries out of the restaurant.

I think on my feet about an excuse, then tell them I accidentally handed her my credit card last night to buy drinks and need to grab it off her. I chase her down the street before she hops into a cab.

"What was that back there?" I ask out of breath.

"I'm tired."

"You're not getting off that easily."

She motions her eyes across the street where a man stands with a camera taking photos of us. I smile, pretending everything's okay then grit through my teeth asking again.

"I don't know, Logan. Try sitting at a table hearing about the woman who's the love of your life suddenly wanting you back."

"C'mon." I brush it off like it's nothing because it is *nothing.* "Are you seriously believing what Ash said?"

"Why would he lie, huh?" She laughs to herself. "Why would Ash make that stuff up? You know what, don't even answer."

"Emerson, c'mon..." I beg her to stop.

"No, Logan. You've got the love of your life waiting for you. Better go find her."

The window winds up and the cab drives away, leaving me standing alone on the sidewalk. The paparazzi run across the road, dodging traffic and almost getting run over by a bus. They demand answers to their impromptu questions, and I answer only to distract myself.

"How did it feel to win last night?"

"Is it true that Real Madrid have offered you a position next season?"

"Are you and Emerson Chase an item?"

The last question strikes a nerve. *People are onto us.*

I could expose our relationship, come out to the world and tell everyone how I feel about her.

But that will damage us more than it would bring good.

"She's engaged to Wesley Chase. She's like my sister."

I pretend it doesn't hurt, and that the anger doesn't consume me while walking back to the restaurant where I'm forced to pretend Emerson Chase means nothing me.

When in reality—I'm in love with her.

NINETEEN

"Another woman may have caught your eye,
but ultimately,
the heart is what matters the most."
~ *Emerson Chase*

Wes packs his final suitcase, zipping it up and placing it near the door.

I sit at the dining table, crunching numbers and emailing our lawyer about the contracts we signed for the fitness line launching in Europe. It's tedious work and something I have been putting off. I also busy myself looking at other properties to purchase building my portfolio and branching away from Wesley.

There's a pot of coffee beside me—cold and stale from when I made it earlier this morning.

"You know where to reach me?"

"I have your number," I remind him, staring at this impossible equation on my screen.

"Will you be okay by yourself?"

I can hear the worry in his voice. This isn't the first time he's gone away for the weekend, but after what happened in London, he's been extra protective watching my every move. He's even made Jimmy, our bodyguard, follow me around town.

The stalker has been arrested, but nothing else can be done. He hasn't breached any laws and the guy just needed a visit to the looney bin to regroup. Nina held bits of information from me so as to not stress me out.

"I'll be fine. Tayla flies in tomorrow morning so we're gonna hang out."

"You never told me Tayla would be in town."

I sigh, shutting the lid of my laptop to give him my full attention. "Mom was supposed to come but had something last minute pop up, so she's sent Tayla instead. I didn't tell you because I figured you didn't care."

"I care, Emerson." He moves closer to me, resting his hand on my cheek.

Without hurting his feelings, I turn my face away allowing him to pull back. Since we got back from London last week, our schedules have been busy with no time to unwind. We have two more shows to film before final edits. We did a round of interviews, appeared as guests on talk shows, and had meetings with our business partners. Each night I've come home utterly exhausted, fitting in small workouts here and there then crashing as soon as I hit the pillow.

It leaves little time to think about Logan and how we left things off, despite the thousands of texts he sends each day which I continue to ignore.

"I should go."

"Have fun."

"Do you really mean that?" he asks in a civil tone, a small smile appearing on his tired face.

"I do." I offer a small smile in return, hoping to reconcile our constant fighting. "We'll get through this, okay? Just have fun with the boys."

"I never meant to hurt you, Em. I don't know what happened that night," he admits quietly. "I know we're not together, but it doesn't stop me from loving you."

Letting out a sigh, my eyes meet his with forgiveness. "It's done, Wes. We need to move on with our lives. We have two episodes left to film. Cliff said they'll show our argument at Scarlett's party. The cracks are already there for those who want to read between the lines."

"I know. But you know that season won't air until the fall. In the meantime, the network doesn't want to show any cracks in our relationship. They want it to be a surprise. Ratings soar higher that way."

Of course, they would.

Stuck between a rock and a hard place, I fight the urge to start another argument and remain tight-lipped. Wes pulls out his phone and stands behind me, leaning down and kissing my cheek as the camera clicks.

"Let's ease the rumors."

He types away, then places his phone in his back pocket. "We both have committed ourselves to the show. Just do this for me, Em. Finish it off with high ratings and then you can walk away." He says goodbye and disappears, closing the door behind him as I move to the balcony and watch Wes drive off.

With my phone in hand, I log on and see the photo he's posted on Instagram.

How beautiful is my fiancée? Love this woman so

much, and can't wait to make her my wife. #Beautiful #FutureBabyMama

Great. That last comment will start the rumor mill. It feels like it's one thing after another, never time to relax without drama.

As predicted, the comments go nuts and Nina's number flashes on my screen within minutes.

"Are you pregnant?"

"No," I tell her. "Wes posted that to ease the rumors about us splitting up."

"Jesus fucking Christ." I hear the relief in her voice. "Thank God. My phone's blowing up."

"Sorry. I had no idea he wrote that. Call him and get him to post something to shut everyone up. I don't know... I'm so over it."

"I get you're over it..." she responds with frustration, "... but you still have a job to do and I'm busting my ass to get things tied up. Don't give me extra work to do by posting silly little lies like this."

"Nina..." my tone is sharp, my patience wearing thin, "... I didn't do this. Take this shit out on Wesley. I need to go."

"Em..." she calls out, apologetic, "... I'm sorry. I have a lot on my plate. Tomorrow's the magazine article and feature spread of your engagement. The photos of the ring and possible dresses will be made public. Don't forget to share the article online. We need to push hard or the magazine will retract future deals if we don't make target."

"I don't feel right about this. What's going to happen when everything's called off?"

"Then the tabloids get what they want... the controversy, the drama. C'mon, Em, you know how it all works."

"I know. I just don't agree." I remain sullen, feeling

sorry for myself. "How much longer do I need to stay here... with Wes?"

"Look. I know it's hard. It can't be easy to stay with a man you don't love—"

"I never said I didn't love him," I interrupt. "It's just a different love."

"Then what are you saying? You want to marry him? This changes the whole game."

The game.

Two words that impact my already-fragile emotions.

I want to run away from it all. Give up and just move to some country town in the middle of nowhere where nobody gives a shit about who I am. Where I can walk down the street dressed in the grungiest of clothes and people simply don't care or judge me.

"Nina, Wesley and I are over. I know what's going to happen when this story breaks... I'll pretty much have to go into hiding till it all dies down. I just don't get why this article is still going forward? It might not sit well with some people."

It won't sit well with Logan.

His jealous streak has only gotten worse—a side of him I've never seen. In some ways, it terrifies me. I don't know what he's capable of. He isn't the Logan Carrington I once knew. He's this obsessive creature who doesn't know how to express his feelings.

A quick phone call turns into an hour-long conversation about our upcoming commitments. I can hear the constant beep in the background, knowing everyone's chasing my tail to see if it's true.

I could kill Wesley with my bare hands right now.

When we hang up the call, so I reluctantly check my

screen and see only Logan's name. You received 10 missed calls from Logan Carrington.

> **Logan:** *Why won't you pick up your fucking phone?!!*

> **Logan:** *I'm dead serious Emerson. Answer my calls.*

> **Logan:** *If this is your way of paying me back, we're fucking over. I never pegged you to be this vindictive, but apparently you are. Have a nice fucking life, Mrs. Rich.*

I don't know how to react to such a snarky message. I could call him. Set the record straight. But I told him to trust me, although we did leave things in the air back in London. Several times I find myself on the verge of dialing his number but quickly retract, knowing that any communication between us won't end well. I need time to think about us, away from him, because he has a way of confusing my state of mind with his charm and irresistible body.

Sitting on the large wicker chair, I tuck my legs beneath me with George snuggled into my side. The day is slightly overcast with a chance of rain in the late afternoon. The wind picks up a little, yet still warm and refreshing, as we continue to sit in silence.

The temptation's too great.

With my phone resting on my lap, I grab it and Google Logan Carrington and Louisa Hemmings.

Several images appear of the two of them—mainly at dinners and charity events. Remembering Ash's comments,

I study the photos looking for traces of happiness. Something in Logan's face which indicates she was or still is the love of his life. *Dammit—where's Poppy when I need her?*

I hit dial, and ring her number wanting her to do another one of her face readings.

"Em?" She sounds surprised to hear from me. "Is everything okay? What's with Wes' baby mama comment? Everyone's going nuts. I was filming with Farrah when she read it, and the cameras caught Farrah's very colorful opinion of his post."

"I didn't realize he'd do that. I'm too tired to think about it. Let people think what they want. The truth will come out in nine months when no baby is on that vagina log ride."

Poppy's infectious laugh barrels through the speaker. "Your brother, honestly." She sighs.

"Are you okay? You sound a bit off."

"Who me? I just have... a nasty bug. Must have picked it up from traveling."

"Oh, I'm sorry..." I can tell she's distracted.

"Listen, Em... can I call you back? I need to grab some painkillers or something."

I tell her to call me back whenever she feels up to it. Quickly hanging up the call, I dial Ash's number next.

"What?" he answers agitated.

"Nice greeting. What's crawled up your ass and died?"

"Nothing," he stalls, then continues, "What's been happening?"

"Same old. And you?"

"Training, you know, same stuff. So, are you knocked up?"

"What do you think, moron? So... how did training go today... for you and, um... Logan?"

"Since when did you care so much?" Ash snickers.

"Logan bailed. He had something to do that was more important. The cunt pisses me off anyway."

I scowl at Ash's choice of words but wonder why Logan would ditch training. "That's odd of him."

"Fuck, yeah. I bet he's off screwing Louisa since she turned up at our apartment last night."

My stomach flips, followed by a rapid burning sensation which stops my regular breathing. I can't believe this. He's run back to her and here I am feeling so sorry for myself because he screwed me over.

What happened in London was purely to get me into bed.

All those words—meant *nothing*.

Everything we did—nothing.

"Anyway, just wanted to see how you are."

"You okay, Emmy?"

"I will be."

I tossed and turned, lost in a sea of nightmares all involving Logan. When the sun came up, I went for a long run along the beach, attempting to clear my head. George came with me, chugging along and not impressed at all with an early morning run.

I'm never one to meditate but sit on the beach with my eyes closed searching for my Zen. I establish right there and then that I have no Zen.

Zen could only be achieved with a bottle of tequila.

Since it's just after 7:00 a.m. I figure it might be too early for that and opt for a fruit smoothie. It certainly doesn't have the same effect.

Tayla turns up just after midday, dressed in denim

cutoffs and an oversized black tee. Already bored, she begs me to go out so she can explore LA. "Let's go out, Emmy. Shopping, drinks…"

I smile at her eagerness to grow up. "Shopping yes, drinking no. You're only sixteen."

"Sixteen these days is like twenty-one. Besides, I've drunk before."

Not long later we're driving to The Grove with the top down and allowing our skin to soak in the sun. I'm happy to spend time with Tayla, chatting away and talking about all the things girls love to discuss. A nice distraction from my fucked-up love life. Despite it being only us girls, Jimmy said he'll be close by in case something happens.

"I don't want to know why you've drunk, or how it's possible, but no drinking on my watch. I need to return you to Mom and Dad in one piece."

"Argh," she drags beneath her shades. "You're just like Mom. What about tonight? Can we at least do something fun?"

"Sure. What do you have in mind?"

"A party?"

I laugh. "Most parties involve alcohol which means no one underage. Leave it with me, I'll see if Scarlett knows of anything going on tonight."

"Wow! Do you think she'll be there?"

I shrug, driving in the parking lot where I pull the car into the first spot I see available.

We spend the afternoon shopping like crazy. I enjoy spoiling my sister. Granted Mom will give me an earful for the clothes I allow her to purchase. Paparazzi follow, but they aren't too invasive and allow us to do our own thing.

Inside Barneys New York, a few shoppers stop me to take photographs and sign autographs, something I haven't done in a while since fans are more eager for pictures than my signature.

When my feet become sore and tired, I suggest we stop at Groundwork Coffee for a much-needed caffeine pick me up. I order myself a double-shot espresso and something less strong for Tayla.

"So, I spoke to Ash yesterday." She grins, blowing on the foam that steams from the top of her cup. "Logan's been a bit down in the dumps."

"Maybe he has his period."

Tayla laughs, almost spilling her drink all over her phone that sits on the table in front of her. "What happened in London? You don't need to sugar coat it for me. I'm a big girl."

"I don't want to talk about it."

"I thought what happened at home was a one-time thing? You only have to stalk the two of you online to see something's going between you guys."

The bitter taste of espresso goes down my throat the wrong way causing a coughing fit. When I finally come for air—despite the whole restaurant on edge waiting to see if I'm okay—I bow my head wanting to keep this conversation confidential. "I don't believe that."

"Here." She shows me a ton of photographs, many of Logan and I together in London that I didn't realize had been taken. Most sites make no reference to us being any more than family friends, aside from one. A small blogger from London who's documented our every move and suggested we're having an *affair*.

"We need to get out of here," I say panic-stricken, the anxiety creeping in as heat rises beneath my skin.

"Are you okay?" Tayla asks, worried.

"I will be." My throat closes in, and with force I pull her

along, my other arm full of shopping bags until we've reached the car and are sitting inside just the two of us.

"What the hell happened back there?"

"I... I don't know," I cry openly. "It's so messed up. I don't know what to do. Whichever way I look at it, I'm hurting someone."

"But you knew this," Tayla reminds me softly. "Your life is not ordinary. Whatever you do is seen by everyone. Can I ask you something?"

I nod quietly, grabbing the tissue she hands to me.

"How serious are things with Logan?"

Letting out a long-winded sigh, I tell her about my feelings while not holding anything back. "I think I love him. I mean, I've always loved him as family but not like this."

"Do you think he loves you?"

"I can't answer that." I fall into a silence, closing my eyes and remembering his words in London. "He's really complicated, and to be honest, I just don't know."

"It's hard for me to even think of Logan in any way besides a brother figure. Him and Ash are douches, you know. This side of him that you see, I can't even imagine it."

I can't hide my smile. "When we're alone there's this spark. Like we're battling but it's a good battle. Does that make sense?"

Tayla frowns, pulling her hair out of the bun that sits on top of her head, only to place it in a bun again. "Ah, not really. Like a sex battle?"

"Sometimes." I chuckle softly.

"La, la, la, la," she sings, pressing against her ears. "Are you done with the sex talk?"

I roll my eyes at her, blowing my nose at the same time. "There was no sex talk."

"Listen..." she shuffles to her side, grabbing my hand

and squeezing it tight, "... we've got a ton of new dresses and shoes. Let's go out tonight and pretend Logan and Wesley don't exist. Just a girls' night out with dancing and no drinks, at least for me. You can get wasted if you want." She laughs.

"You know what?" I smile through my tears. "It sounds like the perfect plan."

After talking with Scarlett, she hooks us up with a party, but it's all the way in Orange County. We arrive late to find the party's in full swing and hosted by a popular DJ who frequents celebrity hot spots.

The house is a mansion. All white with glass windows everywhere you look. It sits on the beach, surrounded by a massive garden with an Olympic-sized pool.

I've never seen Tayla so excited with her phone in hand Snapchatting the whole night. She tried to explain to me how it works, but I was only half-listening, eager to unwind and get my hands on the blue cocktails the waiters are handing out. With a cocktail in hand, I quickly remind her to stick by me and no drinking whatsoever. It's somewhere into my second cocktail that a familiar voice calls my name.

Farrah.

"Oh my God... look who it is. Without Wesley, of course."

She kisses my cheek—a kiss of *death*.

Farrah reeks of perfume and plastic, dressed in a skimpy strapless red dress that makes her tits look like watermelons. Her body's drowning in jewels with well over a million dollars draped around her neck.

"Wesley's in Cabo."

"I think he may have mentioned it." Her normally confident manner is slightly off. Her fingers nervously fidgeting with her necklace. "So, you're here... alone? No man to keep you warm?"

"My sister, Tayla," I briefly introduce them and notice Tayla already has on her resting bitch face. I know she doesn't like Farrah, after all not that many people do.

"Right. Nice to meet you. You'll have to excuse me, I have people to mingle with."

I'm glad she leaves us alone, walking away to another crowd desperate for her presence—making her the center of attention.

We hang out near the front lawn where the marquee's set up and beats blast through the massive speakers. Losing ourselves to the music, we dance for a long time, letting loose and feeling free. My purse is hung across my body and begins to vibrate against my hip. I pull out my phone while trying to sway my body, to see missed calls from Logan.

Ignore.

Ignore.

Ignore.

There's a group of guys and girls beside us who look about Tayla's age. One guy, in particular, takes to Tayla and begins dancing with her. To prove I'm not at all like Mom, I let her move away and dance with him while I continue to dance with a very handsome older man who happens to be near me. He's kinda sexy and reminds me of McDreamy from *Gray's Anatomy*—a silver fox with ripped muscles and a cocky grin.

My purse continues to vibrate.

Ignore.

Ignore.

Ignore.

He appears harmless, a flirtatious smile and what's even better is he's keeping his hands to himself.

I've only had a few cocktails and won't take him to bed. Screw the fucking tabloids. I'll dance with this man and that's that.

The DJ mixes some awesome tunes, a remix of Lady Gaga's *Telephone*. I sway my body to the rhythm of the music until harmless man places his hands on my hips. I ignore his touch and use my vibrating purse as an excuse to ask him to move his hand away.

I place my finger on my ear, trying to listen to the call. "Hello?"

"Emerson..." My name is said in a cold and heartless tone, but the noise makes it difficult to hear anything else. "Walk. Away. Now."

"Huh?" I pull the phone away from my ear and see the caller ID—*Logan*.

Jesus, even from England he has the worst timing. *What the hell is his problem?* Doesn't he understand I don't want anything to do with him after the Louisa love-of-his-life over-breakfast incident?

The whole purpose of going out tonight is to have fun with Tayla who's conveniently disappeared. I tell handsome man I need to go find my sister, walking away from him and out of the marquee until I'm on the lawn where it meets the sand. I can see her with the group of friends she's made, waving back as they all sit in a circle near the shoreline. A few of them chase each other on the sand, laughing and carefree like typical teenagers.

I continue to watch them, inhaling the salty air and remembering the last time I felt like this. The night back at home, the night I found out about Wesley. The night my entire world flipped upside down and changed forever.

"When I tell you to pick up your fucking phone, do it."

My body remains rooted, frozen by the voice who spoke only moments ago. I close my eyes, blaming the cocktails for my imagination running wild.

"Open your eyes and look at me."

I open my eyes instantly, keeping silent as my chest begins to tighten, and in reverse my stomach weakens by the possibility that this is real. In a deadly slow pace, I turn around and see Logan standing right beside me. *How is this even possible?* He was in England yesterday.

My tongue is twisted, unable to speak coherently as he continues to stand beside me. His eyes glare at my chest, stunned to see me dressed in a short, white dress with a plunging-low neckline. My breasts remain secured by a ton of Hollywood tape, careful not to parade the twins in public. My self-confidence is amiss, but I don't let it show or allow it to steer us from the situation.

"What are you doing here?"

"Nice," he says like a stranger, callous and much like the old Logan I used to know. "I flew all the way here and not even a 'nice to see you'?"

I don't have any words for him, not after what Ash had just told me and his obsessive behavior of late.

My head moves swiftly. "Is there a reason you're here? Don't you have a new girlfriend back home who needs attention?" I cross my arms, folding them beneath my breasts then realize that a nip slip is imminent. Slowly, I move my arms down so they're by my side. "And how did you even know I was here?"

"It doesn't matter." He keeps his voice firm, and his stare cold. "I don't like other men touching you."

"What other men?"

"The man on the dancefloor," he grits.

"Oh, please," I retort, insulted he thinks I would have taken it further because that's what he's insinuating. "It was nothing but harmless dancing."

"Nothing..." he bellows with his lips tight, "... is harmless when it comes to you."

I'm not sure what to say. The man you love is standing beside you as jealous as hell and all you can think about is how good he looks in the pair of jeans and the white tee he's wearing. His face is unshaven but so handsome and rugged, only making it harder for me to concentrate.

"You make it sound like I'm trouble. And I take offense to that," I tell him, getting on my high horse and switching the blame. "God, Logan. You fucking make all these promises in London then I find out your almost-fiancée wants you back. The so-called love of your life." I air-quote with resentment.

"Are you still sleeping with Rich?"

"What?" I say in shock. "How many fucking times do I have to tell you... no? Jesus, why can't you just believe me? I've never, ever given you a reason not to trust me. Unlike you and Linda what's-her-face."

"Louisa."

"Yeah," I reply, hurt. "Thanks for reminding me."

"Reliable sources say you're pregnant."

Reliable sources are never reliable.

Logan should know that.

I'm not sure why he continues to believe the lies floating around.

"Does it look like I'm pregnant to my ex-fiancé?"

He bows his head, chin down with his voice low yet full of rage. "Why didn't you pick up my calls? Or answer any of my texts?"

I begin to walk away where the guests can't see us,

annoyed at having to defend myself once again to a man who knows the real me. "Because it doesn't warrant a response. We've been over this and yet, you refuse to trust me."

"You don't leave me many options," he shouts back, startling me. "I fucking have to live with watching the two of you. Do you even know what that's like?"

"Probably the same as being told that Louisa dropped by your apartment." I laugh out of spite. "And knowing you, you would have lapped that up. Taken her to your room and shown her a good ol' time."

"I can't do this." He shakes his head while running his hands nervously through his hair. "I can't even think straight anymore. You're on the front of a magazine... happily engaged Emerson Chase... how the hell do you want me to deal with that?"

"I don't know, okay? Everything's against us. We are oh, so very wrong for each other. We're like fire and gasoline. A deadly combination."

"We should stop this, all of this."

"We should," I say quietly, swallowing the lump in my throat and keeping my head low, so he doesn't see the pain that tears through me when he said those words.

Outside the property there's a gap between the house and the neighbor's yard. There appears to be no one home next door as the lights are off and there's nothing but darkness. In between the houses we stand in the dark with a full moon above us. Although he's standing an arm's length away, his scent is smothering all my senses and allowing my body to drown in his presence.

The music is loud and plays around us. I make the decision to tell him we're over, that I need to sort everything out before anything else. The next few weeks will be stressful enough and I don't need a complicated love triangle to be confusing the situation.

I begin to open my mouth when the cold hits my back and Logan has slammed me up against the concrete wall. I draw his lips to mine, kissing him deeply and losing myself in his touch. He makes me come alive with a simple kiss which ignites all of me despite the wrong that follows us around. The heat of his hands wrap around my ass, lifting me up, as his strong kisses ravage my neckline soothe me.

"Logan," I pant, straightening my back, trying to gather some clarity. "We shouldn't do it here."

"I can't wait," he responds between kisses with the sound of his belt hitting the ground as he pulls me into him, sliding my panties to the side. "Arms against the wall." He lifts and places them flat, demanding they stay there. "Why do you keep torturing me?"

The desperation in his voice echoes in my ears, accelerating the beating of my heart until there's nothing to say but the honest truth.

"Because you torture me with your obsessive need to control what I do."

He bows his head, running his tongue down the middle of my chest. A slight moan escapes between his perfect lips.

"I'm not going to ask you..." his tone changes to more rough and demanding, "... I'm going to be the only man in your life. No more bullshit. No more questions. It's just us now. You, me, and no one else."

The weight of his words kick-starts my emotions, and with him buried inside me penetrating that persistent ache, the intensity of what we're both feeling drives me into a blissful orgasm, my body screaming in delight as I ride it out through his deep thrusts.

The rise and fall of my chest consumes me, my eyesight

blinded by the stars that shine brightly during my explosive finish. He rests his body against mine, keeping himself inside as he kisses my breasts.

I push him off with care, adjusting my dress and panties while he pulls his jeans up and buckles his belt. When our breathing stabilizes, he holds my face with his hands and kisses my mouth softly.

"I thought I'd find you here." The sound of Wesley's voice breaks our moment.

It's finally come to this—no more lies, no more secrets.

Instinctively, I position myself between Logan and Wesley. Even behind me, I can hear the growl escaping Logan's throat.

"What are you doing here?" I ask nervously, watching Wesley move closer. He's a complete mess. Shirt half unbuttoned and hair in a shamble. In one hand, he holds a bottle of bourbon and brings it to his mouth, drinking straight from the bottle.

"Why am I here?" An evil laugh escapes his drunken lips. "Because I need to see for myself. You see, your perfect new boyfriend isn't so perfect."

"Wesley, it's over. You've seen it now."

"Oh..." he mouths, stumbling forward, "... I've seen it all right. I saw the way he fucked that tight little pussy of yours against the wall. You did that nice moan, the one when you're just about to cum. I just wish I could have joined in, you know, double team you."

I shake my head, shocked at his callous words. "You're drunk."

"Yeah." He lowers his head with a smirk, his body inches away which only intensifies Logan's growl behind me. "C'mon, Em, you want two cocks inside you? You're a slut just like the rest of them."

The rage consumes me, my arm ready to swing until Logan holds me back. I wriggle out of his grip.

Why the fuck is he just standing here doing nothing?

"Control your woman, Carrington. Or I'll have to tell her how you tried to pay me to walk away."

What did he just say?

There's a high-pitched scream for help which sounds in the distance. I push Wesley aside and run toward the sound. A large group on the beach surrounds a body on the sand. I run through the grit with difficulty, my feet sinking in making my pace slow.

A man yells for someone to call 911.

The panic urges me to run faster until I'm amongst the crowd pushing everyone away. When it's all clear, I see two bodies lying on the sand, unconscious—Tayla and another girl.

I fall to my knees and scream louder for help, placing my mouth on hers in a state of panic with no clue what I'm doing. I begin to sob, helpless as everyone else who watches on.

Logan and Wesley push everyone out of the way including me and begin resuscitating the both of them. In Wesley's drunken state, he manages to revive the other girl until she's coughs up water and opens her eyes, dazed and confused.

Beside her, Logan is on his knees, panicked. I pray through loud sobs for her to wake up, call her name and beg her to hang on. My legs begin to shake, desperate to give way, yet I somehow muster up the strength to remain alert because losing my sister is not an option.

And then, as if the Lord above listens to my loud prayers, her eyes spring open and her body jerks forward as she purges all the water from her lungs.

The crowd lets out a huge gasp of relief.

Logan falls back into a crumpled heap, tired and wornout by his efforts to save her.

I should thank him for saving her.

But instead, I embrace my sister and ignore him beside me, wishing nothing had ever happened between us.

TWENTY

"Tick. Tick. Boom."
~ *Logan Carrington*

I fall to the ground, desperately trying to revive Tayla. My brain scrambles to remember CPR training clouding my fear of losing her because I've gone completely blank. One look at Wesley reviving the unknown girl jogs my memory. I open her airway and give her two rescue breaths, then compress her chest, ignoring the cries surrounding me.

Thirty fucking times.

Do this thirty fucking times.

Don't panic.

The other girl gains consciousness, distracting me for a moment until my focus is back on Tayla. Her pale face and gray lips haunt me as I lay my own lips onto hers and give her another two rescue breaths. Warm air rushes against my lips, it's a sign she's breathing and within seconds, her eyes open wide with her body following in shock.

The relief washes over me.

Adrenalin running through me spiked by fear and the unknown. Emmy is leaning over Tayla, murmuring through tears, making sure she acknowledges her and isn't suffering from any permanent damage.

The paramedics arrive and check both girls over. Tayla explains that the other girl was mucking around in the water and underestimated the current. When the group saw her panicking, Tayla ran in to help her but got dragged into a rip. Thankfully, two guys were late-night surfing and heard the screams just in time.

The party has stopped and all eyes are fixated on where we stand. It angers me that many have their phones out, eagerly taking photos of what happened. Emmy doesn't care, avoiding me and not saying a word despite Tayla thanking me over and over again before being carried to the ambulance.

At the hospital, Wesley and I wait outside the room sitting on the hard, plastic chairs. We keep our distance, not saying a word to each other. The doctors check Tayla as a precautionary measure and with that, one of us had to call Chris and Abbi to inform them of what's happened.

Emmy is still in a state of shock by her sister's side, and still refusing to talk to Wesley or me. Even Wesley looks remorseful, standing up and pacing the corridor with blood-shot eyes, coming down from whatever substance he's taken.

When Chris answers the phone, I tell him and Abbi that Tayla's okay now, but of course, explain what happened. He asks a million questions in a state of panic, and most importantly why I'm in LA.

I promise him I will answer everything later, but for

now, I'll make sure Tayla rests and gets better. It doesn't ease his worries with both of them catching the next flight over to see their daughter.

The paparazzi caught wind of the situation, camped outside the hospital as security tried to restrain them. When it's time to leave, Emmy's bodyguard escorts her and Tayla through the underground entrance and into a black tinted SUV. Wesley decides to jump in with them, much to my annoyance, and I follow the car alone and still reeling from what's happened.

Outside Emmy and Wesley's apartment, the paparazzi are stationed with their cameras. When the cars pull up, the frenzy begins. The cameras are out snapping away, journalists running across the street knocking on the glass window of the car screaming out personal questions. I thought I could get away with driving behind them, but soon the attention diverts to my window.

"Is it true you and Emerson Chase are having an affair?"

"Will you leave the Royal Kings to move back to the States to be with her?"

"Is Emerson Chase pregnant with your baby, or is it Wesley Rich's?"

The window is wound up, with my focus on the garage door opening. When both cars are parked, Jimmy yells at all of them to back the hell off as it's private property. They reluctantly do so, retreating to their spots across the street and waiting for any activity which will give them the scoop they need.

I follow them upstairs and into the apartment, suddenly realizing how familiar this place feels. Then, I remember, watching all three seasons of the show they were often filmed in this apartment.

This is *their* home.

Everything looks exactly as it does on the screen, although slightly bigger.

It doesn't feel right being here, it's a wake-up call of the life Emmy lives without me. This is her *world*. A world built on lies, deceit, and fame.

Emmy disappears with Tayla to the bedroom, shutting the door behind them.

Wesley's less accommodating, ignoring my presence and disappearing to another room.

Walking to the balcony, I open the door and step outside. The sun's about to rise, and with the exhaustion hitting me fiercely, I sit on the wicker chair and close my eyes.

I've been to hell and back since Emmy left me at the restaurant.

No matter what I do or try, I can't erase her from my thoughts.

I isolated myself from Ash, spending countless hours watching Emmy's every move through various social media accounts. For days, I'd call her every thirty minutes, greeted with nothing but an empty line. The desperation consumed me to the point that I'd contacted Wesley and offered him cash in exchange for walking away. It was a massive risk sending a text message that could ruin my career but I no longer cared.

I am willing to do anything for her.

He agreed but on one condition. He'd go on his trip to Cabo and if he came back and Emerson still wanted out, he'd accept the money and leave her alone. I agreed because I had no choice as I was clutching at straws and anxious to have her all to myself.

The jerk posting on Instagram had me reeling. I was fucking stupid and didn't think straight. Scared she'd run back to him, my insecurity ate at me despite my phone ringing regularly with ex-lovers trying to hook up. It meant nothing since the girl who consumed me wanted nothing to do with me.

Then in walked Louisa.

She wanted what Ash had warned me about—to get back together. I hated that I thought about it for just a moment, it seemed easy and a ticket out of this drama.

But she isn't Emerson.

Everything about Louisa was wrong. I didn't have to tell her I was in love with someone else. My body language said it all being so withdrawn and closed in. It was enough for her to walk away with a bruised ego.

My eyes open wide with the sun shining against my skin. There are voices inside the apartment—sounds like Chris and Abbi have arrived.

This is it.

The cat's out of the bag, and either this makes or breaks us.

Abbi's sitting on the sofa, twisting her hands and staring at the shaggy rug. She's quiet and withdrawn, not even acknowledging Emmy's presence.

Chris is the exact opposite. Pacing up and down while mumbling to himself—the same thing he does when watching our games—and stops mid-step to spin and face all of us. "I want the full story," he demands, glowering with a stiff pose. "Tell me what the hell happened tonight."

"We went out, Dad," Emmy says quietly. "I was watching her, they were sitting on the sand having fun. Another girl thought it would be fun to go for a swim, but she got swept out. Tayla tried to save her."

"And you didn't think to warn your sister to not go in?" he questions anxiously.

"I was... um... busy."

"You were busy?"

Emmy nods, tilting her head as our eyes meet. It's the first time she's looked at me all night, and in just that one gaze I want to apologize for my irrational behavior which got us into this mess in the first place, but she quickly turns away avoiding me once again.

"It doesn't explain why you're here." Chris points to me rudely. "You should be in England training for the goddamn game tomorrow. This makes no sense to me."

"It makes perfect sense," Abbi speaks up calmly, still avoiding eye contact with everyone. "We've been lied to, Chris."

"Mom, I'm sorry but—"

"Emerson. I didn't raise you this way," Abbi begins, then stalls, a look of discontent spreading across her tired face. "I'm disappointed in both of you. After what happened with Ashley, I thought you knew how I felt about secrets in our family. What did you think I would honestly say to you?"

"It's my fault," Wesley jumps in, quick to defend her. "Things got out of hand in Amsterdam, and I let it ruin our relationship. Just don't blame, Em. Everything she's done is out of revenge against me, not you."

I remain tight-lipped. Angry we're even here. All of this could have been avoided if she'd simply fucking left him. He's the reason we're here. His fucking dick running loose with whores. Yet, if he didn't hurt her to begin with you wouldn't have realized that the person in front of you is the only woman you want to be with.

"And you?" Chris points again at me. "I still don't get why you're here."

"Chris," Abbi raises her voice in frustration. "They're sleeping together."

"Who?"

"Emerson and Logan."

Emmy keeps her head low, then raises it to meet mine with a tear falling down her exhausted face. Wesley moves over to where she sits, comforting her as I stand watching, wondering why the fuck I'm allowing any of this. His hands are all over her again. My anger paralyzes me, my emotions wild and out of control.

"Is that true?" Chris questions, disturbed by the reality of the situation.

"I love her," I say out loud for the first time.

In the arms of the man who offered her a life of happiness, her conflicted gaze confuses me. Isn't this what she wants to know? What all women want a man to confess? There's nothing else I can say or do. That's all my cards, laid flat on the table for everyone to see.

"You're damn right you better love her if you're willing to jeopardize your goddamn career!" Chris shouts. The sound echoes through the apartment until Abbi asks him to keep it down. "Your whole life you've worked to get where you are. Ashley's back home training his ass off to win this game and you're here because of what?"

"Because I fucking love your daughter, and watching her with someone else is torture." I stand, raising my hands as I yell in frustration. "The game means nothing to me if the one thing I want is fucking engaged to someone else."

Abbi moves her gaze to meet mine, a look of astonishment mixed with relief. Chris is not so forgiving, he's still full of rage and shares no empathy for our fucked-up situation.

"Now you listen to me..." His pointed finger comes out

again, stern and warning me I have no say in what he's about to command, "... you *will* go back to England. You *will* win your games and prove you're still the best. I did *not* spend the last fifteen years raising you as my son for you to let me down despite who the girl is."

"Chris, you don't get it—"

"Oh, I get it all right," he interrupts unapologetically. "She's my daughter. You want my respect? You want my approval to date her or whatever your plan is? Then get the hell out of here and leave her alone. Focus on your game then deal with this when you're done winning. That's the end of it."

Chris tells Abbi to grab her bag and pack Tayla's belongings so they can fly home. The two of them disappear into the bedroom leaving the three of us alone.

Rubbing the back of my neck, I struggle to even think about walking away right now. How the fuck does he expect me to focus on the game? My fingers are restless, moving of their own accord until they're bunched up into a ball, clenched and ready to smash into something, anything for relief.

"I don't have words for either of you." Emmy removes herself from Wesley, moving toward the balcony with her back facing us. She's changed into sweats and a tank with her hair propped up in a messy ponytail.

"Did you try to pay him off?"

I nod at the same time she turns around. There's nothing but hatred in her expression. No signs of love or any compassion even though I've just told everyone in this room I love her.

Her angered stare shifts to Wesley. "And, you so willingly accepted that?"

Wesley tries to move to her but is stopped as she holds

her palm up and demands he doesn't take another step forward. Emmy bows her head, focusing on her hand, and removes the diamond ring from her engagement finger. She extends her hand and motions for Wesley to take it.

The tension releases from my muscles. The sudden lightness curing the doubt which washed over me only moments ago. Her ending their relationship for good in front of me means only one thing—she's ready to commit and I can walk away and win our finals knowing the woman I love is waiting for me.

Wesley takes the ring from her silently with his shoulders slumped. His body shakes, again, his reaction to the drugs I know he takes quite often despite Emmy thinking he's clean.

Finally, she meets my stare. I wait, holding my breath for her overdue smile and words to ease my insecurity.

"I want you both out of my life." She grits her teeth with an arctic glare. "I don't care what happens with the rest of filming... I almost lost my sister today because of this mess. It's not worth it. Neither of you is worth losing my family over."

"Emerson," I call, panicked. "I am your family."

"You..." the fire burns in her eyes, wild and out of control, fueled by exhaustion and anger, "... especially you."

"Don't do this," I warn her.

"You know what?" she shoots back with a bitter stare. "You did this. Not me. I was looking for a friend that night at the lake. You took advantage of the situation. You had your fun, you played your game, and you won. Game over, Carrington."

"It wasn't a game, Emmy."

"It's always been a game with you. That's what you do. You play, you aim to win. In this game, you've won. I call defeat." Without any more words she walks to her bedroom and slams the door shut behind her. My chest is aching, desperate to follow her and fix us. But I know who I'm dealing with. Emmy isn't one to easily forgive. She's headstrong and determined. Chasing after her will only hurt me more right now. And she doesn't realize she's done just that.

I can't stand being here a second longer. Without saying goodbye, I leave the apartment and head to the car downstairs. The paparazzi are animals, they have multiplied in those few hours that we've been here.

I drive the car out of the garage as they attack me like a swarm of bees. With my foot on the pedal, I rev the engine and get the fuck out of here hoping to never see this place again.

The last plane to Heathrow is boarding in twenty minutes. I fly through customs, avoiding the questions despite their need to pat me down like a drug lord fleeing the country, and run to the boarding gate with only minutes to spare.

Settling in my seat on the plane, I finally pull out my phone. Twenty-three missed calls from Ash.

It will be like pulling off a Band-Aid, painful at first but worth it in the end. Before the pilot warns us to switch our phones to airplane mode, I hit dial, dreading this call.

"What the fuck happened to my sisters?" he barrels through the phone.

"Ash," I strain.

"No!" he yells, causing me to retract the phone from my ear. "You thank your lucky stars Tayla's alive. But Emerson... I can't fucking believe you. How dare you disrespect our friendship that way? And you lied to me. I'm your

fucking best friend and you screw my sister over? You don't think I know what you're like? You manipulate women to suit what you want. But guess what, buddy? You messed with the wrong person."

"Are you done?"

"Yeah," he confirms with a baneful laugh. "I'm fucking done. Don't come back to the apartment. Consider yourself gone from my life."

And that's what it takes.

A moment of insanity to make Emerson Chase mine, turned into losing everything important to me. Instead of realizing how lucky we are to have each other after Tayla's brush with death, it broke us.

I've lost the two people who willingly took me in as if I were their child.

I've lost my best friend—my brother.

But most importantly, I've lost the woman I love.

That's what hurts the most. Despite all we've been through, she doesn't want anything to do with me. She told me I'd won, when in fact, I've lost everything.

It isn't a competition, it's our lives at stake.

And without her in mine, it's pointless to move on.

TWENTY-ONE

"When he feels like home,
that's how you know he's the one."
~ *Emerson Chase*

"**A**nd... cut!"

This was the hardest episode I have filmed. Not only did I have to tell Wesley on camera things had to end between us, but it will be the last time we're together in this apartment.

Saying goodbye is never easy, even when it's what you so desperately need to happen to move on. It's hard to tell if Wesley's equally affected, but I gather through his late nights and excessive drinking he isn't coping well either.

The camera crew and Cliff pack up their equipment, along with the makeup artists, wardrobe, and assistants. We started filming at 6:00 a.m. and finish five hours later.

It's bittersweet in so many ways, yet finally, it's time to wrap up this difficult season.

"So, this is it?"

"This is it." I choke back the tears with my wavering voice barely heard amongst the silence. Even George looks sad, his face is planted on the floor with his paws strategically covering his face.

"I never really expected us to be here, Em. It's odd, you know? Three years of our lives together and now what?"

"We go on. It's for the best. We were never meant to be, Wes." I sigh loudly. "George will miss you."

He bends down, patting George's head and squeezing his mouth in the palm of his hand. "It'll be nice to leave my shoes out without having to worry about them being eaten."

I smile, gently. "He'll have to move on to stinky soccer boots or something."

The small smile graces his worn-out face disappears.

What happened between us has taken a toll on his well-being, a reason I didn't pressure or push him out of my life like he deserves.

"So, you're together?"

I shake my head, sullen and withdrawn. "No, but I love him. If it's meant to happen, it'll happen."

The answer is enough to ease his tension. Leaning into where I stand, he asks for a goodbye hug. It isn't the greatest of ideas given the circumstances, but I don't want to upset him further and find the courage to say goodbye properly to someone who was a huge part of my life.

Inside the arms of the man I once loved, I realize what I need to do. We pull apart and I grab my purse with George's leash linked in my hand.

I scan the apartment one more time, there's boxes stacked high and ready to go.

This was never my home, it was a place where we enjoyed our time. Made memories, good and bad.

But now, someone else can make the memories for themselves.

I have to go back to where it all began.

~

The trip to Connecticut is exhausting and long and gave me time to think...

When Tayla almost drowned two weeks ago, the media went nuts over the Emerson Chase love triangle, at least, that's what the headlines referred to it as.

Nina quit, telling me the stress had finally gotten to her and she needed a break from the industry. I didn't blame her one bit— her phone was off the hook since it all unfolded.

Every magazine, entertainment program, and radio station wanted the inside scoop.

We couldn't go anywhere without being followed. Jimmy even recruited an extra few bodyguards to assist him because things wouldn't die down.

The network told us re-runs were rating extremely high, and despite their need to control our relationship, they didn't care it all broke loose. They got what they wanted in the end.

The hardest part was covering up the sadness which seemed to follow me wherever I went. Deep circles carved beneath my eyes. I'd lost an enormous amount of weight from not eating anything besides the food Poppy or Scarlett would force down my throat. I had to hand it to them, the two of them tried their best to keep me smiling despite the media hounding them for answers.

What hurt the most was how I so easily destroyed the

relationships that meant the most to me because I was too afraid of letting people down.

Tayla was the only family member communicating with me. According to her, Dad had flown to England to make sure the boys were solely focused on training because Logan had moved out and he and Ash weren't on speaking terms.

Coach intervened, but nothing could curb their stubbornness. I hated their friendship was in jeopardy because of me, but Ash refused to take my calls and so I stopped trying hoping soon he'd forgive us both. At least Logan for the sake of their careers.

Mom and I hadn't spoken since she left the apartment with Dad and Tayla. Tayla said she was distraught and locked herself in her office all day and night writing. I knew better than to disturb her creative flow, and settled on talking to her when I got home.

The toughest pain came from how I left things with Logan. I was angry, beyond livid, the night Tayla almost drowned. I couldn't stand being near him or Wesley. I'd never felt so degraded, like a pawn in their sick and twisted game.

Exchange me for money?

That had me seeing red.

How dare they treat me like that.

Then Logan said he loved me. A pity 'I love you' to smooth the mounting tension in the room that day. The words meant nothing to me because I didn't feel they came straight from the heart. They came from this ugly, jealous place which wanted to prove a point to Wesley.

It wasn't until the morning after, when everyone had long gone, that the guilt of my actions sunk in. My heart had splintered into a thousand tiny pieces, followed by long, drawn-out sobs. In my entire life I'd never felt so alone.

Battling to keep breathing and finding a purpose to wake up every morning.

I was stupid.

Caught up in the game just as much as Logan.

I knew how important soccer was to him, yet I teased him for my own benefit because I felt insecure and needed some sort of validation. But all of it—the greed, the selfishness, and the games we played—almost cost him everything he'd worked so hard for.

And all because of me.

I'd let him down.

Once I realized it was my fault as much as it was his, I fell into a deeper funk. I wanted to reach out to him but knew it would be another selfish act. He needed to concentrate, and I proved to be a distraction of the worst kind.

The only thing I could do was move out of the apartment and say goodbye to Wesley Rich.

My baseball cap is down low, covering my eyes and gaunt face. It doesn't stop the paparazzi recognizing me, flashes going crazy until airport security need to restrain them. I walk past the noise and to the doors where Dad's waiting outside in his car.

Dad helps me with my bags, raising his eyebrow without a single word as he places George's carrier on the back seat. He mumbles something about the dog making a mess, but doesn't direct his words at me while he slides into the driver's seat and speeds off.

The drive to Green Meadows seems longer than usual, despite the small amount of traffic heading out of town for the weekend. I know Dad's not impressed about my affair with Logan, and as much as it's painful to talk about it, I need to apologize to him.

"I'm sorry, Dad," I whisper, staring out the window, restraining my tears from falling.

There's only music between us. The sounds of U2. It's so depressing, yet the perfect song to capture my mood.

"I'm disappointed in you, Emerson. I didn't raise a daughter to behave like this. What were you thinking?" He keeps his eyes steady on the road.

"I wasn't... I can't explain it."

He lets out a sigh, shoulders slumping. "When Ash came home and told us he got married I was furious. He had his whole life ahead of him. He worked himself to the bone to achieve his dreams. I didn't want some woman taking that away from him. Someone he'd known for five minutes. Marriage is a wonderful thing when it's done at the right time. It wasn't the right time for your brother and it isn't the right time for you."

"Why didn't you say something? Convince us not to get married if you saw the signs?" I wonder out loud.

It's funny how when you break up with someone, everyone voices their opinion on how wrong you were for each other yet, prior to that, no one breathed a single word.

"I did," he tells me. "I wasn't going to let either of you ruin your lives. But neither of you listened. What would I know? Just an old man out to ruin your life."

"Dad," I say softly. "You're not an old man. You're just my daddy."

The sentiment makes him smile, placing his hand on top of mine. "Despite our earlier arguments, I'm proud of you, Emmy. You took the best of the situation and built it to bigger things. You're an astute businesswoman, and if

Forbes magazine named you the next best thing, you know you're going places."

"I was going places... this separating our assets is trickier than I thought."

"So, you'll get a good lawyer, pay your dues, then build yourself back up."

Wesley and I had been tied financially in every way. The lawyers recommended we split everything fifty-fifty from our cash, investments, properties, and businesses. I'd hired a woman suggested to me—a shark in Hollywood who will fight to make sure everything's divided equally and fairly.

"Thanks, Dad, for the confidence. I need to take it one day at a time."

"You're a smart woman. You never needed to be on that show to prove that to me. Sometimes I wish your brother would have fed off your brain cell."

I laugh. Dad often put Ash down, but deep inside he's so proud of him.

"Ash has his own way of thinking."

"Yeah." Dad grunts. "Know a good divorce lawyer?"

"Excuse me?" I stumble out my words. "Him and Alessandra?"

Dad nods, clearly not pleased with the outcome. "When you commit, Emmy, you commit for life. Remember that."

I'm shocked but also not surprised. Alessandra and I rarely spoke since my stay in London. She was often busy with work, and to be honest, Ash didn't seem invested in their relationship. I love my brother but he has no idea how relationships work let alone marriage. Not that I'm one to talk, obviously I have no idea either.

"So, um... how is Logan?"

"Busy. Training. You know they won their semi-finals? Tough game but they did it. A lot of mistakes, so they need to work their asses off to win premiership this year."

I know they won. I've been following the game and watched it live. It's my only way of seeing Logan, and every time the camera zoomed in on him, my heart retreated into hiding with a box of tissues and tub of ice cream playing *Endless Love* on repeat.

A masochistic cycle I can't break.

I stare out the window, quiet and ignoring the pang which continually reminds me how much I miss him. There's such an adverse reaction to us being together. Wesley's followers didn't hold back their opinions—slut, whore—you name it, I was called it. Logan's hoard of passionate women did the same.

I've stepped away from all my social media accounts because despite my tough exterior, at times, I'm a crumbling mess inside.

We drive up the driveway while I hold back my tears when the house is in full view.

There's no usual welcome from Mom. No knock me down until I'm almost on the ground, full of excitement and smiles. Nothing but an empty greeting which is exactly what I deserve.

We walk inside to find the house strangely quiet.

Dad places my bags down and opens the carrier. "What do you want me to do with George?"

Dad has taken to George, bending down and squashing his face with a baby voice. This man seriously needs grandchildren or something else to keep him busy besides our fucked-up love lives.

"Whatever you want, but best not to show him your closet. He has a fetish for male shoes."

Dad pats his thigh, calling George to follow him outside. George seems relieved—a long flight with another puppy on board was way too stressful for him. The bitch had the audacity to tease him the entire flight with her Louis Vuitton carrier and Gucci collar.

Sucking in the air with a pile of guilt nesting in my stomach, I walk to Mom's office to find the door shut. I knock gently, with no response, then open the door with caution. She doesn't look up to see me, her concentration focused on the screen. Although it's daylight, her blinds are drawn with a small lamp directed on her desk.

"Mom," I whisper, like a lost little girl.

She doesn't say a word, eyes still glued to the screen.

"Please say something." The tears fall one by one, the salty liquid against my dry lips. "I can lose everything I have but I can't lose you."

She bows her head with a sigh, placing her glasses on the desk. "You'll never lose me, kid."

"I have lost you," I sob. "I got caught up in it all... the whole—"

"Romance."

"Romance..." I repeat quietly. "I'm not sure it was all romance, though."

"Bad romance. The best kind." She finally smiles, motioning for me to sit on her lap like I'd always done as a kid.

I position myself on her lap and rest my head on top of hers, hugging her real tight. Her familiar scent is home, comforting me at this very moment. It's exactly what I need and with that feeling, I allow myself to cry in her embrace.

"As a romance writer what's your take on this?" I ask as the tears subside enough to talk. "Tell me what your characters would do right now?"

She thinks for a moment, resting her head against my chest. "Well, they always need that time apart to re-evaluate what's important and what they're willing to give up."

"Go on..."

"Then they meet. Somewhere unexpected, but of meaning. A place close to their hearts. It makes the moment even more romantic."

"Like at Tiffany's?" I joke softly, smiling through my dried-up tears.

"Or, like the field on Benson's Corner."

It takes a moment for the penny to drop.

Benson's Corner is the biggest field in Green Meadows. Ash and Logan would play there every day, sometimes twice a day, for as long as I could remember. I remembered telling Dad one day to build me a cubby house in the big oak tree because we practically lived there.

"That's Ash and Logan's field."

She nods.

"What are you trying to say, Mom?"

"I'm trying to tell you that I'm sure you'll find an equally devastated man on that field kicking the ball around aimlessly."

I shuffle on her lap, anxious yet eager. "Logan's here?"

Mom's face remains placid, nodding again to assure me she's not lying.

"How... um... is he?"

"A mess," she states truthfully. "You did a number on him, kid."

I'm about to defend myself until Mom stops me. "I meant..." she points to my heart, "... in here."

"Mom, I don't know how to fix us. We've kinda always been a broken unit. It's just so hard."

"The two of you never saw eye to eye. You were

constantly fighting for Ash's attention. Both headstrong and extremely competitive."

"And that's what got me into this mess to begin with. I signed up for the show because they were doing great things. I wanted to be better, and look at the mess I created for myself."

"And look at where it brought you... here."

"I'm sorry, Mom. I hurt you and lied, and just wasn't thinking about anyone else but that moment."

"I get it, kid. You had that moment. We've all had it..." She pauses, then drives her mouse around the screen. "I want to show you something."

I scoot off her lap to allow her to navigate on the screen without too much trouble. She clicks out of the word document she's in, then opens another. There's a title on the screen which says, *Bad Romance.*

"What's this?" I ask, unsure of what she's trying to show me.

"My next book. You see, for a while now, I had this story in my head but it wasn't right. Something wasn't flowing. Then, I started to witness something. Something I'd never witnessed before. *A bad romance.* One I knew would end up with broken hearts."

I still don't quite get what she's saying especially with my exhausted mind barely functioning.

"I knew long before it broke that you and Logan were in this bad romance. I watched, I observed, and it became my story." She smiles, touching my hand. "Don't worry, names and places have been changed. But I wrote this, for you. I wanted you to look back at this one day and remember a time in your life when love consumed you. When nothing else mattered besides this one man."

"I don't know what to say."

"Say you'll read it?"

"Of course, I'll read it, but how did you know?"

"How?" She raises her brow with a grin. "Because you're my children. I know everything. Remember when you were seventeen and told me you went to the shop to buy Mrs. Cambridge a going-away present because it was her last day working in the library? I knew you went to the drugstore and bought rubbers for Ashley."

"Mother!" I raise my voice in amusement.

"I was merely grateful your brother was being safe. Plus, I was glad he ran to you for advice on girls and not me."

We both laugh, letting out a sigh as we finish.

"Thank you, Mom. For putting up with me. For writing this so I can see it from the eyes of the world rather than my own."

"I love you, kid. No one can ever change that."

"Ditto." I smile.

It's late. The darkness settling in with no lights surrounding us but the few street lamps and the moonlight. It's eerily quiet, not even the sounds of the summer crickets pounding my eardrums. There's only one sound dominating the space around us, the constant echo of a bouncing ball.

Logan's standing in the middle of the field, dressed in a pair of white training shorts and a black tee, dribbling the ball with his feet. I watch on the sidelines for a while, admiring the way he concentrates on his footwork. His face scrunches up when he's concentrating, repeatedly blinking until he aims the ball which lands straight in the net.

My footsteps feel like lead weights—heavy and dragging

across the grass. I'm terrified he will tell me to leave him alone, exactly what I did to him in my apartment.

"You're here." My voice is barely above a whisper.

"You're here."

"Well, it's my home."

"It is your home," he answers coldly.

"It's your home, too. Always has been."

He won't make eye contact with me, staring at the goal with a hard glare on his face. I want to tell him I miss him. That I love him, and somehow need us to work out. But I'm terrified he'll break me in a revenge attack for how I broke him, by telling him to leave me the hell alone and never talk to me again.

"I was wrong," I admit. "We were both wrong."

"I did what I had to do."

"Honestly Logan, you don't make it easy to forgive you!" The anger comes out of nowhere, perhaps from the built up fear and the unknown. *I hate that I want him so much.*

"Why?" He turns around and faces me, eyes blazing and full of pain. "Because I fucking love you and you couldn't see that. You were happy to continue tormenting me with your fictional relationship."

"But I told you—"

"Yeah... yeah... heard it a million times. You're contractually obliged to star in the show. I guess I'm the fool for thinking the smallest part of you felt the same."

"You don't think I feel the same? You don't think I love you?" I grab my phone and dial the number of the head of the network—Jeffrey Marsh. It goes straight to his secretary, so I place her on speaker phone.

"Mr. Marsh is no longer with the company."

"Huh?"

"He was dismissed today."

"Well then, tell me who I need to speak to regarding my contract?"

"I'm not sure, Miss Chase."

I hang up and call Cliff. "Cliff, I'm done with the show. I don't care what it costs me to get out of my contract, I'm willing to pay whatever even if that means every last dollar I have."

"Are you out of your mind, Chase?" he yells into the receiver.

"I've never been saner." I hang up the call and will deal with the ramifications later. "No more excuses. That's it. Now what?"

"God, Emmy. It's more than that."

"Then what is it?" I drag out in pure frustration, throwing my hands in the air.

"There's no turning back with us. We're either all in now or nothing. We can't ever go back to the way we were... friends or whatever you call it."

"I know that," I tell him. "You're part of my family. You always have been. And now I know why. This was in the cards all along, we just needed to play the game in order to realize what we'd be willing to give up. We both lost, but we can both win."

This is it.

All or nothing.

My heart's pounding so hard, ready to combust from the pressure of waiting for him to decide. If he tells me he's not in, I don't know what I'll do. I've never wanted anything as much as I want him right now and that frightens me.

His head is bowed, eyes closed with his mouth tight. I watch him anxiously, the way his hands slowly open and unleash the tight fists he's been holding. The base of his jaw lifts until his eyes mirror mine, the desperation matching my own. He moves his body in front of me, raising his hand to touch my cheek, and the second it does the spark between us stills our troubled hearts.

"I meant what I said," he murmurs with the air escaping his lips. "No turning back. All or nothing. Marriage, babies... that whole growing-old-together thing." He gets down on one knee and runs his fingertip from my stomach down my thigh until it stops at the scar on my knee.

"Wait," I whisper, unsure as my heart accelerates from his actions. "Is this a proposal?"

He shakes his head with a beautiful smile. "No. Trust me, if I propose marriage there'll be fucking fireworks and you'll be crying like a baby."

"I don't cry like a baby," I tell him with a pout, easing the nerves.

"When I pushed you off the zip-line that day, I wanted you to soar. You always amazed me with your fearless attitude. So, when I saw you scared for the first time, I was sad. It wasn't you, and I'll be damned to see you become that person. This is who you are... you take risks and sometimes they pay off and sometimes they don't."

I fall to my knees at eye level with him, wrapping my arms around his neck, desperate to close the gap between us. "You scarred me that day. A piece of you always on me. I should have known."

"Neither one of us knew, but it doesn't matter we know now."

"We know now." I beam with happiness. "So now what?"

"We show the whole world what we're about." His grin is infectious, spreading all over me like a warm security blanket.

How can this man be so beautiful? And mine... *finally*.

"And how do we do that?" I tease him with a smile.

He grabs his phone from his pocket and holds it up in the air, positioning it before he plants the softest kiss on my lips. I don't break free, not even when the camera clicks. When the cold air touches my face and he pulls away, a smirk plays on his devious lips.

The phone is turned around so I can see the photo and in the space of seconds, he's uploaded it.

It's us.

Me and him.

Logan Carrington and Emerson Chase, with the caption beneath the photo saying #Love.

We head back to the house holding hands, laughing about the time Ash got stomach cramps from drinking a can of beer he stole from Dad's man-cave fridge when he was twelve, and ran home with a shit stain on the back of his jeans.

Mom and Dad are sitting in the living room, curled up by the fireplace reading books. The two of them are polar opposites—Mom's reading a romance novel titled *Chasing Love* and Dad's reading about the most celebrated sporting heroes of all time. They still manage to bond over their love for reading, snuggled into each other's side on the big cream sofa with pillows surrounding them.

Tayla is lying on her stomach across the shaggy brown rug, no surprise, on her phone with her headphones on. She's grinning at the screen, typing quickly then taking a selfie with George.

I swear that dog's a traitor.

Logan places his arm around me as we sit on the sofa adjacent to my parents. Part of me wants to giggle like a teenager bringing her boyfriend home for the first time despite him practically living here. I knock into his ribs on purpose, goading some sort of reaction from him. He kisses the top of my head as I curl into his chest, listening to his heartbeat.

"Family meeting," Dad commands, placing his book down.

"It's weird without Ash," I say.

Tayla removes her headphones and rings Ash, placing him on video call. "Now we're all here."

"Hey." I wave over the phone cautiously, reminding myself we haven't spoken in weeks.

"Is that your new boyfriend?" he questions, deadpan. "Looks like a dick."

Logan laughs as Mom interrupts, "Ashley Christopher Chase... behave."

"We all know the truth now. Have you talked about how it will work? Emmy is in LA and Logan is contracted to England," Tayla asks, keeping her tone neutral to avoid interrogating us.

"Actually, I've requested to pull out of the show. Dad's right. I enjoy business and my heart isn't in acting anymore. I'm sure another opportunity will present itself."

"About Logan..." Dad announces. "I have news for you and Ash but I wanted to wait until we were all together."

We all wait on edge, Dad taking longer than usual to reveal his news.

"The US team has picked both of you up on one condition..." he trails off to clear his throat. "You have to win this premiership. Royal Kings will negotiate your contract on those terms."

Logan's face beams with enthusiasm. "Are you kidding me? Because that's great. A chance to represent our country in the World Cup trials. Shit! Ash, did you hear that?"

"Uh, yeah." He seems less enthused, distracted by someone beside him.

"Bro, c'mon. We've been waiting on this for like... forever."

"Yeah." He rubs the back of his neck nervously. "I just kinda like England. Emmy, don't be mad, please."

I exhale a laugh. "What would I be mad about?"

He whispers to someone beside him and then suddenly Poppy's face is on the screen, smiling wide with a persistent wave.

"Uh... why are you with Poppy?"

Logan's mouth is wide with a smirk. I turn to him for an answer and he continues to watch me like I'm on a short fuse. "I don't get it."

"I think your brother and Poppy are an item," Mom says with a playful smile.

"But... but..." My words don't come out. "When? How? This is insane..."

"Back when you guys visited London, over drinks and terrible dad jokes. Insane, yes... but fuck, I love this woman." He kisses her cheek and it's hard to ignore how happy he looks. I don't actually think I've ever seen him this happy. It's frightening, yet I'm overcome with joy at the same time. "You always said we didn't have the ESP thing going on. Twenty-six years later, it's finally kicked in."

"Oh yeah," I challenge. "What am I thinking now?"

"You're in love with the goof beside you, and want this phone call to end so you can get laid because it's been two weeks."

I gasp, eyes wide in shock. "Ashley!"

Everyone laughs, even Mom and Dad despite the awkwardness of me getting laid.

When the laughter dwindles I relax enough to respond

back to him, "You're right... I do love the goof beside me." I nudge Logan with my elbow again. "And that's all I'll say."

"It's good to see you happy, sis, even if it's with him." Ashley smiles through the screen. "You'll always be my bro. Just make it official already. If you like it then you should have put a ring on it," he chants, mimicking Beyoncé.

Logan grins, kissing my finger and leaning into the call as if it was only him and Ash.

"Soon, bro..."

One week later—they won their premiership.

And when the crowds cheered like maniacs, there in the middle of the stadium covered in mud and sweat, Logan pulled out a ring and asked me to marry him.

Fireworks and all.

My brother's best friend, my rival, my lover.

The man who was always meant to be mine.

EPILOGUE

"Lights, camera, action!"
~ Emerson Chase

S eason three aired and the ratings soared with the
drama which had unfolded.

It had been a difficult six months, and this was
the final wrap-up—the live reunion show.

Kyle and Kelly are the first to be interviewed in front of
a live audience.

Anthony Carron hosts all the reunion shows on the
network. An over-the-top host with a vivacious attitude and
thirst for gossip. He flaunts his homosexuality like a pair of
new shoes, never one to shy away from drama in his own
life. He knows how to bring out the real stories, make light
of situations that appear too heavy, and stands center ring
when the boxing gloves come out.

I've been too wrapped up in my own scandal to see
what others around me have been going through.

Kyle and Kelly focused on a business venture this season which went horribly wrong. Their partner bailed, taking all their life savings and investments. Luckily, the camera caught some of the fraudulent activity, and now it's with the courts to decide what will happen.

Harley's sexuality finally came out. A surprise to many including myself, but nevertheless, a positive step forward. He speaks about his battle with depression and how coming out has helped him deal with that. When the cameras rolled back and showed some of the pivotal scenes in this season, it's hard to watch and even more difficult when he fights to hold back the tears on stage. Poppy and I intervene, joining him on the couch and holding his hand while he openly speaks about his struggle to finally accept himself.

There's a short interlude until Poppy comes on. I love how excited she is, dressed in a yellow and white polka dot 1950s-style dress with white wedges. Her bright smile lights up the room, and when they call Ash out to join her, the two of them sit on the couch like lovesick fools.

"This season had lots of drama, and we can't forget the moment in London when Ash takes Poppy to the Royal Kings stadium and she kicks the ball in. How about we watch this clip." Anthony points to the camera and footage of the two of them roll.

I remember Poppy switching flights, leaving later which she said was because she wanted to spend more time with her family. I had no idea this went on. And when Ash gave Poppy a lesson on how to kick the ball in the net, she kicks the ball accidentally too hard and straight into his nuts. Every male in the room cringes at the sight, squeezing their thighs as the women laugh in hysterics.

"Have you recovered?" Anthony manages to question through his fit of laughter.

"Yes, the boys are back to normal." Ash grins.

Jesus. Did he have to talk about his boys? I'm grossed out —too much information makes my stomach queasy.

"Explains why Poppy's always smiling," Anthony quips, the audience following with a short chuckle. "What's happening now, with the both of you?"

"Ash is training here in the States, so we get to spend a lot of time together." Poppy smiles.

"Is this serious?"

"C'mon, Anthony, silly question. I love this chick." Ash moves off the sofa and gets down on one knee in front of the audience and pulls out a small box.

Oh my God!

I don't even know if his divorce is final.

I'm glued to the screen and it's like watching a train wreck about to happen. I can't turn away, eager to know what happens next.

"Poppy Rose Clark... you're the craziest woman I've ever met. When I'm with you, life is just better... it's perfect. No one else can kick me in the nuts and make me smile at the same time."

And there it is, classic Ash with non-filtered words.

"Will you marry me?"

Poppy's face lights up with utter delight, extending her hand as he slides a unique pink diamond ring on it. The two of them kiss at the same time my phone buzzes in my hand.

Mom: *FYI. Dad and I already knew this was going to happen. Calm your titties, we love Poppy.*

I'm not sure what disturbs me more, the fact I didn't know Ash was going to propose or that Mom told me to calm my titties.

"Did you know?" I question Logan as he stands beside me.

He bites his lip, keeping quiet, then caves when I use my whiney voice and tell him to answer me.

"Yes. He's my best friend. I promised not to tell anyone."

I exhale, annoyed. "Nice to know where your loyalty lies."

Their segment lasts longer than scheduled, and when they walk off the set Poppy runs into my arms as I wait for her long-awaited embrace.

"Jesus, Pop." I grin. "Are you sure you wanna marry that dork?"

"I've never been so sure."

Ash follows, elated, hugging me with a small sniff.

"Are you crying, Ashley?"

"Just glad she said yes."

"You better treat her right or you have me to answer to," I warn him gently, hugging my brother before I'm called on to the set.

Nervous about appearing in front of a live audience, my hands repeatedly pat my thighs while I breathe in and out to curb the anxiety which follows me. Nausea lingers in the pit of my stomach, only adding more stress to the situation.

Logan senses my trepidation, rubbing my shoulders to calm my nerves. "You'll do great. I'm here, okay?"

I nod, wanting to get this over with. I haven't seen Wes since the day I left the apartment, but according to the tabloids he did a stint in rehab and has moved in with another actress.

I step onto the stage, dressed head to toe in designer labels. The wardrobe crew want me in a similar dress to the one I wore when Wes and I first went out to dinner. I told them, no, settling for a white off-the-shoulder blouse and black pants. My shoes are Louboutin—a pair I want to steal and take home.

Wesley follows me on the stage and sits beside me on the sofa, keeping his distance. He looks much better, tanned and with his hair slightly longer. Rehab agrees with him, his eyes no longer clouded by dark circles.

"This was an explosive season for the two of you. Let's watch some of the highlights from season three."

The footage rolls of our many moments. Some sweet, and some of our brawls. I knew Logan won't take kindly to seeing this again, he's already watched season three despite me warning him not to. It only angers him and sent him on a jealous hissy fit, but the positive came from the extremely heated sex that followed.

"How do you feel watching these moments?" Anthony asks, crossing his legs with his cue cards in hand.

"It's not easy. It was a difficult time for both of us," I answer honestly.

"And for you, Wesley?"

"The writing was on the wall."

It's never leaked out about Wesley's night in Amsterdam. As much as it hurt me at the time, I understood how damaging it could be for him and his career. So, I never breathed a word of it, allowing people to conjure up their own theories as to why we started to fall apart.

"You and Logan Carrington had quite an affair," Anthony says with a wicked smile. "We've got some unseen footage of the two of you."

They show the party at Scarlett's house with the two of us leaving in the limousine together. Then they show some paparazzi shots of us in the Indian restaurant with Ash, us in London leaving the pub, and then they show footage from afar of us arguing on the street of London when I'd just found out about Louisa. The network has never asked my permission to show this footage, but I don't care, it's all out in the open anyway.

"And Logan's here?"

I nod. "Backstage."

The producers asked if Logan could sit in, but I flat out refused and said no. I don't want him dragged into this any further, we've moved on and that's that.

The media already follows us around like crazy wherever we go. We keep a low profile, but they come up with ridiculous stories and publish them time and time again for attention.

"Wesley, you had a difficult time this season and ended up in rehab. Are you out now?"

"Yes, clean and sober."

"There's also been some other controversy following you. Can we bring out Farrah?"

Farrah walks onstage dressed in gold skimpy number with matching heels. Her hair is platinum blonde, styled in heavy curls which rest at her waistline.

She sits on the other side of Wesley, away from me.

"Welcome Farrah," Anthony greets her. "On several occasions this season you were filmed talking about their relationship. It's clear that you had an issue with Emerson which could be taken as jealousy."

"You're wrong, Anthony. I wasn't jealous of her. What's there to be jealous about?"

Bitch. That's a low blow.

The words are desperate to leave my tongue, but I cross my legs and look away from her while trying to ignore her childish comment.

"You were also seen out with Wesley quite a bit. Was something going on there?"

"Yes," she admits as the audience gasps. "We had something on the side."

Wesley shakes his head, disapprovingly. "One time doesn't count as something on the side. I was drunk and high. Clearly, my judgment was clouded."

The two of them get into a heated exchange which Anthony diffuses. I don't know what to say, still trying to control my emotions. I know he cheated on me, it was impossible for Wesley to go without sex for such a long time. But honestly, I thought he had better taste than Farrah Beaumont.

"What do you think of this?" Anthony directs the question at me.

"Wesley and I had an agreement. He was free to do whatever he pleased. If you lay with dogs, you're going to catch fleas."

"You fucking bitch," Farrah swears, raising her voice. "Did you know your fiancé knocked me up? Huh? Yeah, right in your bed."

"Jesus Christ, Farrah." Wesley bows his head between his knees.

"I lost that baby. So, call me whatever you want. At the end of the day I carried his child not you."

Wesley raises his head and begs me to look at him, apologizing through a single stare. No matter what happened, it's all irrelevant. It's utterly pointless dwelling on the past when my future is waiting backstage.

Anthony asks more questions which result in Farrah storming off. When the segment is done, he thanks us both as we leave and walk backstage.

Wesley pulls my arm back, asking me to stop. "I'm sorry, Em."

"I forgive you, okay. Just take care of yourself." I pat his arm then walk away to where Logan is standing in the back room. As soon as he sees me, the worry on his face subsides and is replaced with a smile.

"You did well."

"Barely made it."

He brings me in for an embrace, the scent of his cologne making it all better.

"I know that was hard for you to watch."

He smiles into my hair. "It's fine... I know how to take it out on you."

I laugh at his naughty answer but stop midway to breathe out the sick feeling in my stomach. He pulls me back, searching my eyes until a smile plays on his lips.

"Go. Now."

I don't say a word, running past the backstage crew and straight for the bathroom where my stomach unravels and empties into the basin just in time. I take a deep breath, peeling myself away from the basin and splashing my face with cold water.

Morning sickness—the bane of my existence.

Why do they even call it that when it happens all day long?

Checking my reflection in the mirror one more time, my skin seems to have evened out in color again. If I'm lucky, I might make it home without having to use the sick bags that Logan keeps in the glovebox.

Walking out of the restroom, Logan's just outside the door, pacing with his usual worried expression. "Are you okay?"

"Take blueberry Danish off the list of things that I could eat but now repulse me."

Logan takes my hand, rubbing the back of it with his thumb.

"We're running out of food for you to eat. I hope this doesn't last much longer," he pauses, a small smile playing on his lips. "What trimester is the horny stage where you won't be able to keep your hands off me?"

"The same trimester where you will need to feed me grapes while fanning me with banana leaves."

Logan laughs, pulling me into an embrace. "You're impossible."

"Pregnant, Logan," I remind him happily. "I think that's the word you're looking for."

BONUS SCENE - ASHLEY CHASE

"Babe, just one more minute," I beg her through strained vocals, "... not even... like twenty fucking seconds."

She's doing that thing with her mouth, wrapping her tongue around me while she literally has me by the balls. Holding them delicately in her hand, she tugs on them with enough force to make me crumble in pleasure which sends signals to every fucking part of my body that shit's gonna get real.

I love watching her—sexy with her hair a wild mess in the palm of my hands. Her eyes divert to the coffee table again, distracting me slightly. I rein her in to focus on me, selfish I know, using my hands to put her focus back on my dick. The most important thing in the room right now.

The warm feeling disappears as she withdraws, disconnecting the heat that comes from her twister tongue.

"Ashley, you really should see what's on your phone in case it's important," she suggests, catching her breath and licking her lips.

My girl is sexy on her knees. Well fuck, she's sexy every which way I look at her.

Bending down, I cup her chin in my hand and stare into her eyes. She's always grinning, cute dimples that distract any rational thoughts I have because I can't turn her mischievous face away.

My dick won't let up, begging to be finished off despite the constant interruptions.

"Fuck," I mumble under my breath, leaning forward to grab my phone with frustration.

There's several missed calls, messages, and emails that have come through in the space of ten minutes. I don't know what to look at first, but go for Logan's messages since he only messages me a million times if it's important.

Logan: *I'm sorry. Talk to me first before you read anything.*

What is this fucker going on about? I'm about to ignore him since I'm still massively pissed he bailed somewhere without telling me a single thing. His actions of late have been out of character and I suspect it has something to do with Louisa turning up at our apartment dressed in this skimpy black dress with no bra on. Even for her, it was wild and nothing like her usual uptight attire.

I log into my social media account to see the thousands upon thousands of tags until I follow a link to a media article posted an hour ago.

Drowning at LA Party

Tayla Chase (sister of Generation Next star Emerson Chase and Royal Kings defender Ashley Chase) almost drowns at a party in LA. The sixteen-year-old had been seen drinking with older sister Emerson, before hanging out on the beach with an unknown crowd.

The drunken teen was found at the scene unconscious and revived by Logan Carrington.

Another unidentified girl had been saved by Wesley Rich.

Earlier, witnesses saw Emerson Chase in a heated kiss with childhood friend Logan Carrington. The two were seen arguing until Wesley Rich found them outside the home of LA's hottest DJ —Mikey Gee.

According to a reliable source, the love triangle erupted in an explosive fist fight between Logan and Wesley because Emerson Chase is rumored to be pregnant. Neither party has commented on the pregnancy. However, the baby is said to belong to Wesley Chase.

A large lump has formed inside my throat constricting my ability to yell or even breathe. *What the fuck did I just read?* My eyes scan the article again with my stomach churning and leaving me feeling ill something happened to my little sister.

"Ashley?" Poppy calls my name, worried. "What's wrong? It looks like you've seen a ghost."

I don't answer, ringing Dad's phone which goes straight to voicemail. I try Mom, the same thing. If anyone will pick up her phone it's Tayla.

"Ash," she greets with a shaky voice.

"Tayla," I almost scream down the phone. "What the hell happened?"

"I'm okay." I can hear the exhaustion in her voice. "I went to help someone who was drowning and got caught myself."

"Why the fuck were you drinking? Did Emerson let you fucking drink?"

"I wasn't drinking, Ash. Emerson wouldn't let me drink."

"But the tabloids—"

"C'mon, don't believe what you read." She chuckles softly but it's followed by a raspy cough. "You should know that."

I grit my teeth, barely able to control the rage. "Really? Because I'm reading *shit* about Logan and Emerson."

Silence falls over the phone.

"Ash, it's not my place to comment. Talk to them." She reassures me she's okay but is tired and needs to sleep. We hang up, and in a confused state I sit back on the sofa with my dick still hanging out though flaccid from the shock.

"Is this true?" I ask the question to myself even though Poppy is beside me caressing my hair.

"Speak to them, Ashley. Though Emerson's not pregnant with anyone's baby. That is complete rubbish."

"Just fucking tell me." I close my eyes, rubbing my face with the palms of my sweaty hands. "Is my best friend fucking my sister?"

"I think it's more than that."

"You knew about this and didn't tell me?"

"Hey!" she hollers, pulling away and folding her arms. "It's not my business. And it's not exactly like we're honest with everyone either. You're technically still married to Alessandra. Your family has no clue you've separated."

She has a point. A valid one at that.

My marriage to Alessandra had disaster written all over it. She may have been beautiful and smart, but she wasn't the woman I envisioned spending my life with. In fact, I never envision settling down at all—until *Poppy*.

"But it's my best friend and my sister."

She nods, eyes wide goading some sort of reaction from me.

"My best friend and my sister," I repeat.

She nods again, remaining quiet.

"I don't understand... how long? When? The questions pour out as my mind is unable to comprehend such an absurd thing.

They hate each other.

This must be a joke.

"Ashley." Poppy calms her voice while unfolding her arms and placing her hands flat on her lap. "This is a good thing."

"No, it's not," I say adamantly, pulling my pants up and walking away from the sofa, pacing back and forth. "Logan is a bastard. He treats women like yesterday's trash. He takes what he wants and that's it. God, I can't even... and to top it off Emmy *hates* him. She's always hated him. This won't last, or work. They'll just screw each other over then I'm left in the middle. Nothing will ever be the same after this."

"Let them be. You never know, Ashley, this could be the real deal for them."

"The real deal?" I laugh, ridiculing her. "This will *never* work. Jesus! I can't fucking believe this. All the lies.... how did I not fucking see this coming? And Logan bailing on our most important training session and risking our game so he could fly over and fuck my sister! What's with that?"

"Calm down," she begs of me. "You've gone mad. Can you hear yourself? They're a good fit, the two of them. Let them sort out their relationship without you being a factor."

"You don't get it, it's always been the three of us. And if they do work out then what? What about me? I'll be left behind."

Poppy walks over to where I'm standing, stretching on her tiptoes and wrapping her arms around my neck.

"You've got me, you silly twat."

I can't hide the smile that appears unwillingly. "Your British name-calling is very distracting. So are your tits."

"Well, they feel neglected because your pecker's getting all the action."

I bury my head in her neck, thankful I have her.

I never expected this eccentric, gorgeous woman to come into my life and just complete me. She is a mirror of me, understands me better than I understand myself sometimes. A scary thought since we've only been in each other's life for a week.

She was everything I needed that night when Alessandra left.

Some could say it was rebound, but I wasn't rebounding from Alessandra. I didn't love her like she needed to be loved. I wasn't husband material and our living together proved that. I felt relief when Alessandra wanted out—she brought the giant elephant into the room that night and finally set it free.

"I fucking love you, woman." I laugh, slapping her ass causing her to squeal in delight.

"Oh, bollocks, I give good head."

"Yes," I agree with a smirk. "Fucking good head."

"You're crazy, you know that?"

"As crazy as you."

She lets out a sigh and stares into my eyes. I love the way her eyes twinkle when she smiles, switching between green and blue depending which way you look at her.

"I don't care what happens between us. I have fun when I'm with you. I don't want that to stop."

"Why does it have to?"

"You know..." she trails off. "Feelings and stuff get in the way."

I cup her chin again, bringing her face into mine until my lips are planted on her sexy mouth.

"So, let it."

With an infectious grin, she kisses me back deeply which switches me into aroused mode. Pulling back, her stare is full of lust and follows with her falling to her knees again.

We celebrate the moment with what Poppy does best—an excellent blow job.

When she's finished and I'm sitting on cloud nine, she reluctantly leaves the apartment to fly back home, but not before asking me for the millionth time if I'm okay.

I tell her I am in the end, simply to shut her up.

But I'm not.

How can I be?

Alone, in the dark, my head begins to conjure up things. Things that won't go down well if Logan shows his face anywhere near me. He lied, he betrayed my trust, and he stole my sister ready to use her like he does every woman who enters his life.

He shouldn't have messed with me.

I know every dirty little secret of his, everything but this.

And now I need answers.

I pick up my phone and dial his number—voicemail.

My rage intensifies with every missed call until finally, an hour later, his name appears on my screen.

I clutch at my phone with the tightest of grip, watching the color drain from my hand until it's almost all white. I do my best to control my ill feelings toward him, but the second I answer and the call connects, I lash out at the one man I've trusted my life with.

Logan fucking Carrington—my ex-brother.

BONUS SCENE - LOGAN CARRINGTON

"Should George be eating that cracker?" I yell into the bedroom while watching George with one eye as he devours a cracker in the corner of the kitchen. I know he doesn't like to be watched it's another quirky habit of his that baffles me.

Inside the bedroom, Emmy's sitting on our bed reading.

"Can you not scream that in front of George? It's diet doggy crackers. Ever since you hit the scene, George has put on a few pounds."

"A few?" I laugh. "The dog can't fit through the doggy door. Last night, I had to save him from an embarrassing failure as he tried to pass through it."

"You're not helping his ego right now," she complains, pouting her lips looking all cute and shit.

I grab the remote from the nightstand and climb into bed. I love the sheets are warm and that inside the bed is this sexy woman who belongs to me—my fiancée.

She's engrossed in reading, wearing her new glasses which she complains make her look like a grandma. I think she looks like a hot librarian—a virgin at that—one who's never had her clothes ripped off by any man.

"Are you still reading Abbi's manuscript?"

Emmy nods, barely acknowledging me.

"And?"

She places it down, annoyed at my interruption. "It's so good. I haven't put it down since I began two hours ago. Except for now, because you're needy and crave attention."

I bury myself into her side, sliding my hand into my favorite spot—the crevice just beneath her tits. Her scent is intoxicating, and I feel myself becoming instantly hard. "I am needy," I tell her, rubbing myself against her hip. "I need you on all fours and your ass in my face... now."

She smacks me with the manuscript, bruising my ego only. I pull away and lie on my back. My head's against the soft pillow, so I switch the television on until she yanks the remote out of my hands and switches it off.

"I'm ready." There's a nervous smile on her face and a sudden burst of energy. Odd, coming from a distracted woman who was busy reading only moments ago.

"Ready?"

"Yes." She removes her tank exposing her tits. Fuck, they're so fucking perfect I could cry. Seriously—tit heaven. "Oh, and I have something special."

"A swing?"

"No."

"Anal beads?"

"No..." she hesitates. "But I guess you could use it in my ass if you want."

She removes something from under the bed and places it in front of me. It's a black box. I open it and find a vibrator inside. It's blue with pink polka dots all over it.

"Apparently, it has multiple speed settings and can get you off in less than a minute. Plus, it's pretty, don't you think?" she rambles on.

I can hear the anxious tone in her voice. Something isn't quite right, and rather than lead with my dick, I watch her with curiosity. She's on her knees, topless with her eyes wide staring back at me. The corner of her lip is trapped beneath her bite while she twists the end of her hair around her finger almost fidgeting.

"I can get you off in less than a minute," I remind her, gazing longingly at her chest. "And your nipples are hard."

"Yeah, they're sensitive."

"You're hiding something."

She's quick to open her mouth. "No, I'm not."

I know her too well, she's definitely hiding something. But what? Then, it dawns on me.

The day of the week. Monday night. The deadliest night of the week.

"Wow, you think you're gonna get off so easy?"

"C'mon, you do this every Monday night, and then I have to deal with sour and jealous Logan."

"Funny, you weren't complaining when you came three times in a row."

"No..." she trails off. "But still, why the hell do you watch? Who cares! It's over with him now. I want no part in this."

We have this argument every Monday night. I know she's already watched the episodes when her producer couriers them over. I don't know why I can't stop. It drives me fucking insane having to watch her fool around with Wesley onscreen.

I don't want to talk myself out of it, ignoring my raging dick and her half-naked body. With just one press of the remote the television comes on and I stare at the screen waiting.

Emmy lets out a loud huff, falling back onto the bed

and covering her face with a muffled scream. I ignore her overdramatic behavior and spend the next forty minutes with my stomach in knots, bile rising in my throat, and my blood pumping so fucking hard I'm on the verge of a migraine.

It's the episode when they went to London. I should seek solace in the fact she'd been fucking me behind his back yet, that doesn't seem to make it any easier watching them with each other and the way the episodes are edited to make them so united.

I switch off the television and stare blankly at the black screen.

"You're your own worst enemy," she says stubbornly. "You can either sit there and sulk like you always do, and not talk to me for the rest of the night until you crack because, again, you're your own worst enemy, or... you can turn around and keep perfectly still, quiet if you want to brood and I'll just give you a show."

It piques my attention, yet I maintain my broody persona because I don't want to jump the gun so quickly and look like a pussy.

And speaking of pussies, there's one staring at me when I turn around.

She's lying on the bed, two pillows propped up behind her, so her body is angled perfectly. Her long, lean legs appear even longer in that position. Smooth and irresistible. Her knees are resting against each other, but when she notices she has my undivided attention, she spreads them enough for me to see the full view.

"I realized when we began our steamy affair you enjoy it when I try new things."

My lips remain still, desperately trying to hide my smirk. "Well, you didn't like anal play."

"I didn't." She shakes her head. "I think we can both agree that I do now."

"You certainly do." I lick my lips, crawling toward her until I'm close enough to smell her arousal. "So, what's left?"

"What did you tell me last week was a fantasy of yours?"

This is a trick question.

My male instinct tells me not to answer, yet I do because I have some sort of death wish.

"A threesome?"

She snorts. "Two guys and me?"

"Is that a joke?"

"Much like your answer."

"Fine." I roll my eyes at her and continue to play this ridiculous game hoping I'd get a 'happy ending' soon. "Bondage?"

"No, but I'm not opposed to it."

"Fisting?"

"Oh, my God!" she yells, wincing. "No."

I give up in frustration because her naked body is begging to be fucked.

"Honestly, do you know how much I say during sex? You're catching me at a weak moment. I can barely remember my name half the time."

"Squirting," she responds with a satisfied smile. "You told me you wanted to watch me squirt. Now, I can't make any promises but this bad boy over here is supposed to do the trick."

With a wide grin, I lean my head in far enough to rub the tip of my nose against hers. Our lips are inches away from each other.

"Do you know how much I love you?"

"Uh-huh," she says with a straight face until her mouth widens into a smile. "Talk to my vagina because the face don't wanna hear it."

I slap the side of her thigh which causes her to squeal, then straighten my back. My woman is about to give me the show of a lifetime.

I realize then that she'll do anything for me, as silly and boundary-pushing as it may be. And so, I will do the same for her.

Tonight, after all is said and done and I'm completely covered in her juices, I will sign the dotted line on the contract that's been sitting on our dining table for weeks. A contract that causes this huge divide between us every time we try to discuss it.

Our own reality television show.

Eight episodes.

One season.

All us—completely raw and unscripted.

BONUS SCENE - WESLEY RICH

The words are coming out of her mouth but they don't make any sense. Farrah continues to talk while standing in front of the mirror—wearing only her pink lace thong—applying fresh red lipstick onto her fake pout.

"I mean really, Wes, did you honestly not see that Emerson was fucking Logan behind your back?"

I saw. *I watched.* I felt completely helpless after my own actions.

Despite our somewhat turbulent relationship, Emerson had a way of standing her own ground. She got what she wanted indirectly even if I didn't know it at the time. I had controlled her wild spirit as much as I could over the years, but even then she had a way of making me feel like I had zero control over her.

And perhaps—that's why I proposed marriage.

Yeah, I loved her.

She was convenient.

We worked together, and it was either her or some Hollywood bimbo like Farrah who would end up as my wife. At least Emerson was hot and intelligent. She had an annoying family though, who I had planned to get rid of. Distance her from them as much as possible because I couldn't stand them stealing her attention away from me. That and her brother's a fucking moron.

"What do you care anyway, Farrah? You sucked my dick, hell, you even shoved it up that tight ass of yours. Let it fucking go already."

The shrill in her laughter is disturbing. "How can you let it go? You got played in front of the whole world!"

This bitch is riding my tail and it's time to cut her loose. I don't need anyone else shoving my failures in my fucking face.

"You've always been jealous of Em. The whole world saw that," I respond too eagerly.

Her face remains stiff. Emotionless from the Botox injected into her once-youthful skin. I know she's threatened by the truth. Finally, it's enough to shut her up already.

Moving to the bed, she crawls toward me until she's straddling my body with her tits against my chest. They're massive, an eyesore, great for a tit-fuck but not as good as the real deal.

Not as soft as Emerson's.

Don't torture yourself.

"Funny, Wes. I was never jealous of Emerson Chase... I just don't like her. In fact, I despise her. Enough to make sure that big dick of yours got in trouble in Amsterdam."

"Excuse me?"

"Let's just say it was my idea those two whores visited your hotel room, and maybe, it was the network's idea to break the two of you up. You know, for ratings and all."

My memory jogs back as quick as it can to that night.

Some boys and I had been at the club, drinking hard

and hanging with some girls. It was innocent until the last drink when things got blurry and I lost control of my actions. I remember being in the room with these women and on the biggest high ever. Yeah, I'd sniffed coke before but that was years ago. These women came to my room with the goods and I caved. I don't know why I did.

"Are you telling me it was a setup?"

Farrah laughs while caressing my cheek. "Sweetie, Emerson isn't right for you. So, you fucked two whores? Even if I didn't send them to your room you would've fucked someone else anyway."

I never cheated on Emerson. Okay, like when we were first dating I scored some head from some random women, but I hadn't cheated on her since we moved in together. It was only when I had my suspicions about Logan that I let Farrah fuck me. Purely because she offered and I needed a release.

"Get off me," I demand, angry and uncontrolled.

"Why are you so worked up? She moved on to Logan."

"Why?" I ask loudly. "Because this would have *never* have happened if you didn't fucking get involved. You're telling me it was a setup and you expect me to fucking act like my whole world didn't fall apart?"

I push her off me, her body losing balance as she tumbles off the bed and onto the floor. With a yelp followed by small cries, she manages to stand up examining the bump on her head from hitting the table.

"You'll pay for that Wesley Rich."

"Fuck off, Farrah."

"You've got a choice..." she composes herself and fixes her hair with a calm smile planted on her unreadable face, "... you can tell the world that the baby inside me is yours and not Jeffrey Marsh's or, I can take a snap of this beautiful bruise and share your dark little secret."

"What the *fuck* are you going on about?" I spit out with frustration.

"That Wesley Rich is an abusive drug addict who tried to hurt me when the cameras aren't around."

"You wouldn't dare..." I warn her.

She walks to where I'm standing and wraps her arms around my waist. Her naked torso disturbs me because underneath the plastic lays a cold and bitter heart. One so dark and twisted that nothing else could taint it.

"Try me, Wesley. When I don't get what I want, everyone gets hurt."

I have no choice—*again.*

My life is being dictated by a woman driven by greed, money, and power. Jealous of everything that brings me happiness. Out to destroy anyone in my life who I love.

A replicate of my mother.

The person I hate most in this world.

ALSO BY KAT T. MASEN

The Dark Love Series

Featuring Lex & Charlie

Chasing Love: A Billionaire Love Triangle

Chasing Us: A Second Chance Love Triangle

Chasing Her: A Stalker Romance

Chasing Him: A Forbidden Second Chance Romance

Chasing Fate: An Enemies-to-Lovers Romance

Chasing Heartbreak: A Friends-to-Lovers Romance

The Forbidden Love Series

(Dark Love Series Second Generation)

Featuring Amelia Edwards

The Trouble With Love: An Age Gap Romance

The Trouble With Us: A Second Chance Love Triangle

The Trouble With Him: A Secret Pregnancy Romance

The Trouble With Her: A Friends-to-Lovers Romance

The Trouble With Fate: An Enemies-to-Lovers Romance

The Office Rival: An Enemies-to-Lovers Romance

The Marriage Rival: An Office Romance

Bad Boy Player: A Brother's Best Friend Romance

Roomie Wars Box Set (Books 1 to 3): Friends-to-Lovers Series

ABOUT THE AUTHOR

Born and bred in Sydney, Australia, **Kat T. Masen** is a mother to four crazy boys and wife to one sane husband. Growing up in a generation where social media and fancy gadgets didn't exist, she enjoyed reading from an early age and found herself immersed in these stories. After meeting friends on Twitter who loved to read as much as she did, her passion for writing began, and the friendships continued on despite the distance.

"I'm known to be crazy and humorous. Show me the most random picture of a dog in a wig, and I'll be laughing for days."

Download free bonus content, purchase signed paperbacks & bookish merchandise.
Visit: **www.kattmasen.com**

61359962R00203